Praise for *Erasure*

"*Erasure* demonstrates the folly of racia[l] ... [show]s
how our culture alters its past—how we ... [are] ... [to]o
quick to assume and we're too quick to f[orget] ... [defi]-
nitely keep an eye on."   —*Playboy*

"Oases in what too often feels a dreary desert of literary mediocrity, Everett's
books . . . are unfailingly intelligent and funny, formally bold and intellectually
ambitious. . . . [The novel-within-the-novel] is a truly vile and very, very funny
piece of writing, mocking the clichés of ghetto genre-writing with all possible
viciousness."   —*L.A. Weekly*

"A tour de force for Everett, who cheerily blasts apart our notions of political/
racial correctness in a story that is sharp-edged yet lyrically tender-hearted. It's a
brilliant book that can only benefit from word of mouth and is virtually guaran-
teed to be even better than you've heard it is."   —*The State* (Columbia, SC)

"Short, tight, and nasty, [the novel-within-the-novel is] as fast and funny as a
modern-day *Candide*."   —*San Francisco Chronicle*

"The sharp satire on American publishers and American readers that Everett puts
forward is delicious, though it won't win him many friends among the sentimen-
tal educated class who want to read something serious about black inner-city life
without disturbing any of their stereotypes."   —*Chicago Tribune*

"*Erasure* deserves the attention of anyone—black or white—interested in sophisti-
cated fiction that subtly questions the phrase 'black and white.'"
                                                —Tom LeClair, *Book Magazine*

"*Erasure* is probably Everett's most wryly humorous and disturbingly semi-
autobiographical and metafictional novel."   —*African American Review*

"An over-the-top masterpiece. . . . Percival's talent is multifaceted, sparked by a sa-
tiric brilliance that could place him alongside Wright and Ellison as he skewers the
conventions of racial and political correctness."   —*Publishers Weekly*

"A scathingly funny look at racism and the book business: editors, publishers,
readers, and writers alike."   —Vanessa Bush, *Booklist*

"More genuine and tender than much of Everett's previous work, but no less impressive intellectually: a high point in an already substantial literary career."
                                                           —*Kirkus Reviews*

"Everett makes good use of his literary antecedents, most notably Richard Wright and Ralph Ellison, reworking their themes in intriguing ways. This is an important novel from a well-established American author."   —*Library Journal*

"*Erasure* is just that—a revelation, the heart and mind of a writer laid bare. Percival Everett has accomplished that rare thing, a novel at once emotionally moving and outrageously satirical. Shocking, tender, brainy, honest."

—Josephine Humphreys

"The prospect of reading anything from Percival Everett's pen is thrilling. He is a total original, someone whose work one reads with that marvelous sense of familiar discovery which we get from reading only the best writers. *Erasure* is no exception. What a great pleasurable ride, what a read!"   —Richard Bausch

"Why do I love Percival Everett's new novel, *Erasure*? Because, like all of his fiction, it is audacious. Its audaciousness consists not only of a wildly engaging story, but of describing the most indispensable worst and best of people. In plot, dialogue, sheer inventiveness, Everett is stupendously one of our least compromised writers. The construction of this novel is genius; *Erasure* refracts the American experience, then powerfully re-shapes it. Thelonious Ellison—a writer—is one of the edgiest, most savvy, indelible characters I've encountered in decades!"

—Howard Norman

"The most refreshingly alive novel I've read in a long time. It's funny and serious and sad and strong and courageous. . . . This one will last. And that is what counts."

—Clarence Major

"A parody within a parody, intricately cross-hatched as a double-crostic, *Erasure* may be the most irreverent take on matters racial since—well, since nothing. It's what Ellison's *Invisible Man* would look like if he crawled out of his dark hole and said, 'Yo mamma.'"   —Lisa Zeidner

"The anger and brilliance of Percival Everett's *Erasure* puts you in mind of *Invisible Man*, but the satirical wit is all Everett's own. Half the time I wanted to laugh until I cried and the other half I wanted to fly into a righteous rage and go and start . . . never mind."   —Madison Smartt Bell

erasure

Also by Percival Everett

erasure

A NOVEL

percival everett

Graywolf Press

Copyright © 2001 by Percival Everett

This publication is made possible in part by a grant provided by the Minnesota State Arts Board, through an appropriation by the Minnesota State Legislature from the Minnesota arts and cultural heritage fund with money from the vote of the people of Minnesota on November 4, 2008, and a grant from the Wells Fargo Foundation Minnesota. Significant support has also been provided by the National Endowment for the Arts; Target; the McKnight Foundation; and other generous contributions from foundations, corporations, and individuals. To these organizations and individuals we offer our heartfelt thanks.

Published by Graywolf Press
212 Third Avenue North, Suite 485
Minneapolis, MN 55401

All rights reserved.

www.graywolfpress.org

Published in the United States of America

ISBN 978-1-55597-599-9

18 20 22 23 21 19 17

Library of Congress Control Number: 2011930487

Cover design: Kapo Ng @ A-Men Project

I could never tell a lie that anybody would doubt,

nor a truth that anybody would believe.

—*Mark Twain*, Following the Equator

erasure

My journal is a private affair, but as I cannot know the time of my coming death, and since I am not disposed, however unfortunately, to the serious consideration of self-termination, I am afraid that others will see these pages. Since however I will be dead, it should not much matter to me who sees what or when. My name is Thelonious Ellison. And I am a writer of fiction. This admission pains me only at the thought of my story being found and read, as I have always been severely put off by any story which had as its main character a writer. So, I will claim to be something else, if not instead, then in addition, and that shall be a son, a brother, a fisherman, an art lover, a woodworker. If for no other reason, I choose this last, callous-building occupation because of the shame it caused my mother, who for years called my pickup truck a station wagon. I am Thelonious Ellison. Call me Monk.

I have dark brown skin, curly hair, a broad nose, some of my ancestors were slaves and I have been detained by pasty white policemen in New Hampshire, Arizona and Georgia and so the society in which I live tells me I am black; that is my race. Though I am fairly athletic, I am no good at basketball. I listen to Mahler, Aretha Franklin, Charlie Parker and Ry Cooder on vinyl records and compact discs. I graduated *summa cum laude* from Harvard, hating every minute of it. I am good at math. I cannot dance. I did not grow up in any inner city or the rural south. My family owned a bungalow near Annapolis. My grandfather was a doctor. My father was a doctor. My brother and sister were doctors.

While in college I was a member of the Black Panther Party, defunct as it was, mainly because I felt I had to prove I was *black* enough. Some people in the society in which I live, described as being black, tell me I am not *black* enough. Some people whom the society calls white tell me the same thing. I have heard this mainly about my novels, from editors who have rejected me and reviewers whom I have apparently confused and, on a couple of occasions, on a basketball court when upon missing a shot I muttered *Egads*. From a reviewer:

> *The novel is finely crafted, with fully developed characters, rich language and subtle play with the plot, but one is lost to understand what this reworking of Aeschylus'* The Persians *has to do with the African American experience.*

One night at a party in New York, one of the tedious affairs where people who write mingle with people who want to write and with people who can help either group begin or continue to write, a tall, thin, rather ugly book agent told me that I could sell many books if I'd forget about writing retellings of Euripides and parodies of French poststructuralists and settle down to write the true, gritty real stories of black life. I told him that I was living a *black* life, far blacker than he could ever know, that I had lived one, that I would be living one. He left me to chat with an on-the-rise performance artist/novelist who had recently posed for seventeen straight hours in front of the governor's mansion as a lawn jockey. He familiarly flipped one of her braided extensions and tossed a thumb back in my direction.

The hard, *gritty* truth of the matter is that I hardly ever think about race. Those times when I did think about it a lot I did so because of my guilt for not thinking about it. I don't believe in race. I believe there are people who will shoot me or hang me or cheat me and try to stop me because they do believe in race, because of my brown skin, curly hair, wide nose and slave ancestors. But that's just the way it is.

Saws cut wood. They either rip with the grain or cut across it. A ripsaw will slice smoothly along the grain, but chew up the wood if it goes against the grain. It is all in the geometry of the teeth, the shape, size and set of them, how they lean away from the blade. Crosscut teeth are typically smaller than rip teeth. The large teeth of ripsaws shave material away quickly and there are deep gaps between them which allow shavings to fall away, keeping the saw from binding. Crosscut teeth make a wider path, are raked back and beveled to points. The points allow the crosscut saw to score and cleave the grain cleanly.

I arrived in Washington to give a paper, for which I had only moderate affection, at a conference, a meeting of the *Nouveau Roman* Society. I decided to attend out of no great affinity for the organization or its members or its mission, but because my mother and sister still lived in D.C. and it had been three years since my last visit.

My mother had wanted to meet me at the airport, but I refused to give her my flight information. For that matter, I also did not tell her at which hotel I'd be staying. My sister did not offer to pick me up. Lisa probably didn't hate me, her younger brother, but it became fairly clear rather early in our lives, and still, that she had little use for me. I was too flighty for her, lived in a swirl of abstracts, removed from the *real world*. While she had struggled through medical school, I had somehow, apparently, breezed through college "without cracking a book." A falsehood, but a belief to which she held fast. While she was risking her life daily by crossing picket lines to offer poor women health care which included abortions if they wanted, I was fishing, sawing wood, or writing dense, obscure novels or teaching a bunch of green California intellects about Russian formalism. But if she was cool to me, she was frozen to my brother, the high rolling plastic surgeon in Scottsdale, Arizona. Bill had a wife and two kids, but we all knew he was gay. Lisa didn't dislike Bill because of his sexuality, but because he practiced medicine for no reason other than the accumulation of great wealth.

I fancied occasionally that my brother and sister were proud of me, for my books, even if they found them unreadable, boring, mere curiosities. As my brother pointed out once while my parents were extolling my greatness to some friends, "You could rub your shit on a shingle and they'd act like that." I knew this before he'd said it, but still it was rather deflating. He then added, "Not that they don't have a right to be proud." What went unsaid, but clearly implied, was that they had a right but not a reason to be proud of me. I must have cared some then, because I was angered by his words. By now however, I appreciated Bill and what he had said, though I hadn't seen him in four years.

The conference was at the Mayflower Hotel, but as I disliked meetings and had little interest in the participants of such affairs, I took a room at a little B&B off Dupont Circle called the Tabbard Inn. The most attractive feature of the place to me was the absence of a phone in the room. I checked in, unpacked and showered. I then called my sister at her clinic from the phone in the lobby.

"So, you're here," Lisa said.

I didn't point out to her how much better *So, you made it* might have sounded, but said, "Yep."

"Have you called Mother yet?"

"No. I figured she'd be taking her afternoon siesta about now."

Lisa grunted what sounded like an agreement. "So, shall I pick you up and we can swing by and get the old lady for dinner?"

"Okay. I'm at the Tabbard Inn."

"I know it. Be there in an hour." She hung up before I could say *Goodbye* or *I'll be ready* or *Don't bother, just go to hell.* But I wouldn't have said that to Lisa. I admired her far too much and in many ways I wished I were more like her. She'd dedicated her life to helping people, but it was never clear to me that she liked them all that much. That idea of service, she got from my father, who, however wealthy his practice made him, never collected fees from half his patients.

My father's funeral had been a simple, yet huge, somewhat organic event in Northwest Washington. The street outside the Episcopal church my parents never attended was filled with people, nearly all of them teary-eyed and claiming to have been delivered into this world by the great Dr. Ellison, this in spite of most of them being clearly too young to have been born while he was still practicing. I as yet have been unable to come to an understanding or create some meaning for the spectacle.

Lisa arrived exactly one hour later. We hugged stiffly, as was our wont, and walked to the street. I got into her luxury coupe, sank into the leather and said, "Nice car."

"What's that supposed to mean?" she asked.

"Comfortable car," I said. "Plush, well appointed, not shitty, nicer than my car. What do you think it means?"

She turned the key. "I hope you're ready."

I looked at her, watched as she slipped the automatic transmission into drive.

"Mother's a little weird these days," she said.

"She sounds okay on the phone," I said, knowing full well it was a stupid thing to say, but still my bit in all this was to allow segue from minor complaint to reports of coming doom.

"You think you'd be able to tell anything during those five minute check-ins you call conversations?"

I had in fact called them just that, but I would no longer.

"She forgets things, forgets that you've told her things just minutes later."

"She an old woman."

"That's exactly what I'm telling you." Lisa slammed the heel of her palm against the horn, then lowered her window. She yelled at the driver in front of us who had stopped in a manner to her disliking, "Eat shit and die, you colon polyp!"

"You should be careful," I said. "That guy could be a nut or something."

"Fuck him," she said. "Four months ago Mother paid all her bills twice. All of them. Guess who writes the checks now." She turned her head to look at me, awaiting a response.

"You do."

"Damn right, I do. You're out in California and Pretty Boy Floyd is butchering people in Fartsdale and I'm the only one here."

"What about Lorraine?"

"Lorraine is still around. Where else is she going to be? She's still stealing little things here and there. Do you think she complained when she got paid twice? I'm being run ragged."

"I'm sorry, Lisa. It really isn't a fair setup." I didn't know what to say short of offering to move back to D.C. and in with my mother.

"She can't even remember that I'm divorced. She can recall every nauseating detail about Barry, but she can't remember that he ran off with his secretary. You'll see. First thing out of her mouth will be, 'Are you and Barry pregnant yet?' Christ."

"Is there anything you want me to take care of in the house?" I asked.

"Yeah, right. You come home, fix a radiator and she'll remember that for six years. 'Monksie fixed that squeaky door. Why can't you fix anything? You'd think with all that education you could fix something.' Don't touch anything in that house." Lisa didn't reach for a pack of cigarettes, didn't make motions like she was reaching for one or lighting one, but that's exactly what she was doing. In her mind, she was holding a Bic lighter to a Marlboro and blowing out a cloud of smoke. She looked at me again. "So, how are you doing, little brother?"

"Okay, I guess."

"What are you doing in town?"

"I'm giving a paper at the *Nouveau Roman* Society meeting." Her silence seemed to request elaboration. "I'm working on a novel, I guess you'd call it a novel, which treats this critical text by Roland Barthes, *S/Z*, exactly as it treats its so-called subject text which is Balzac's *Sarrasine*."

Lisa grunted something friendly enough sounding. "You know, I just can't read that stuff you write."

"Sorry."

"It's my fault, I'm sure."

"How is your practice?"

Lisa shook her head. "I hate this country. These anti-abortionist creeps are out front every day, with their signs and their big potato heads. They're scary. I suppose you heard about that mess in Maryland."

I had in fact read about the sniper who shot the nurse through the clinic window. I nodded.

Lisa was tapping the steering wheel rapid fire with her index fingers. As always, my sister and her problems seemed so much larger than me and mine. And I could offer her nothing in the way of solutions, advice or even commiseration. Even in her car, in spite of her small size and soft features, she towered over me.

"You know why I like you, Monk," she said after a long break. "I like you because you're smart. You understand stuff I could never get and you don't even think about it. I mean, you're just one of those people." There was a note of resentment in her compliment. "I mean, Bill is a jerk, probably a good butcher, but a butcher nonetheless. He doesn't care about anything but being a good butcher and making butcher money. But you,

you don't have to think about this crap, but you do." She put out her imaginary cigarette. "I just wish you'd write something I could read."

"I'll see what I can do."

I've always fished small water, brooks and streams and little rivers. I've never been able to make it back to my car before dark. No matter how early I start, it's night when I get back. I fish this hole, then that riffle, under that undercut bank, that outside bend, each spot looking sweeter and more promising than the last, until I'm miles away from where I started. When it's clear that the hour is late, then I fish my way back, each possible trout hiding place looking even more exciting than it did before, the new angle changing it, the thought that dusk will make the fish hungry nudging at me.

My mother had just awakened from her nap when we arrived at her house on Underwood, but as always she was dressed as if to go out. She wore blush in the old way, showing clearly on her light cheeks, but her age let her pull it off. She seemed shorter than ever and she hugged me somewhat less stiffly than my sister had and said, "My little Monksie is home."

I lifted her briefly from the floor, she always liked that, and kissed her cheek. I observed the expectant expression on my sister's face as the old woman turned to her.

"So, Lisa, are you and Barry pregnant yet?"

"Barry is," Lisa said. She then spoke into our mother's puzzled face. "Barry and I are divorced, Mother. The idiot ran off with another woman."

"I'm so sorry, dear." She patted Lisa's arm. "That's just life, honey. Don't worry. You'll get through it. As your father used to say, 'One way or another.'"

"Thank you, Mother."

"We're taking you out to dinner, madam," I said. "What do you think of that?"

"I think it's lovely, just lovely. Let me freshen up and grab my bag."

Lisa and I wandered around the living room while she was gone. I went to the mantel and looked at the photographs that had remained the same for fifteen years, my father posed gallantly in his uniform from the war in Korea, my mother looking more like Dorothy Dandridge than my mother, and the children, looking sweeter and cleaner than we ever were. I looked down into the fireplace. "Hey, Lisa, there are ashes in the fireplace."

"What?"

"Look. Ashes." I pointed.

The fireplace in the house had never been used. Our mother was so afraid of fire that she'd insisted on electric stoves and electric baseboard heat throughout the house. Mother came back with her bag and her face powdered.

"How did these ashes get here?" Lisa asked, sidling up to the subject in her way.

"When you burn things, you make ashes," Mother said. "You should know that, with your education."

"What was burned?"

"I promised your father I'd burn some of his papers when he died. Well, he died."

"Father died seven years ago," Lisa said.

"I know that, dear. I just finally got around to it. You know how I hate fire." Her point was a reasonable one.

"What kind of papers?" Lisa asked.

"That's none of your business," Mother said. "Why do you think your father asked me to burn them? Now, let's go to dinner."

At the door, Mother fumbled with her key in the lock, complained that the mechanism had become sticky lately. I offered to help. "Here," I said. "If you turn the key this way and then back, it turns easily."

"Monksie fixed my lock," she said.

Lisa groaned and stepped down ahead of us to her car.

Mother spoke softly to me, "I think there's a problem with Lisa and Barry."

"Yes, Mother."

"Are you married yet?" she asked. I held her arm as she walked down the porch steps.

"Not yet."

"You'd better get started. You don't want to be fifty with little kids. They'll run your tail into the ground."

X X X

My father had been considerably older than my mother. In June, when school ended, we would drive to the house in Highland Beach, Maryland, and open it for the summer. We'd open all the windows, sweep, clear cobwebs and chase away stray cats. Then for the rest of the summer we would all remain at the beach and Father would join us on weekends. But I remember how the first cleaning always wore him out and when it came time to take a break before dinner and play softball or croquet, he would resign to a seat on the porch and watch. He would cheer Mother on when she took the bat, giving her pointers, then sitting back as if worn out by thinking about it. He had more energy in the mornings and for some reason he and I took early strolls together. We walked to the beach, out onto the pier, then back, past the Douglass house and over to the tidal creek where we'd sit and watch the crabs scurrying with the tide. Sometimes we'd take a bucket and a net and he'd coach me while I snagged a couple dozen crabs for lunch.

Once he fell to his butt in the sand and said, "Thelonious, you're a good boy."

I looked back at him from the ankle-deep water.

"You're not like your brother and sister. Of course, they're not like each other either. But they're more alike than they're willing to admit. Anyway, you're different."

"Is that good, Father?" I asked.

"Yes," he said, as if figuring out the answer right then. He pointed to the water. "There's a nice fat one. Come at him from farther away."

I followed his instructions and scooped up the crab.

"Good boy. You have a special mind. The way you see things. If I had the patience to figure out what you were saying sometimes, I know you'd make me a smarter man."

I didn't know what he was telling me, but I understood the flattering tone and appreciated it.

"And you're so relaxed. Hang on to that trait, son. That might serve you better than anything else in life."

"Yes, Father."

"It will also prove handy for upsetting your siblings." Then he leaned back and proceeded to have a heart attack.

I ran to him. He grabbed my arm and said, "Now, stay relaxed and go get help."

That turned out to be the first of four heart attacks he would suffer before just out and shooting himself one unseasonably warm February evening while Mother was off meeting with her bridge club. His suicide apparently came as no surprise to my mother, as she called each of us, in order of age, and said the same thing, "You must come home for your father's funeral."

Dinner was typical, nothing more or less. My mother said things that made my sister roll her eyes while she smoked an entire pack of imaginary cigarettes. Mother told me about telling all her bridge buddies about my books, asking as she always did if there wasn't a better word for *fuck* than *fuck*. Then my sister dropped me at my hotel and perfunctorily committed herself to lunch with me the next day.

I was scheduled to present my paper at nine the next morning, so my intention was to get to bed early and maybe sleep through it. However, when I entered my room I found a note that had been slipped under the door that told me to return a call to Linda Mallory at the Mayflower. I went to the lobby for the telephone.

"I was hoping you would come to the conference," Linda said. "The secretary in your department told me where you'd be staying."

"How are you, Linda?"

"I've been better. You know, Lars and I broke up."

"I didn't know you were together. I suppose asking who Lars is at this juncture is pointless."

"Are you tired? I mean, it's early yet and we are still on California clock, right?"

"Is that Bay area talk? *California clock?*" I looked at my watch. 8:20. "My paper's at nine in the morning."

"But it's only eight o'clock," she said. "That's five for us. You can't expect me to believe you're going to bed at five. I can be over in fifteen."

"No, I'll come there," I said, fearing that if I declined completely, she would show up anyway. "I'll meet you in the bar."

"There's one of those little bars in my room."

"In the bar at eight-forty-five." I hung up.

Linda Mallory and I had slept together three times, two of those times we had sex. Twice in Berkeley when I was doing some readings and once in Los Angeles when she was down doing the same. She was a tall, knock-kneed, rather shapeless-however-thin woman with a weak chin and a sharp wit, a sharp wit when men and sex weren't involved at any rate. She zeroed in on male attention like a Rottweiler on a porkchop and it became all she could see. In fact, before her ears perked to male attention she could be called attractive, dark eyes and thick hair, lean and with an easy smile. She liked to fuck, she said, but I believed she liked saying it more than doing it. She could be pushy. And she was completely without literary talent, which was both irritating and, in a weird way, refreshing. Linda had published one volume of predictably strange and stereotypically *innovative* short fictions (as she liked to call them). She'd fallen into a circle of *innovative* writers who had survived the sixties by publishing each others' stories in their periodicals and each others' books collectively, thus amassing publications, so achieving tenure at their various universities, and establishing a semblance of credibility in the so-called real world. Sadly, these people made up a good portion of the membership of the *Nouveau Roman* Society. They all hated me. For a couple of reasons: One was that I had published and had moderate success with a realistic novel some years earlier, and two, I made no secret, in print or radio interviews, what I thought of their work. Finally, however, I was hated because the French, whom they so adored, seemed to hold my work in high regard. To me, a mere strange footnote to my obscure and very quiet literary career. To them, a slap in the face perhaps.

Linda was already in the bar when I arrived. She wrapped me up in a hug and I remembered how much like a bicycle she had felt in bed.

"So," she said, in that way people use the word to introduce beating around the bush. "We had to come three thousand miles to see each other when we live in the same state."

"Funny how things work out."

We sat and I ordered a scotch. Linda asked for another Gibson. She played with the onion in her glass, stabbing it with the red plastic sword.

"Are you on the program?" I asked. I hadn't seen her name, but then I hadn't looked.

"I'm on a panel with Davis Gimbel, Willis Lloyd and Lewis Rosenthal."

"What's the panel?" I asked.

"'The Place of Burroughs in American Fiction.'"

I groaned. "Sounds pleasant enough."

"I saw the title of your paper. I don't get it." She ate the onion off her sword just as our drinks arrived. "What's it about?"

"You'll hear it. I'm sick of the damn thing. It's not going to make me any friends, I'll tell you that." I looked around the bar and saw no familiar faces. "I can just feel the creepiness here."

"Why did you come then?" she complained.

"Because this way my trip is paid for." I swallowed some scotch and was sorry I hadn't requested a water back. "I'd rather admit to that than say I came here because I care about the proceedings of the NRS."

"You have a point." Linda ate her second onion. "Would you like to go up to my room?"

"Smooth," I said. "What if we don't have sex and say we did?" After an awkward spell, I said, "So, how's Berkeley?"

"It's fine. I'm up for tenure this year."

"How does it look?" I asked, knowing full well it couldn't look good for her.

"Your family's here," she said.

"My mother and sister." I finished my scotch and became painfully aware that I had nothing to say to Linda. I didn't know enough about her personal life to ask questions and I didn't want to bring up her recent breakup, so I stared into my glass.

The waitress came over and asked if I wanted another drink. I said no and gave her enough for the two Gibsons and my scotch. Linda watched my hands.

"I'd better get some rest," I said. "I'll see you tomorrow."

"Probably."

The center of the tree is the heartwood. It does little to feed the tree, but it is the structural support. The sapwood, which feeds everything, is weak and prone to fungi and insect damage. The two look the same. But you want the heartwood. You always want the heartwood.

I grabbed breakfast alone in the cozy hotel dining room and then walked down Connecticut Avenue to the Mayflower. It was a chilly, gray morning and that shaded my mood, but also I simply felt lost, failing to understand why I had made the trip at all. I of course didn't care about the meeting and I had already seen enough of my family. There were more people than I expected to see at my session and I felt suddenly just a little nervous. There was really nothing at stake for me, or so I had convinced myself, in reading the paper I had written. Still, I was serious about it and knew that I would step on a few toes, though I was near as sure that it would take them a couple extra beats to actually become insulted.

The first paper read was a surprisingly easy-to-follow, albeit boring and inconsequential, discussion of Beckett and what he would have written had he lived longer and been met with a different kind of acceptance. Then it was my turn and I was greeted with a certain clearing of throats and not-quite-muttering, showing me, at least, that my reputation had, if not preceded me, then arrived with me. I read my paper:

F/V: PLACING THE EXPERIMENTAL NOVEL

F/V: a novel excerpt

(1) S/Z * The title perhaps answers any question before it is raised, making it in some sense an anti-title, but a title nonetheless, thus offering the suggestion of negation. So, is the title the name of a work or the name of a mere shadow of a work? In establishing its own subject, ostensibly Balzac's Sarrasine, it raises the question of whether that text is indeed its subject. And of course it is not, as S/Z tells us, its subject is the elusive model of that thing which Sarrasine might be argued to be a representation. Like Barthes, let us designate as hermeneutic code (HER) "all the units whose function is to articulate in various ways a question, its response and the variety of chance events which can either formulate the question or delay its answer; or even, constitute an enigma and lead to its solution." ** The S/Z refers no doubt to the unvoiced and voiced, but the enigma pales in consideration of the slash which separates them. The "/" at once combines the S and the Z into the title/anti-title and divides them, equally, but not so, as the S precedes the Z. The "/" is also that line which we have come to accept as the greasy and shifting mark, however dimensionless, between the signifier and the signified. The slashed whole connotes the cut text, the injured text or perhaps merely the fragmented text (which is either a lie of the writerly or a necessity of the readerly). The separated letters hold together as an indication of the containment of opposites and the necessity of their union in context, illustrating the impossibility of the individual consideration or the definitional bounding of the two, the "slash" or "/" being not only glue, but wedge. The "/" itself becomes a signifier and in each reference to the title it will be a sliding, conflicting element which behaves similarly to its function between S and Z, which is to say, any way it pleases or does not please. We shall indicate this element of the "/" as a signifier or seme or any tacit or voiced reference to its notion by using the abbreviation SEM, designating each time a concept (word) contains in it an implied "/," e.g. sick (SEM. well) or sick (SEM. crazy).

(2) There are said to be certain buddhists whose ascetic practices enable then to see a whole landscape in a bean. * There are "certain" buddhists, even two might be enough, and we are not to read the majority of buddhists or common, usual buddhists. Is it the perjorative "certain" as in, "There are certain people in this room who are not wel-

come?" Or perhaps, "certain" means to say that those buddhists are assured, without doubt, steadfast in the beliefs. Before we enter the first sentence fully we are trapped by our first puzzle (HER. certainty). "Certain" is a word, the connotative import of which we cannot be certain. Unless, of course, given its possible meanings, we are to attend to only certain ones.

Pausing and backing up we have before the first sentence I. Evaluation. Is the "I" the Roman numeral one or is it the English pronoun I. "I" followed by a period (HER. period), connoting an extremely short sentence or, a mark of finality connoting the end of the self (SEM. self), thus casting away responsibility for the text to follow. And of evaluation, are we to attach this word to I which precedes it or to the text which follows? If the former, does it reiterate the shedding of culpability?

The "ascetic practices enable them" is curious as it seems to personify and give credit to the practices of the buddhists as if they exist in the world apart from their practitioners. It is because of these things we call practices that it is buddhists who are enabled and not catholics or muslims. Though the term practices is vague here, we might reasonably take it to mean "certain practices," so practices (SEM. buddhists) becomes attached via the "I," in that special way, to those whom it enables (SEM. practices) . . . to see a whole landscape in a bean. * What must it be to see a whole landscape anywhere, as our vision must stop somewhere, peripherally left and right, and away from us at the horizon. So, is the whole landscape always a fragment of a greater landscape? Or are we to understand that all landscapes exist as fragments and that those fragments are in themselves whole? A landscape can only be seen whole "in a bean" and therefore the trick which is enabled by the practices is really not so special at all. And why "in a bean" and not in a glass marble or within the footprint or in a close-up photograph of a face. The bean is present and therefore means something (even if it means nothing [SEM. Zen]) and we shall refer to units in this symbolic area with SYM. The bean of course implies the seed which it both is and contains, being what it is and that from which it comes. It is its own birth, complete and whole, from the ground, the land and so, is complete as a picture of itself, a landscape. This growth from the self while being the self is the ultimate action. We shall refer to such actions with ACT and we shall number each of the terms which constitute it as they appear (ACT. in a bean: (1) what is seen; (2) the seed of itself; (3) the idea of itself . . .). Finally, it is not the buddhist whom we should find interesting, but the bean.[1]

---

1. A pause here, as within the subject text, to make clear what has in fact already been offered, that being the five major codes under which all the textual signifiers

(3) Precisely what the first analysts of narrative were attempting: to see all the world's stories. * Precisely is terribly imprecise, as the "first analysts" were not trying to see a landscape in a bean, but rather define the necessary and sufficient conditions for calling a story a story. So, "precisely" is ironic, quietly claiming that the subject text is above the pedestrian efforts of the "first analysts" (SEM. precision). What is implied by reference to the likeness in mission of the buddhists and the first analysts is that the buddhists are not in fact among the first analysts. Those bean-gazing, fat boys have no need for the establishment of narrative model because the model is already contained in the bean. Precisely—the buddhists do not look to the bean for a representative landscape, but for the landscape therein contained. Theirs is not to extract the essential quality which makes that thing what it is, but to see it completely, in which case attention to particular features might well destroy the achievement we have been told we should admire. Is our first analyst to be Aristotle and his concern with praxis and proairesis? Or shall we wonder about the prehistorics who must weigh the telling of two descriptions of events and decide which is true and which is fabrication, the assumption here being that telling the truth requires only remembering, while offering a fabrication requires a picture of what

------

can be categorized. They are, in no order of importance, but of appearance: The hermeneutic code comprises terms which imply, suggest, embody, contain, protract, disclose and/or solve enigma. Semes exist without connection to character, place or thing, and are listed to achieve some semblance of thematic congregation: We are instructed to allow them "the instability of dispersion, characteristic of motes of dust, flickers of meaning." (In other words, free associative mumbo jumbo is not a bad way to install or jumpstart meaning or, more to the point, interest.) As well, there is to be no structuring of the symbolic grouping, but generous allowance for multivalence and reversibility. The opposite might well be the meaning of the text, since every positive carries with it some understanding of its negation. Actions (terms of the proairetic code) are merely listed, as any sequence of the terms is "never more than the result of an artifice of reading," the reading accumulating a list of generic titles for those things done (sitting, dying, exploding, nodding off), such titles embodying sequences, the sequence existing because it is named, revealing itself in and by the very process of naming, the title is not the product of logical deduction or induction, and empirical only in the sense that the title is established for some reason (logic aside). Finally, and rather easily defined, the cultural codes are references to a system of knowledge or type of knowledge (medical, literary, historical . . .), indicating the body of knowledge without expression of the resident culture (REF. culture).

a telling of the truth might sound like. But maybe we are simply to choose the Russian formalists and leave it at that (SYM. analysts). And they are attempting (ACT. attempting) to undercover this model, the obvious implication being that they have failed. One never says of a man who has struck the motherlode, "He is attempting to find gold." (SEM. attempt) . . . to see all the world's stories * Embedded here is already the conclusion that there is this universal story (REF. story). The naming has done either the damage or the work and cannot be undone. The naming has created the thing itself and to then go look for that which makes it that thing is to fail to acknowledge that in the first place its existence must be verified; having been named not constituting the same as really being (REF. unicorn).

(4) . . . (and there have been ever so many) within a single structure: we shall, they thought, extract from each tale its model, then out of these models we shall make a great narrative structure, which we shall reapply (for verification) to any one narrative . . . * As if there have been stones of which it has been said, "Is this story?" and really meaning it, instead of meaning what a lousy story it in fact is. At best, the effort seems a response to the commercial picture of the publisher saying to the writer, "You call this a story?" But this digression takes the whole of the notion (though a fragment of the text) and falls outside the spirit of the analysis. so many (HER. many SEM. many) ** seems ironic, even contentious, seeming to laud the productivity of the makers of stories, yet offering the comment parenthetically, thus compartmentalizing the writers of stories without ever mentioning them. they thought (SEM, thought HER they REF. they) *** an obvious announcement of the failure to complete their mission. The rest tells us what they expect from the beans into which they stare, but "they thought" renders their beans blank. And so we come to dismantling of the endeavor as the endeavor of the text at hand, Sarrasine, not being chosen as a model at all, but accepted as one treated in a way which in turn is a model for the treatment of other texts, as is this text. A reiteration of the obvious is never wasted on the oblivious.

When I was done, there was a tentative smattering of applause and then a nerve-dulling silence while people tried to figure if they were offended and why. As I stepped back toward my seat a ball of keys flew past my head and hit the flocked wallpaper. I looked into the audience to find Davis Gimbel, the editor of a journal called *Frigid Noir.*

Gimbel shook his fist in the air and shouted, "You bastard!"

I could tell immediately that he hadn't understood a word of what I had read; his reaction seemed inappropriate and extreme. But he was eager to appear as though comprehension had come quickly to him.

Linda Mallory was in the audience and we shared a look. She indicated with a nod that she thought my paper was all right and offered a single, quiet, continued applause. I picked up Gimbel's keys and tossed them back to him.

"You will no doubt need these," I said. These words too were taken as an insult and Gimbel, a man who fancied himself a kind of Hemingway, moved toward me as if to fight. He was restrained quickly by his entourage, a changing but constant stable of four young, aspiring writers who would evaporate and be replaced by the next crop.

"I didn't mean to hurt your feelings, Gimbel," I said. I could already tell that the session was going to be the talk of the meeting, that it was going to take on a life of its own and become the kind of thing these talentless puds thrived on. "Which part bothered you most?"

"You, you mimetic hack," Gimbel spat at me.

"A mimetic hack," I repeated his words. "Okay." I glanced at the door and saw people already bolting for the outside, where they would offer their versions of *the fight* and say, "I was sitting right next to Gimbel when it all started" or "I couldn't believe it when Ellison hurled the keys right back at him." Anyway, I left the room, everyone giving me a wide berth, out of fear or reverence, I could not tell.

I arrived back at my hotel to find a death threat scrawled across the back of a bookmark. It said: *I'll kill you, you mimetic Philistine*, signed: *The Ghost of Wyndham Lewis.* I wasn't worried about the acting out of any such threats, as the clowns who had taken me as their enemy were as unlikely to actually do something as they were to actually write something.

Story idea. A woman gives birth to an egg. She goes in for a normal delivery and what comes out is an egg, a six-pound-three-ounce egg. The doctors don't know what to do, so they slap a diaper on it and stick in an incubator. Nothing happens. Then they have the mother sit on it. Nothing happens. The egg is given to the mother to hold. She falls in love with the egg, calls it her baby. The egg has no limbs to move, no voice with which to cry. It is an egg and only an egg. The woman takes the egg home, names it, bathes it, worries about it. It is unchanging, ungrowing, but it is her "baby," she says. Her husband leaves. Her friends don't come over. She talks to the egg, tells her she loves it. The egg cracks . . .

Went to my sister's clinic over in Southeast. Washington hides its poverty better than any city in the world. Just blocks from the mall and Capitol Hill, where thousands of tourists mill about each day, people cover their windows with towels to keep out the rain, and nail boards across their doors when they lock up at night. Though my sister lived up above Adams-Morgan, she practiced in Southeast, "where the people lived." She was tougher than I could ever be.

I walked in through the front door and ten women's faces turned to me together, demanding to know what I was doing there. I went to the receptionist's desk.

"I'm Thelonious Ellison, Dr. Ellison's brother," I said.

"You're kidding me." The receptionist was not fat, but there was plenty of her. She got up, came around her desk and gave me a squeeze. I sank into her, thinking that was what a hug should feel like. "The writer brother," she said, stepping back to look at me. "And fine." She called back down the hall. "Eleanor, Eleanor."

"What?" Eleanor asked.

"We got us a real writer in here."

"What?"

"Dr. E's brother."

Eleanor came and hugged me too. She was wearing her stethoscope, but that melted into her ample bosom as she crushed me. "Doctor E's with a patient right now."

"Yeah, honey," the receptionist said, beside herself with smiling. "You have a seat and I'll tell her you're here. If you need anything, you call my name, Yvonne, okay?"

I sat in an empty, thinly upholstered, orange chair beside a young woman with curling, blue fingernails. She had a little boy with a runny nose sitting on her lap.

"Handsome boy," I said. "How old is he?"

"Two years," she said.

I nodded. The chair was more comfortable than I expected a waiting room chair to be and I felt the artificial pressures of my day fading away, trailing off to a whisper in that din of reality.

"So, what are you doing here in Washington?" Yvonne asked me from her desk.

"Came in for a meeting," I said.

"You must be important to be coming into Washington for a meeting like that," she said.

I shook my head and laughed. "No, it's just a meeting of the *Nouveau*

Roman Society. Hardly important. I read a paper this morning and now I'm done."

Yvonne looked at me as if my words were getting lost in the space between us. She nodded her head without looking directly at me and went back to her work on the desk. I felt awkward, out of place, like I had so much of my life, like I didn't belong.

"You write books?" the woman with the child asked.

"Yes."

"What kind of books you write?"

"I write novels," I said. "Stories." Already feeling out of place, I now didn't know how to sound relaxed.

"My cousin gave me *Their Eyes Were Watching God*. She had it in a class. She goes to UDC. I liked that book."

"That's a really fine novel," I said.

"She gave me *Cane,* too," the young woman said, adjusting her son on her lap. "That one's my favorite."

"Great book."

"It ain't a novel though, is it?" she asked. "I mean, it ain't just one story and it's got them poems in it. But it seemed like one thing, know what I mean?"

"I know exactly what you mean."

"I think about that story 'Box Seat' and I think I'm in that theater all the time, watching them midgets fight." She shook her head as if to come back around, wiped her child's nose.

"Have you gone to college?" I asked.

The girl laughed.

"Don't laugh," I said. "I think you're really smart. You should at least try."

"I didn't even finish high school."

I didn't know what to say to that. I scratched my head and looked at the other faces in the room. I felt an inch tall because I had expected this young woman with the blue fingernails to be a certain way, to be slow and stupid, but she was neither. I was the stupid one.

"Thank you," I said to the girl.

She didn't respond to that and, luckily, was called back to an examination room at that moment.

Lisa came out in her white jacket and her stethoscope slung around her neck. I'd never seen her in her element before. She seemed so calm, at ease, in charge. I was proud of her, in awe of her. I got up and though her half of the hug was stiff, mine was not and it worked to soften the whole thing. She was taken by surprise and even blushed a little.

"I've got to see two more patients and then we can go," she said. "You're lucky, no picketers today. They must be in church or at a coven meeting. You're okay out here?"

"Yes, Yvonne is taking care of me," I said, but the receptionist had cooled to me. She offered a mechanical smile and wagged the eraser of her pencil in the air. "I'll be waiting."

When I was fifteen, my friend Doug Glass, that really was his name, asked me if I wanted to ride over to a party with him. This was during the summer in Annapolis. He was a year older and had his own car. I was excited to go. When we got there the music was loud and unfamiliar, the bass thumping. The air was full of male voices trying to dig down another octave and girls' giggles. We stood out on the lawn first and I held onto a beer in a plastic cup until it was warm. I hadn't acquired a taste for it yet and, to tell the truth, I was afraid it might make me throw up. We were in a part of Annapolis I'd never visited before, but I could see the spire of the capitol building, so I knew about where I was.

"Yo, brother, what's yo name?" a tall boy asked me, blowing cigarette smoke not quite in my face. "I'm Clevon."

"Monk," I said.

"Monk?" he laughed. "What the fuck kind of name is *Monk?*"

Right at that second I didn't want to tell him my real name was Thelonious.

Another guy came up and the tall one said, "Hey, Reggie, this here is, now get this, *Monk.*"

"Kinda looks like a monkey, don't he?" Reggie said.

"What's your real name?" Clevon asked.

"Ellison," I said.

"That your first name or your last name?"

"Last."

"What's your first name?"

"Theo," I lied.

Clevon and Reggie looked at each other and shrugged, as if to say Theo was an okay name not worthy of ridicule.

"Why they call you Monk, little brother?" Reggie asked.

I didn't like the way "little brother" sounded. "Just a nickname," I said.

Doug came back over to me and said, "Come on, Monksie, let's go inside."

"Monksie," Clevon and Reggie repeated into their cupped hands as they chuckled.

"Let's go back to the beach," I said to Doug, following him toward the house. "This is boring."

"Let's go inside first. Don't you want to see some girls?"

As a matter of fact, I did want to see girls, more than anything. But what I was going to do when I saw them was anybody's guess. I just hoped none of them would call me *little brother* or ask me my name.

The lights were dim inside and the center of the floor, of what I took to be the living room, was studded with gyrating dancers. Doug started bopping and pointing at people as we moved across to the other side. I didn't know Doug all that well, but still I was amazed that he was familiar with so many people. He stopped beside a couple of girls. They had to nearly shout to be heard over the music.

"Some party!" Doug said.

"Yeah," the girl said.

"This your sister?" Doug asked.

"Yeah."

Then they watched the dance floor for a while. Doug was now my hero, the way he had talked to that girl was amazing to me. Then he turned to her when a slow song came on and said, "Dance?"

"Yeah."

I was left with the sister. She was pretty, wearing a skimpy sundress which showed her shoulders. There was a turning light somewhere and every few seconds her neck and thighs became clear to my view. Her skin was beautiful. She caught me looking and I apologized.

"I'm Tina," she said.

"Ellison," I said.

"Dance?"

"Okay."

I worried about more things in the following three minutes than I ever had in my life. Had I put on deodorant? Had I brushed my teeth? Were my hands too dry? Were my hands too moist? Was I moving too fast? Was I actually leading? Was my head on the correct side of hers? I held her loosely, but she pulled me close, pressing into me. Her breasts were alarmingly noticeable. Her thighs brushed my thighs and as it was summer I was wearing shorts and could feel her skin against mine and it was just slightly too much for my hormonal balancing act. My penis grew steadily larger through the song until I knew that it was peeking out the bottom edge of the left leg of my pants. Tina became aware of it and said something which I couldn't make out, but included the words "baby" and "all right." Then someone switched on the lights and I heard the voices of Clevon and Reggie saying, "Look at Monkey's monkey." I ran out of the house and down the street toward the Capitol.

I made my way to the city dock where I found my older brother with the family boat and some of his friends. He asked if I was okay and I told him I was and asked if I could hang out with him. He looked at the other guys and grudgingly, he said yes. They were awkward with me there and didn't say much and one by one they peeled away and left us.

"Climb out there and untie us," Bill said. "How'd you get over here?" He started the motor and got us moving.

"Doug drove me. Took me to a party. We got separated."

"Oh."

"Did I mess up your party?" I asked.

"No, don't worry about it." I listened to the familiar thumping of the Evinrude and began to relax. The water of the bay seemed so peaceful to me. I looked at the sky.

Lisa and I drove over to the Capitol Grill and found a booth under an elk's head. "Why do you like to eat here?" I asked her.

"I don't know, something about all these boys making decisions." She sipped her tea. "Okay, I've got one for you. You're in a boat and your motor cuts out, but you're in shallow water, but you're wearing two-hundred-dollar trousers, but your ride to the airport is just about to drive away from the beach. Why is this a legal issue?"

I shook my head.

"Because it's a matter of Row versus Wade." She smiled a smile I hadn't seen in many years. "Lame, eh?"

"Did you make that up?"

"I stay up late, what can I say." Lisa looked about the room, then back at me. "It's good to see you, little brother."

"Thanks. It's good to see you, too. You know, I'm really proud of you. Dad would be proud of you as well. That clinic."

"It's not very glamorous."

"I don't know what that has to do with anything." I noticed a man at the bar staring at us. "Do you know him?" I asked.

Lisa turned to see and the man looked away. "Nope. Why?"

"He just seemed interested in you for some reason."

"That would be nice."

"I'm sorry about what happened with Barry. I always thought he was a joke."

"You said as much way back when." Lisa laughed. "Remember how mad I got at you?"

The waiter came and took our orders. He smiled at Lisa as he put away his pad. "How's it going, Doc?"

"Fine, Chick, what about with you? Chick, this is my brother, Monk. He's visiting from California."

I shook the man's hand. "Chick." I watched him walk away and smiled at my sister. "He likes you."

"Maybe, but I think he used to date Bill."

"Oh." We sat there thinking about Bill for a while until I felt I'd thought about him long enough and said, "I had a rather nice conversation with one of your patients. I didn't get her name. She had a little boy with her and blue nails."

"I know who you're talking about. That's Tamika Jones. Tamika Jones actually has two children. The little boy with her today is named Mystery."

"Mystery?"

"That's right. And her daughter's name is Fantasy."

"Mystery and Fantasy."

"Named after their fathers. One was a mystery and the other a fantasy."

"You're kidding me."

"I wish."

"I make up shit for a living and I couldn't have come up with that." The man from the bar was staring again, but when I caught him he got up, left the bar and headed for the door. "Sometimes I feel like I'm so removed from everything, like I don't even know how to talk to people."

"You don't," Lisa said. "You never have. It's not a bad thing. You're just different."

"Different from whom?"

"Don't get defensive. It's not a bad thing. Actually, it's a good thing. I've always wanted to be like you."

It used to be that I would look for the deeper meaning in everything, thinking that I was some kind of hermeneutic sleuth moving through the world, but I stopped that when I was twelve. Though I would have been unable to articulate it then, I have since come to recognize that I was abandoning any search for elucidation of what might be called subjective or thematic meaning schemes and replacing it with a mere delineation of specific case descriptions, from which I, at least, could make inferences, however unconscious, that would allow me to understand the world as it affected me. In other words, I learned to take the world as it came. In other words still, I just didn't care.

When I was thirteen and my sister was sixteen, she caught me masturbating with a magazine in the front basement. When she asked me what I was doing, I said, "Masturbating."

My response was so casual that it gave her pause. As I was fastening my belt, she said, "You're a pervert."

"I might be," I said. "I don't know what a pervert is."

"Well, you'd better not let Mother and Father catch you doing that. That's all I have to say."

"I hadn't planned on it. And what if they did? Would they take it away

from me?" My point made, I turned my attention back to the centerfold of
my magazine.

"Where did you get that?" she asked. She glanced up the stairs at the
closed basement door.

"I bought it." Then to make her relax, "Father's at the office and
Mother won't come down here because of the spiders."

"It's normal," Lisa said, as if suddenly concerned about my scarring
psychically.

"What's normal?"

"Masturbation."

"Do you do it?"

"No," she said and turned red, leaned to start up the stairs.

"Thanks," I said.

"For what?"

"For telling me it's normal."

"Okay," she said.

"It's normal if you don't do it, too," I said.

I gave a long look at Lisa's cheeseburger as she pulled off the onions
with her fork and set them at the side of her plate.

"Still not eating meat?" she asked.

"I eat it occasionally," I said.

"One burger won't kill you."

I poured the oil and vinegar on my salad and nodded. "I appreciate
that you have to do everything here with Mother," I said. "I know it's not
fair."

"The way it worked out."

"Can I help in any way?"

"Yeah, you can move to D.C." She looked me in the eye and then
smiled. "If I need you, I'll call you. There is one thing." When I looked at
her, she put down her fork and remembered cigarettes. "Mother's running
out of money."

"But I thought—"

"So did I, but it's running out anyway."

"I don't have much. I don't make anything on my books."

"Don't sweat it," she said. "I was just letting you know."

Now, I was feeling awful, like a failure, letting both my sister and my mother down. Living in my own little bubble I had never thought about these things. I felt myself sinking.

After lunch, my sister asked if I'd stop at a bookstore with her, said she wanted to pick up something for one of her staff who had just had a baby. I asked if she wanted to give her one of my books and Lisa said that she'd prefer to give the woman something she could read. Then she laughed and I guess I laughed with her.

While Lisa wandered off to the garden book section, I stood in the middle of Border's thinking how much I hated the chain and chains like it. I'd talked to too many owners of little, real bookstores who were being driven to the poorhouse by what they called the WalMart of books. I decided to see if the store had any of my books, firm in my belief that even if they did, my opinion about them would be unchanged. I went to Literature and did not see me. I went to Contemporary Fiction and did not find me, but when I fell back a couple of steps I found a section called African American Studies and there, arranged alphabetically and neatly, read *undisturbed*, were four of my books including my *Persians* of which the only thing ostensibly African American was my jacket photograph. I became quickly irate, my pulse speeding up, my brow furrowing. Someone interested in African American Studies would have little interest in my books and would be confused by their presence in the section. Someone looking for an obscure reworking of a Greek tragedy would not consider looking in that section any more than the gardening section. The result in either case, no sale. That fucking store was taking food from my table.

Saying something to the poor clone of a manager was not going to fix anything, so I resigned to keep quiet. Then I saw a poster advertising the coming reading of Juanita Mae Jenkins, author of the runaway bestseller, *We's Lives In Da Ghetto*. I picked up a copy of the book from the display and read the opening paragraph:

> *My fahvre be gone since time I's borned and it be just me an' my momma an' my baby brover Juneboy. In da mornin' Juneboy never do brushes his teefus, so I gots to*

remind him. Because dat, Momma says I be the 'sponsible one and tell me that I gots to holds things togever while she be at work clean dem white people's house.

I closed the book and thought I was going to throw up. My sister came up behind me.

"What's wrong?" she asked.

"Nothing," I said, dropping the book back onto the stack.

"What do you think of that book?" she asked. "I read it's going to be a movie. She got something like three million dollars for it."

"Really."

The reality of popular culture was nothing new. The truth of the world landing on me daily, or hourly, was nothing I did not expect. But this book was a real slap in the face. It was like strolling through an antique mall, feeling good, liking the sunny day and then turning the corner to find a display of watermelon-eating, banjo-playing darkie carvings and a pyramid of Mammy cookie jars. 3 million dollars.

My sister offered me the loan of her car for the afternoon if I'd pick her up from work. I dropped her off in front. The picketers were back. They spotted Lisa and began to shout at her. "Murderer! Murderer!" they said. I got out and walked with her through the line and to the door, realizing as I did so that she did it alone everyday, that I wasn't there to be the protective brother, that she didn't need me. Still, she accepted my escort graciously and told me she'd see me later. I started back to the car, catching good looks at the wild, sick, raging faces. One man held a huge poster with the picture of a mutilated fetus. He shook his fist at me. For a second, I thought I saw the face of the man who had been staring at us from the bar in the restaurant, but then he was gone.

Story idea—a man marries a woman whose name is the same as that of his first wife. One night while making love he says her name and the woman accuses him of calling out the name of his first wife. Of course he in fact has called out the name of his first wife, but also he has called out his present wife's name. He tells her that he was not thinking of his first wife, but she says she knows what she heard.

I drove around the city for a while, noting while doing so how it was possible to be comfortable inside an automobile. My sister had taken my compliment about her automobile as an offense and perhaps, in some way, that was how I had meant it. I had never understood spending so much money on a set of wheels. But I had to admit that it was comfortable, quiet and that it made sense that my sister would want to be able to unlock her car and turn on the lights from across a parking lot. Still, I felt out of place behind the wheel of the thing—what else was new. I drove through Georgetown, then up Wisconsin, then back across Massachusetts to Dupont Circle. I went to my mother's house, wanting to catch her before her nap. That way I'd be able to leave because of her coming "down time" and because I had to pick up Lisa.

"My Monksie is home," Mother said again.

We sat in the kitchen and she made tea. "You're looking great, Mother."

"Go on," she said. "I'm an old lady. I don't know about this tea, sweetheart. This woman who used to be one of your father's patients brought it to me."

"That was nice of her," I said.

"She's a sweet woman, but, lord, she's even older than I am. I can't seem to get it through to her that your father has passed away." She put the cups and saucers on the table.

"Where's Lorraine?" I asked.

"She's out doing the shopping."

I looked at the calendar on the wall. It was from last year, but on the correct month. "Mother, that calendar's out of date."

"Lisa keeps telling me that, but I can't remember to change it."

"Tell you what, I'll pick up a new one for you." As I said it, I wondered what kind of grief I might cause Lisa by buying Mother a new calendar. Would the old lady go on and on about where it came from? I could imagine the months peeling by and Lisa having to endure, *Would you look at that picture of the Grand Canyon. Monksie gave me that calendar. He noticed that the old one was out of date.*

"Here you go." Mother set the teapot down between our cups, then sat. "So, how was your meeting?"

"Fine," I said. "The paper went well and now I'm done."

"That's good," she said. She got up and turned the dial of the burner to off a second time, then sat back down.

"You should be careful burning things in that fireplace," I told her. "It's never been used. The flue is probably stuck shut."

"It did get sort of smoky in the living room."

"You shouldn't use it at all."

"I'm finished burning the things anyway." She poured the tea.

"What were you burning?" I asked.

"Just some papers. Your father gave me instructions when he was in the hospital. He said, 'Agnes, please burn the papers in the gray box in my study. Will you do that for me?' I told him I would and then he asked me to please not read them."

"So, did you?"

Mother shook her head. "Your father asked me not to."

I looked at the counter and saw a blue box sitting there. "You're not burning the stuff in that box too, are you?"

"That's what I burned. It did make the living room smoky. I never thought about the flue. That's why we never had a fire in this house. Because I'm afraid of fire."

"I knew that about you, Mother."

"Oh, I didn't offer you milk. Would you like some?"

"No thanks." I blew on the tea and drank some. "So, are you meeting with your club much these days?"

"Not so much. They're all dying off. Young women aren't interested in bridge anymore."

"From what I gathered you ladies never play bridge anyway."

"Is that what you gathered?" She laughed softly. "I suppose that's right."

I looked at her eyes and could see the fatigue. "Maybe you should stretch out for a while."

"I do feel a little tired. Lorraine's making dinner tonight. We'll eat at seven, but you can come at six for cocktails."

"Okay, Mother."

Anyone who speaks to members of his family knows that sharing a language does not mean you share the rules governing the use of that language. No matter what is said, something else is meant and I knew that for all my mother's seeming incoherence or out-of-itness, she was trying to tell me something over tea. The way she had mentioned the smoke in the living room twice. Her calling the blue box gray. Her easy and quick capitulation to what it was she and her cronies actually did at their meetings. But since I didn't know the rules, which were forever changing, I could only know that she was trying to say something, not what that something was.

For my father, the road had to wind uphill both ways and be as difficult as possible. Sadly, this was the sensibility he instilled in me when I set myself to the task of writing fiction. It wasn't until I brought him a story that was purposely confusing and obfuscating that he seemed at all impressed and pleased. He said, smiling, "You made me work, son." He once said to me in a museum, when I complained about an illegible signature on a painting, "You don't sign it because you want people to know you painted it, but because you love it." He was all wrong of course, but the sentiment was so beautiful that I wish to believe it now. What he might have been trying to say, I suppose, though he never would have even thought about it in these terms, was that art finds its form and that it is never a mere manifestation of life.

Lorraine had been the housekeeper since before I was born. She liked me as a child. She liked me as a young adult. But when she opened a book of mine and discovered the word *fuck*, she stopped liking me. From that point on she was polite, but curt, never overtly displeased by my presence, but clearly not anticipating any grief upon my departure. Lorraine, as far as I knew, never had a life away from my family. She had days off, but I didn't know where she went, if she went anywhere. She even went with us to the beach in the summers. But she was not our nanny. If we had a problem, we went to Mother. If we needed rides someplace, we went to Mother. If we needed food or clean clothes, we went to Lorraine.

"Good evening, Mr. Monk," she said as I entered the house with my sister.

"How are you, Lorraine?" I asked.

"Getting older every day."

"You don't look it," I said.

"Thank you."

Lisa took my jacket to hang in the closet as if I were a real visitor. I looked at the house again. I had loved the house as a kid. It was a large two-story with many rooms and nooks and a finished basement apartment in which Lorraine resided. But it now seemed cold, despite how high the heat was turned. The drapes covering the windows were heavy, the wood of the stairway bannister and door jambs dark and somber.

"Mrs. E is already at the table," Lorraine told us and led us into the dining room as if we didn't know the way.

Mother remained seated when we entered. Her eyes were red and weak. We leaned to kiss her and she patted our cheeks.

"Are you feeling okay, Mother?" Lisa asked.

"She missed her nap today, Dr. Lisa," Lorraine said.

We sat on either side of our mother. I poured the wine and Mother waved it off.

"Did you take your medication?" Lisa asked.

"I did. All three thousand pills." Mother fanned her off the subject. "How was your meeting?" she asked me, having forgotten our earlier conversation.

"It's over, that's the important part."

"You presented a paper?"

"Yes, Mother."

"On?"

"Just some stuff about novels and literary criticism. Dry, boring, meaningless stuff. I actually just came to see you."

"That's my sweetheart, Monksie. But why aren't you staying here with me?"

"Since I am at the conference, I need to be near the proceedings." I looked at my sister. "I did go down to Lisa's clinic earlier. She's really doing good work."

"She's just like her father." By the way she said it, it was not clear it was a good thing. Then she aked me, "Are you still driving that station wagon?"

"Yes, Mother."

Lorraine came in with the dinner. The roast beef was lean. The broccoli and cauliflower were overcooked and the grains of rice were so separate and distinct that it was near impossible to pick them up with a fork. Lorraine came in a couple of times to check on us.

Lisa put down her fork and picked up her wine glass, held it over her plate without drinking. "Mother, I've been going over the books and I believe you're going to have to sell Father's office. The upkeep is costing so much that the rent is meaningless."

"That was your father's office."

"Yes, Mother. You've got the other properties," Lisa said.

"Your father started out in that office in nineteen fifty. You weren't born yet. Bill was just a year old."

"Well, I'm putting the office up for sale. It's something we have to do." Lisa was tugging at the corners of her napkin, a tic she'd had since childhood.

"It was your father's office, dear."

"I know that, Mother." Lisa looked at me.

"Mother," I got her attention. "When's the last time you visited Father's office?" She didn't have an answer. "The fact is, you hardly ever went there when Father *was* practicing. Now, it's completely different. It even looks different from the outside." I reached over and took her hand. "Lisa knows what's best."

"Oh, Monksie." Mother sniffed in her tears. "You're such a sweet child, always have been. And so smart. You get that from your father, did you know that?"

I glanced over at Lisa to see that she was eating again.

"Of course, we'll sell the office."

"Just like that," Lisa said. "Monk chimes in and you're hooked on the idea. Christ."

Lorraine stepped into the room just in time to hear her lord's name used in vain. She collected our plates and issued an admonishing "Hmmph, hmmph, hmmmph" as she exited.

Mother complained of a headache and we had dessert without saying much. Then Lorraine came in and mercifully informed us of Mother's approaching bedtime. We kissed the old lady goodnight and watched Lorraine walk her upstairs.

Sitting in my sister's car outside my hotel, I apologized for butting in about the sale of the office at the dinner table.

"No, you helped," she said. "Thanks."

"I'm sorry she always reacts to me like that."

"Monk, you're special. I don't mean just the way Mother, and Father when he was alive, treated you. I've always thought that. I just wanted you to know."

I looked out the window at the street. "I think the same about you, you know."

"Yeah, I know." She smiled. Her smile had always been so confident that I was jealous of it. Her smile always made me relax.

I kissed my sister goodbye, told her I'd talk to her soon and went into my hotel where I found Linda Mallory waiting in the lobby.

"Hi, Linda."

"I've been thinking about your paper."

"I'm sorry."

"Would you like to go upstairs and fuck me?"

"No, Linda."

"I'm having a real crisis," she said. "I really need to have some sex. I need it for self-validation."

"I'm sorry, Linda."

She stormed past me, out the door and into the street. Then I heard my name being shouted from outside. It was a bit embarrassing as I turned to find the hotel staff and a couple of guests staring at me. I stepped out and on the narrow path leading through the yard was Davis Gimbel.

"A screaming comes across the sky. It has happened before, but there is nothing to compare it to now," he said.

The words had little effect on me, save to announce Gimbel's disturbed, certifiable, and agitated postmodern state. Behind the short, bomber-jacketed academic were Linda Mallory, seething with pent-up sexual frustration, and three other intellectually homeless academics aching to see a fight.

"What's this all about, Gimbel?" I asked.

"There's nothing to compare it to now," he said.

"Okay." I stepped down the steps to take the noise away from the stoop. "Listen, I'm sorry you didn't like the paper, but I believe you misunderstood something. I don't even think about you guys, much less write about you."

That really got him mad. He circled me as best he could in the small space and even pounded his chest with a closed fist once or twice. "You don't think much of postmodern fiction, do you?" he said. "Like all avant-garde movements, we never have time to finish what we set out to accomplish."

I looked at his face in the street and moon lights and found it no more or less ugly for its contorted state. "What did you set out to accomplish?"

"You know good and well. You and your kind, you interrupted us."

"My kind?" I let that go. "Interrupted you? By not paying attention?"

"The whole culture. You're just one of the sheep."

"What the hell are you talking about, man? Are you drunk?"

He continued his circling. A couple of unassociated people stopped at the gate to watch. "Of course, if an avant-garde movement ever achieves its purpose, then it ceases to be avant-garde. By the mere fact that it opposes or rejects established systems of creation, it has to remain unfinished. Do you even understand what I'm saying? We are defunct practitioners of defunct art."

"You know what your problem is, Gimbel?" I said, leaning away from him. "You actually think you're saying something that makes sense. Now, if you'll excuse me."

That's when the little Hemingway doll took a poke at me. I sidestepped the swing and watched him roll into an azalea bush. Linda and the other defunct artists rushed to his aid. I offered a shrug to the confused bystanders and stepped away toward the door.

Gimbel was on his knees now and he yelled, "Postmodern fiction came and went like the wind and you missed it. And that's why you're bitter, Ellison."

I stopped, not believing that the man had actually come to fight me because of a paper that I only barely took seriously. Standing over them all on the steps, I said, "I don't mean to disparage or belittle what you do, Gimbel. I don't know what you do."

Gimbel found his legs and stood straight, puffed up his chest. "I have unsettled readers. I have made them uncomfortable. I have unsettled their historical, cultural and psychological assumptions by disrupting their comfortable relationship between words and things. I have brought to a head the battle between language and reality. But even as my art dies, I create it without trying."

His little group applauded.

"Man, do you need to get laid," I said, shook my head and stepped through the door.

✗ ✗ ✗

It's 1933 and Ernst Barlach is cracking his knuckles while the cup of tea on the table in front of him cools. "My hands hurt so much these days," he says.

Paul Klee nods, sips his tea. He is saddened himself. He has just been expelled from the Düsseldorf Academy of Art. "They are calling me a Siberian Jew."

"Who is? Das Schwarze Korps?"

"Who else? And they are burning any books which contain pictures of our work. They call me a Slavic lunatic."

"They're correct about both of us."
Ernst laughs.

Eckhart: You know I have a novel, Adolf.
Hitler: Do tell, Dietrich.
Eckhart: I call it The Morning. *The main character is essentially myself. The character is an unrecognized literary genius who is addicted, but manages quite well the sweet gift of morphine.*
Hitler: I hope it is as powerful as your volume of poems. Such anguish and sheer beauty those verses offer the reader.
Eckhart: It irks me no end that the whole of my recognition rests on the translation of that damn Norwegian. I actually hate Peer Gynt.
Hitler: Oh, but how you transformed it. Now, it speaks to the German soul. That is why it is so popular with the people. And what the work led you to, your patriotic writings and how you've unveiled the Jews for what they are. I will fight the trolls with you.
Eckhart: They will destroy German culture if we let them.
Hitler: Then we will not let them.

Eckhart: I am ein Judenfresser.
Hitler: Me, too.
Eckhart: I can't believe we lost the war. These pamphlets of mine however will show our people why we lost and that the enemy we should fear most was not in the trenches.
Hitler: What is this one called?
Eckhart: I call this one Judaism in and out of Us.
Hitler: I liked Austria under Judah's Star.
Eckhart: Everyone seemed to like that one. I sent This is the Jew *to a professor and he sent it back to me with a note telling me it is full of hate. So, I wrote back. I wrote, "It is said that the German schoolmaster won the war of 1866. The professor of 1914 lost the World War."*
Hitler: You told him.
Eckhart: I have an idea for a newspaper, a weekly that I plan to call, Auf gut

Deutsch. *And I have been thinking. You should join the Thule Society.*
Hitler: I am already a member.
Eckhart: Shall we recite the motto together?
Hitler and Eckhart: Remember that you are German. Keep your blood
pure.

Somehow these notes for a novel came to me on my flight back to Los
Angeles. The faces of those nuts in front of my sister's clinic served as in-
spiration. But I must admit to a profound fascination with Hitler's relationship to art and how he so reminded me of so many of the artistic pur-
ists I had come to know. But those faces, washed with hate and fear,
wanting so badly to control others, their potato eyes so vacant, their
mouths near frothing. I could still hear them calling my sister a murderer.
Their voices had the scratch of overuse, like the twisting of metal.

On the plane I read a review in the *Atlantic Monthly* or *Harpers* of Juanita
Mae Jenkins' runaway bestseller *We's Lives In Da Ghetto:*

> *Juanita Mae Jenkins has written a masterpiece of African American literature.*
> *One can actually hear the voices of her people as they make their way through the ex-*
> *perience which is and can only be Black America.*
>
> *The story begins with Sharonda F'rinda Johnson who lives the typical Black life*
> *in an unnamed ghetto in America. Sharonda is fifteen and pregnant with her third*
> *child, by a third father. She lives with her drug addict mother and her mentally defi-*
> *cient, basketball playing brother Juneboy. When Juneboy is killed in a driveby by a*
> *rival gang, the bullet passing through his cherished Michael Jordon autographed*
> *basketball, Sharonda watches her mother's wailing grief and decides she must have*
> *some voice in the culture.*
>
> *Sharonda becomes a hooker to make enough money to take dance classes at the*
> *community center. In tap class, her athletic prowess is noticed by the producer of a*
> *Broadway show and she is discovered. She rises to the top, buys her mother a*
> *house, but her limitations catch up with her and she comes plummeting back to*
> *earth.*
>
> *The twists and turns of the novel are fascinating, but the real strength of the*

work is its haunting verisimilitude. The ghetto is painted in all its exotic wonder. Predators prowl, innocents are eaten. But the novel is finally not dark, as we leave the story, with Sharonda trying to raise enough money to get her babies back from the state. Sharonda, finally, is the epitome of the black matriarchal symbol of strength.

"Is something wrong?" the woman seated beside me asked.

It was raining when I arrived in Los Angeles. A real Southern California rain, which washed away hillsides and homes, flooded parts of Newport and Long Beach and backed up traffic on every freeway. I found that I was restless during my drive home, not because of the sea of unmoving tail lights in front of me, and not because of my having two more weeks of the semester left to teach, but because something was gnawing at me. I didn't know what it was; I had seen or heard something that struck me as wrong. I let it go; what else could I do? I finally made it to Santa Monica and my house, where I brushed my teeth, not so hard, as per instructions of the dentist, through his hygienist, as I never got to see the big man himself, but just hard enough to interrupt the formation of the plaque that was eating me away from the inside, and went to bed. My head on my pillow, I had a dream. First, of my father telling me the stories of how Paul Robeson once broke into song in Miss Madsen's Tea Room at the beach and how Paul Laurence Dunbar would stroll the pier reciting poetry, and then I was alone on that very pier, younger, but not so young that I was afraid of being alone there so late. The moon was full and bright and there was a corona about it. Way out, under the shine of the moon on the water, I imagined I could see the surface disturbed by a school of bluefish. Then my sister was with me and she was trying to tell me something, but she was, uncharacteristically, beating around the bush. "Are you asking for my help?" I asked her, but she just talked on, saying things I didn't understand, but the quality of them left no question as to her anxiety. "Is it

Mother?" I asked, but this too was met with chatter that, as soon as she spoke it, I forgot it. Until she said, "Did you see him?" I stopped her and asked, "See whom?" But she laughed at me for having said *whom* and would not come back to the subject. Then I awoke.

All propositions are of equal value.

The following morning, after a walk through the large back room that served as my woodshop, I got around to going through my mail and, as I expected, there was a letter from my agent, whom I had for some time been wondering whether to keep, as he seemed painfully, for me at least, resigned to the fact that my work was not commercial enough to make any real money. This was undoubtedly true, but nonetheless it seemed a part of his job to foster some kind of optimistic delusion on my part. Still, he was willing to take my work for what little return he saw. The letter from him was short, merely introducing the letter that had been sent to him, namely a rejection of my latest novel:

> *Dear Yul,*
>
> *Thanks for letting me to take a look at T. Ellison's lastest effort. Who am I kidding? Why did you bother sending it to me? It shows a brilliant intellect, certainly. It's challenging and masterfully written and constructed, but who wants to read this shit? It's too difficult for the market. But more, who is he writing to? Does the guy live in a cave somewhere? Come on, a novel in which Aristophanes and Euripides kill a younger, more talented dramatist, then contemplate the death of metaphysics?*
>
> *Thanks again.*
>
> *All Best,*
>
> *Hockney Hoover*

There are times when fishing that I feel like a real detective. I study the water, the lay of the land, seine the streambottom and look at the larvae of aquatic insects. I watch, look for hatches and terrestrial activity. I select my fly, one I've tied at streamside, plucking a couple of fibers from my sweater to mix with the dubbing to get just the right color. I present the fly while hiding behind a rock or in tall grass and wait patiently. Then there are times when I wrap pocket lint around a hook, splash it into the water while standing on a fat boulder. Both methods have worked and failed. It's all up to the trout.

Classes did end as all things must, and right on schedule, and with the welcome news that my promotion to professor had come through. But the news did nothing to erase my depression over the rejection of my novel, now the seventeenth one.

"The line is, you're not black enough," my agent said.

"What's that mean, Yul? How do they even know I'm black? Why does it matter?"

"We've been over this before. They know because of the photo on your first book. They know because they've seen you. They know because you're black, for crying out loud."

"What, do I have to have my characters comb their afros and be called niggers for these people?"

"It wouldn't hurt."

I was stunned into silence.

"Look at that Juanita Mae Jenkins book. It's sold like crazy. The paperback rights went for five hundred thousand."

In my mind, I had the generous thought, *Good for her*, but I didn't mean it. She was a hack. "She's a hack," I said. "She's not even a hack. A hack can actually write a little bit."

"Yeah, it's shit. I know that, but it sells. This is a business, Thelonious."

I didn't say another word, just set the receiver down in its cradle and stared at the phone.

While I was staring at the phone, it rang again. It was Lorraine and she was very upset.

"Is it my mother?" I asked. "Lorraine."

"No, it's Dr. Lisa."

'What about Lisa?"

"They shot her."

"What?"

"Dr. Lisa is dead."

I put the phone down because I didn't know what to do. My stomach was cold on the inside. I could feel my heart beating. I struggled to recall my brother's telephone number and dialed it.

"Bill, I just got a call from Lorraine."

"Yeah, me, too."

"See you at the house."

Often, I would simply cut wood. The smell of it, the feel of it, the sound of the saws, manual or power, tearing through it. I would practice bevels with the router, miter cuts, add to my pile of tapered legs. I wanted to turn on the table saw and rip a plank, but I had to drive to the airport. I had to go see what Lorraine had meant when she said that my sister was dead. I had to meet Bill at Mother's and figure out why Lisa wasn't there. I'd get on the plane knowing virtually nothing. If the passenger beside me were to ask the purpose of my trip, I'd have to tell him I didn't know. Perhaps I would say, "Lorraine said they shot my sister" and then the person beside me would know as much as I.

It's incredible that a sentence is ever understood. Mere sounds strung together by some agent attempting to mean some thing, but the meaning need not and does not confine itself to that intention. Those sounds, strung as they are in their peculiar and particular order, never change, but do nothing but change. Even if grammatical recognitions are crude, meaning is present. Even if the words are utterly confusing, there is meaning. Even if the semantic relationships are only general or categorical. Even if the language is unknown. Meaning is internal, external, orbital, but still there is no such thing as propositional content. Language never really effaces its own presence, but creates the illusion that it does in cases where meaning presumes a first priority.

A metaphor cannot be paraphrased.

X X X

It wasn't difficult to conclude that Bill was a homosexual, whether it was true or not. He liked being with men in a way different from the way heterosexual men liked being with men. Effeminate behavior, I learned when young, served as no measure of sexual orientation. My gym teacher, whom I imagined eating rail spikes for breakfast, was gay and I knew it not because he held his hands a certain way, not because he made a pass at me, not because he would park himself by the showers and listen to us bathe, but because I saw him late one night walking hand in hand with another man. At first I was shocked, but I caught myself. What I really felt was envy. He seemed so happy, holding his friend's hand, enjoying the evening. I wanted to hold a hand too, albeit a girl's hand, but a hand nonetheless.

Bill would date girls, but was cranky the while. I don't know if Father and Mother ever suspected anything. If they had I'm sure the scene would have been ugly. My parents talked rather badly about the *queens* that paraded the street near my father's office, but, more than anything, thinking of sexual preference, or that there was sexual preference, didn't exist. My father had a term, which I heard once, for a homosexual man and that was *Eye. I* never did discover how the word came to mean anything.

X X X

I was driving up Highway 395 on my way to fish the South Fork of the Kern. At the junction of 178 and 395 I stopped for a bite. It was summer and dusk was coming on and so it was late enough and still eerie enough for the weirdos to be out. I sat in a booth and was called "sugar" by the middle-aged waitress while a couple of guys spoke French to each other in the booth behind me. When traveling, it is best to eat without regard to health or one might not eat at all. I was carving into what was called a chicken fried steak and was unable to detect chicken or steak, but it was clear that it was indeed fried, when a couple of stringy, gimme-capped, inbred bohunks came noisily into the restaurant. Their keen hearing, though it did not allow them to know it was French, picked up the annoying cadence of a "fern" language. They sat at the counter and cast more than a few glances toward the French-speaking men, until they could take it no longer and walked over to them.

"You boys funny?" The skinnier and taller of the two asked.

"Funny?" one of the Frenchmen asked.

"You know, queers," from the second long-fingernailed, backwoods, walking petri dish.

"Ah, queers," the Frenchman said. "Oui."

"Oui," from bumpkin number one, who looked at his buddy and shared a laugh. "Come on outside so we can kick your ass."

"I don't understand," the second Frenchman said.

Bumpkin two must have stepped or leaned closer. I registered the alarmed expression on the face of the waitress, who then called out that she didn't want any trouble.

"Outside, faggots. You ain't chickens, are you? It's two against two. That's fair."

"Actually, it's two against three," I said. I put the bite that was on my fork into my mouth.

Bumpkin one stepped over to look at me, then laughed to his pal, "I think we got the nigger riled."

I chewed my food, trying to remember all the posturing I had learned as an undersized teenager.

"You a faggot, too?" he asked.

I pointed to the fact that I was chewing. This confused him slightly and I could see for a split second his fear. "I might be," I said.

"So, you want to fight, too."

I didn't want to fight, but the fact of the matter was that I was already fighting. I said, and still I am proud of it, "Okay, if we're going to do this, let's do it. Just remember that this is one of the more important decisions you will ever make."

I'd overshot my mark. His fear grew and turned into rage and he hopped back and yelled for me to get up. I was afraid now that I might really have to do something I didn't do very well, throw punches. I stood and though I wasn't a skinny wire, I was not much larger than either of them. The second bumpkin yelled for the gay men to get up, too.

They did and I wished I'd had a camera to capture the expressions of

those two provincial slugs. The Frenchmen were huge, six-eight and better, and healthy looking. The rubes stumbled over themselves backing
away, then scrambled out of the diner.

I was laughing when the men asked me to join them, not at the spectacle of the rednecks running out, but at my own nerve and audacity, to pre-
sume that they needed my help.

C'est plus qu'un crime, c'est une faute.

I imagined my sister treating a patient, a little girl with a name my sister despised, looking into her ears, joking with her, asking her if purple
was her favorite color because that was the color of her throat. The child
laughed and my sister said something stern to the mother, wrote out a
prescription for antibiotics. She walked the mother and child down the
corridor to the front, where a scared teenager fidgeted in her chair on seeing my sister. The receptionist said something to my sister and handed her
a chart. She took the pen from her jacket breast pocket and checked a
couple of places, initialed a couple of places. Then the little girl tugged at
my sister's skirt and all sound stopped while my sister offered the child a
raised-eyebrows glance. The sound came back. Broken glass, screams, the
squawking of chairs against the floor. My sister's mouth formed words
that even my imagination cannot make out and then she was gone.

The police rang the bell of my mother's house. She thought they had
come to read the gas meter. They told her about my sister. The officer, a
woman, said, "She was pronounced dead on the scene."

My mother undid the clasp of her watchband, then fastened it again,
then she said, "Thank you for coming to tell me. Would you mind telling
Lorraine for me?" She called Lorraine into the room.

Lorraine upon seeing the police was immediately in a panic, her hands
starting to shake.

"Lorraine," Mother said, "these nice people have something to tell
you. I'll be upstairs. It's time for my nap."

I took a taxi from National to my mother's house, stared down at the river as the car crossed the Fourteenth Street bridge. I had vague and unsettling memories of everything that had ever gone wrong when I was a child, times when I accidentally hurt my sister, times when I hurt her on purpose, when some boy had crushed her feelings, when her grades weren't what she had wanted, Bill ignored her, I ignored her, Mother paid me more attention. I admired her, but hardly knew her and it was all my fault, had to be my fault, because she was not alive to blame. But that thinking was bullshit and I quickly dropped it, replacing it with consideration of my familial duties.

At the house, my brother opened the door to let me in. Our embrace served only to amplify the distance between us, though our grief was very real.

We stepped back and looked at each other.

"How's Mother?" I asked.

"She's asleep," Bill said. "I gave her something. I got here a couple of hours ago. Lorraine's the one who's bouncing off the walls. I gave her something, too."

"Maybe later you can give me something," I said. "Have you figured out what happened yet?"

"Someone shot into the clinic and killed Lisa," he said. "I talked to the police thirty minutes ago. A rifle."

I walked into the living room and sat on the sofa. "Did they catch who did it?" I asked. It felt like a stupid question, a pointless concern. It really didn't matter. Lisa was dead and nothing would change that. "Do they know why?"

"Some zealot, they think. One of those anti-abortionist idiots."

"Lisa mentioned that murder in Maryland when I was here," I said. "Good lord. I can't believe this. I was halfway expecting Lisa to open the door when I arrived."

"Me, too."

"I should go up and see Mother," I said.

"I guess. She's pretty out of it. After that, we should go over to Lisa's and look at her papers, see if she left any instructions."

✗ ✗ ✗

Mother was, as Bill had said, out of it. She looked up at me through her haze and wondered aloud if I were my father. "Is that you, Ben?" she asked. "They've taken away our little girl."

"No, Mother, it's me, Monk. You just rest, okay?" I helped her back down into her pillow. "Get some sleep."

"My baby is dead," she said. "My little Lisa is gone."

✗ ✗ ✗

Klee: What are you thinking about?

Kollwitz: Why is it that bloody-minded men are such prudes? Why are they so hostile to sexuality and images of the body?

Klee: You're referring to mustache boy.

Kollwitz: You were lucky to leave when you did. I couldn't bring myself to abandon my home. But back to the subject. That monster and those like him are as threatened by those silly nymphettes of Mueller as they are by Kirchner.

Klee: Ferkel Kunst.

Kollwitz: Pardon?

Klee: That is what he calls what we do.

Kollwitz: I lost my son in the first war and I fear I will lose my grandson in this one. All because of a man who is afraid of his pee-pee.

Klee: And other people's poo poos.

Kollwitz: They've established a new bureau. The Commission on the Value of Confiscated Works of Degenerate Art. They're selling our works to foreigners. They sold them for nothing and burned the rest. I want the ashes of the bonfire to mix with my paints.

Klee: That's a lovely idea.

Kollwitz: Imagine the smell of those ashes.

Klee: Indeed.

✗ ✗ ✗

My sister's apartment was full of life. I never knew her tastes in any-thing after she became an adult. She liked pastels. She listened to R&B. She enjoyed color photographs of horses and birds. Her bed was neatly made. Her kitchen was clean. Her bathroom smelled sweet. Beside the sink was the ring box I had made for her four years earlier. There was an inlay of wood on the top. I remembered vividly making the box and hoping the while that she would like it as much I enjoyed constructing it. I lifted the lid and looked closely at the spalted maple inlay. It had darkened with age, but was still considerably lighter than the ebony box. There was one ring in the box and I guessed it had been Lisa's wedding ring.

Lisa wanted to be cremated and that was what we did. We had her body burned and her ashes collected in an urn that we brought home and set on the mantel over the fireplace that was never used. Mother cried. Lorraine cried. Patients and co-workers and colleagues and Lisa's ex-husband-sans-new-wife all came to a service at the Episcopal church my family never attended and they cried, too. When younger, I despised religion. Later, I didn't care, viewing the trappings with vague amusement and almost always finding the practitioners somewhat dull of spirit and thought. They said their words to their god and Lorraine, at least, was made to rest somewhat easier. Then we went home and sat at the kitchen table. Bill and I sat at the table, Bill having given Mother and Lorraine little somethings to help them sleep.

Bill asked me if I was still making chairs.
I told him I was. I finally asked him where Sandy and the kids were.
He told me they were in Arizona.
Bill asked if I had a new book coming out soon.
I told him that I was trying to sell one.
He didn't ask me what it was about.
I asked Bill where his wife and children were.
Bill told me that he admitted to Sandy that he was gay and that she took him to court and took the kids, the house, the money, everything. He told me his practice was failing because everyone now knew he was gay.
I asked how something like that could happen.
He said he lived in Arizona. He said: "Sandy actually deserves everything. I lied to her for fifteen years. I endangered her life, or so she believes. The judge believed her anyway. I've confused my children and it

will take a while for them to be able to understand what's happened. If they ever will. I deserve what I got. Which is, basically, nothing. I can't look my kids in the eye. I owe more money than I make. And I live in Arizona."

X X X

I felt bad for my brother and, truthfully, I was impressed by his understanding response to his wife's anger and his children's confusion. But it was sad that the most significant bit of information in his admission of guilt and failure was that he owed more money than he made. Mother needed caring for and I didn't believe that Bill was up to it. Lorraine was nearly as old as Mother and would perhaps require the same care, as never had I been made aware of any family of her own. The spotlight was falling squarely on me. My skin crawled, my head ached, my neck itched, all as I watched my life as I knew it change before my eyes. While sitting at that kitchen table with Bill, I was already packing up my apartment in Santa Monica.

Poor me! A man without a religion, without a decent lie to call my own. Giving up life for life, loving as I knew I should, and, perhaps most importantly, attempting to live up to the measure of my sister. Time seemed anything but mine, as if I were sleeping, walking and eating with a stopwatch! In my imagination, I told Mother I'd be back, took a leave from my teaching, put things in storage, packed bags, flew east on an L1011 seated next to a woman my mother's age, eighty-two, on her way to a rosarian convention in Georgia, moved in with Mother and Lorraine.

I sat in the living room, the air still and overwarm. I'd made myself a pot of tea and was trying to control my anxiety and my imagination. I listened to the sounds of the old house, the house of my childhood, the house where I'd known my sister. Bill was asleep. Mother and Lorraine were long asleep. The house's creaking found rhythm and I counted the cadence of the groaning, complaints, stiffenings. I considered the possibility that reasoning myself to D.C. and into that house was premature, but I had no success dispelling the thoughts. With the revelation of my brother's woeful personal circumstances, *de jure* absenteeism yielded to *de facto* guilt and so I was as good as there.

There may be space breaks between paragraphs of texts, between lines of text, sentences or words of the text.   That these spaces have some kind of narrative   significance   or charge is not arguable, though the weight of such import might be, and most times is, infinitesimal. What is more interesting is the fact that narrative always travels in the same direction and so the

spaces, the negative   or   white   spaces travel the same way. Never are we dropped into a space and returned to the previous narrative position or into nothingness   .

✗ ✗ ✗

The leave of absence seemed the most logical course. After talking to my mother and determining that she really had little idea what was going on, but enough of an idea, I couldn't simply place her somewhere. She was used to her house, knew her house, knew Lorraine and where the hell was Lorraine going to go. The saddest part of it all was the callousness of my consideration that I would only have to be gone a year because my mother would probably die. I felt like shit when I tracked down and identified that thought.

✗ ✗ ✗

Juanita Mae Jenkins was welcomed by a talk show host named Kenya Dunston who had put Ms. Jenkins' book on her *Book Club* reading list. They hugged and the audience smiled and Ms. Jenkins sat next to Kenya.

"Girl, that is some book," Kenya said.

"Thank you," said Ms. Jenkins.

"Three hundred thousand copies sold," Kenya said, shaking her head and making a ticking sound with her mouth.

The audience applauded.

"I know, I can't believe it," Ms. Jenkins said.

"Girl, you gone be rich. Well, you know I love the book, but tell me, how did you learn to write like that?

"A gift, I guess."

"Sho' nough." Kenya mugged at the audience and they laughed again. "Before we talk about the book, we want to hear a little bit about you. You're not from the South, are you?"

"No, I'm from Ohio originally. Akron. When I was twelve I went to visit some relatives in Harlem for a couple of days and that's what the novel comes from."

"The language is so real and the characters are so true to life. Girl, I just couldn't believe this was your first book. Where'd you go to college?"

"I went to Oberlin for a couple of years, then moved to New York."

"A man?"

"Ain't it always?"

The audience laughed.

"Well, that didn't work out," Ms. Jenkins said.

"Never does."

"Never does. And so I got this job at a publishing house. I watched these manuscripts come by and these books come out and I thought, where are the books about our people? Where are our stories? And so I wrote *We's Lives In Da Ghetto.*"

The audience applauded and the camera panned across their adoring faces and smiles.

"You struck a chord," Kenya said.

"I guess I did."

"Film rights?" Kenya mugged again to the audience.

Ms. Jenkins nodded.

"Millions?"

Ms. Jenkins shyly put off the question.

"But a lotta money, right, girlfriend?" Kenya slaps her guest's knee.

"Why shouldn't *we* get some of that good money, chile," Ms. Jenkins said.

The audience exploded with applause and cheering.

"Let me read a short piece from the middle of the book," Kenya said.

"Yo, Sharonda, where you be goin in a hurry likes dat?" D'onna ax me when she seed me comin out da house.

"Ain't none yo biznis. But iffan you gots to know, I'se goin to the pharmcy." I looks back at my dough to see if Mama comin out.

"The pharmcy? What fo?" she ax.

"You know," I says.

"Naw," she say. "Hell, naw. Girl you be pregnant again?"

"Mights be."

The audience blew out a collective sigh.

"Girl, that is some writing, right there," Kenya said.

"Thank you."

"I don't want to give the story away, but my favorite part is when Sharonda tap dances in a show for the first time. That was just so, so, so moving." Kenya smiled at Ms. Jenkins, then held up her book. "The book is *We's Lives In Da Ghetto* and the author is Juanita Mae Jenkins. Thank you for being with us."

"Thank you."

Young doctors have a lot of debt. This was a fact that I had not known, but knew now. School, a new practice, equipment. Especially, a practice like my sister's. She relied on some grants and was part-time staff at a hospital to help support the place. My sister had taken out an insurance policy on herself, but much of that went to paying off her bills. My mother had some savings, but she was not wealthy. The house was at least paid for. What had been my father's office was a money drain. And until I could sell my sister's share, a third of the Women's Clinic Southeast belonged to me. The two physicians in the clinic with my sister were as young as she, terrified that they were the next targets and unwilling to commit themselves any further into the operation by buying me out.

DOCTOR 1: This whole venture has always been iffy. I'm nearly ready to cut my losses and get out.

DOCTOR 2: We have done some good work here.

DOCTOR 1: What the hell does that mean? We hand out birth control pills and condoms to girls who won't use them. We treat people who act like we owe it to them. What are we doing? Being role models? These kids laugh at us.

DOCTOR 2: We didn't start this to be popular.

DOCTOR 1: But we are popular. We're popular the way a drunken uncle is popular because he falls asleep with money falling out of his pockets.

DOCTOR 2: You're bitter. You're sounding like a Republican.

DOCTOR 1: That's suppose to fill me with guilt. There's a new political correctness. I go to parties and I'm afraid to admit what I do for a living. "I practice medicine at a women's clinic," I say. "Oh, you perform abortions," they say and look at me like I'm the villain.

DOCTOR 2: That's true.

DOCTOR 1: You're damn right. It's okay to say you're pro-choice, just as long as you don't say you're for abortion. (Pauses) I'm terrified.

DOCTOR 2: What about our patients?

DOCTOR 1: They'll divide up and go to the other clinics.

DOCTOR 2: What would Lisa say?

DOCTOR 1: Lisa's dead.

Money was tight. I went over to the English Department at American University and asked for a job. I gave them my *curriculum vitae:*

Curriculum Vitae

```
Thelonious Ellison
Citizenship: USA
Social Security #: 271-66-6961
Address: 1329 Underwood St.
         Washington, DC 20009
```

Education

University of California, Irvine, M.F.A.,
Creative Writing, 1980

Harvard University, A.B., English, 1977

Publications

(books)

Personal Knowledge, a novel, Tower Press, New
York, NY, 1993.

The Persians, a novel, Lawrence Press, New York,
NY, 1991.

The Second Failure, a novel, Endangered Species
Press, Chicago, IL, 1988.

Shedding Skin, short stories, Lawrence Press,
New York, NY, 1984.

Chaldean Oracles, a novel, Fat Chance Press,
Lawrence Press, 1983.

(short works)

"Euripides Alibi," short story, *Experimental
Fiction,* Santa Cruz, CA,v.5, no.3, 1995.

"The Devolution of Twain's Memory," fiction,
Theoretical Ropes, Spring, University of Texas,
1995.

"House of Smoke," short story, *Lanyard Review,*
*v.*7 no.1, New Orleans, LA, 1994.

"The Last Heat of Misery," short story, *Alabama
Mud,* Fall, Dallas, TX, 1994.

"Climbing Down," short story, *Frigid Noir Review*
#45, Santa Fe, NM, Spring 1993.

"Night Deposits," short story, *Frigid Noir Review* #44, Santa Fe, NM, Winter 1992.

"Façon de parler," short story, *Out of Synch,* University of Colorado, Winter 1992.

"Clem's Resolution," short story, *Last Stand Review,* University of Virginia, v.20, no. 2, 1991.

"Another Man's Wife," short story, *Esquire,* New York, NY, September 1990.

Teaching History

Professor of English, University of California-Los Angeles, 1994-95.

Associate Professor, UCLA, 1988-94.

Visiting Professor of English and Honors, University of Minnesota, fall 1993.

Faculty, Bennington Writing Workshops, Bennington College, 1992, 93.

Honors

Timson Award for Excellence in Literature, *The Persians,* 1991.

3 Pushcart Prize prizes, 1990, 92, 94

National Endowment for the Arts, Fiction Fellowship, 1989.

The D. H. Lawrence Literary Fellowship, University of New Mexico, 1987.

Selected Readings and Lectures

1995-Rutgers University
1993-University of Michigan
    -Bennington College

```
1992-Vassar College
    -Pen-American Center, New York, NY
1989-Univerity of Virginia
1988-Rutgers University
```

Member

```
Nouveau Roman Society
Modern Lanquaqe Association
Associated Writing Programs
```

The chair of the department was a large man with a large head and I could not keep from staring at it. He no doubt perceived my fascination with his cranium, but what he told me was what I expected to hear. "Of course, the most I would be able to do is pull together some kind of visiting thing, but the department's all gone for the summer." He looked out his window and scratched that noggin. "We do need a lecturer for a survey of American Lit in the fall."

"How much does it pay?" I asked.

"About four thousand, thirty-nine hundred and something. Not much." He continued to stare at my credentials.

"That's for the whole semester?" I asked.

The big head nodded.

"Thanks."

Brown trout emerge from spawning gravels in spring and soon establish feeding territories. Young browns prefer quieter water than rainbow trout and tend to grow at a slower rate. Some spend their lives confined to headwater streams, but most of them migrate downstream to better habitat and feeding in rivers and lakes. Some brown trout live to be twenty years old. Browns are canny, the most wary of trout.

X X X

Lorraine was in the kitchen, standing over a pot of rice on the stove. She was wearing a yellow apron, perhaps the only one she had, I thought, since I had seen her in nothing but a yellow apron over a dark dress my entire life. When I was a child I imagined she had drawers of yellow aprons, a favorite yellow apron, a yellow apron for weddings and a yellow apron for funerals. I sat at the table.

"How are you feeling today, Lorraine?" I asked.

"Fine, Mr. Monk." She put the lid on the pot and moved along the counter to chop some celery. "It's a good thing you've done, coming home to care for your mother."

I didn't say anything, just watched the motion of the blade through the vegetables.

"I'm sorry if my books offend you, Lorraine."

She was taken off guard by my directness, but kept chopping, peppers now.

"You know, just because my characters use certains words doesn't mean anything about me. It's art."

"Yes, I know."

"Have you ever used the word *fuck*?" I asked.

She stopped cutting, seemed almost ready to laugh. "Yes, I have, Mr. Monk. It's a word which has its uses."

"Yes ma'am." I watched as she stirred the rice again. "Do you have any family in D.C.?" I asked.

"No. I used to have an auntie, but she died a long time ago. This is the only family I've ever known."

"I'm sorry," I said.

"Oh, no," she said. "I don't miss my family. I never knew them."

"No, I mean I'm sorry this is the crazy family you landed in."

"Ya'll aren't crazy," she said. "Ya'll are different, that's a fact. But you're not crazy."

"Thanks. Hey, Lorraine, where would you go if you couldn't live here?"

She put the lid on the pot and stared down at it. "I don't know."

"Do you have any friends?"

She shook her head, but said, "A couple."

"Do you have any money saved?" I knew how much Lorraine was paid because I was now making out her checks. It was not bad considering she had free rent and food. "Do you have anything?"

She cleared her throat. "I've saved a little bit. I've never been much good at saving. Why are you asking?"

"Lorraine, Mother's getting up there. What's going to happen when she dies?"

"I'll stay here and take care of you, Mr. Monk."

I looked at the old woman, nearly as old as my mother, and hadn't a clue what to say next. I got up and started to leave, stopped at the door to the dining room, looked back and said, "That will be fine, Lorraine."

Ernst Kirchner: I'm glad, no proud that those brown shirts are burning my paintings.

Max Klinger: What do you mean?

Kirchner: Imagine how I would feel if monsters like that tolerated my work.

"Monksie, are you feeling okay?" my mother asked. She sat down on the sofa beside me.

"I'm fine," I said. "What about you? How was your nap?"

"Like a nap."

"Would you like me to make us some tea?"

"No, honey, stay where you are. Relax. You can't run yourself ragged because of an old lady." She looked at the fireplace. "Thank you."

"Pardon?"

"For coming to live here," Mother said.

"I love you, Mother," I said, as if to say of course I'd be there.

"I miss Lisa," she said.

"Me, too."

Mother arranged the fabric of her skirt on her lap. "I'm lucky to be able to get around the way I do. I even make it up those stairs without getting winded."

"That's terrific."

"Will Lisa be coming by later today?"

"No, Mother."

"Because I miss her. Did I say something to hurt her feelings? I know she and Barry broke up."

"I don't think so, Mother."

I called my agent to check on the status of my novel and he had no good news for me. Three more editors had turned it down. "Too dense," one had said. "Not for us," a simple reply from another. And, "The market won't support this kind of thing," from the third.

"So, what now?" I asked.

"I don't know what to tell you," Yul said. "If you could just write something like *The Second Failure* again." The ice clinked in his glass.

"What are you telling me?" I asked.

"I'm not telling you anything."

Second Failure: My "realistic" novel. It was received nicely and sold rather well. It's about a young black man who can't understand why his white-looking mother is ostracized by the black community. She finally kills herself and he realizes that he must attack the culture and so becomes a terrorist, killing blacks and whites who behave as racists.

I hated writing the novel. I hated reading the novel. I hated thinking about the novel.

I went to what had been my father's study, and perhaps still was his study, but now it was where I worked. I sat and stared at Juanita Mae Jenkins' face on *Time* magazine. The pain started in my feet and coursed through my legs, up my spine and into my brain and I remembered passages of *Native Son* and *The Color Purple* and *Amos and Andy* and my hands began to shake, the world opening around me, tree roots trembling on the ground outside, people in the street shouting *dint, ax, fo, screet* and *fahvre!* and I was screaming inside, complaining that I didn't sound like that, that my mother didn't sound like that, that my father didn't sound like that and I imagined myself sitting on a park bench counting the knives in my switchblade collection and a man came up to me and he asked me what I was doing and my mouth opened and I couldn't help what came out, 'Why fo you be axin?"

I put a page in my father's old manual typewriter. I wrote this novel, a book on which I knew I could never put my name:

MY PAFOLOGY

by Stagg R. Leigh

Won

Mama look at me and Tardreece and she call us "human slough." That how it all start up. "Human slough," she say, "You lil' muthafuckas ain't nuffin but human slough." I looks at her and I'm wonderin what "slough" means and I don't like the look on her face and so I get up from the chair I been sittin in and I walk across the kitchen and grab a big knife from the counter. She say, "And what you gone do wif that, human slough?" And I stab Mama. I put the knife in her stomach and pull it out red and she look at me like to say why you stab me? And I stab Mama again. Blood be all on the floor and on the table, drip drip drippin down her legs and my baby sister starts screamin and I says, "Why you be screamin, Baby Girl?" And she look at me and she say it because I be stabbin on Mama. I look at my hands and they all covered wif blood and I realize I don't know what goin on. So, I stab Mama again. I stab her cause I scared. I stab Mama cause I love her. I stab Mama cause I hate her. Cause I love her. Cause I hate her. Cause I ain't got no daddy. Then I walk out the kitchen and stand outside, leavin Mama crawlin round on the linolum tryin to hold in her guts. I stands out on the sidewalk just drippin blood like a muthafucka. I look up at the sky and I try to see Jesus, but I cain't. Then I wonder which one of my fo' babies I'm gone go see.

I wake up and I'm just soaked in sweat, been sweatin like a fuckin pig. I throw them sheets off me and pull on some jeans. I tighten up my belt and then yank my pants down on my ass. The tee shirt I'm wearin be funky as shit, but I don't give a fuck. The world be stinkin, so why not me? That's what I says. So, why not me? That's my motto. So, why not me? It be eleben-thirty in the moanin. I check the kitchen floor fo' blood on my way through. That was a fucked up dream, real fucked up. I step on outside and look up at the sky and I wonder which one of my fo' babies I'm gone go see.

Aspireene's mama be keepin company with some nigger they call Mad Dog, so I don't need to be sniffin round her crib. I ain't gonna have some buck pop a cap in my ass. No suh. Tylenola's mama be a crazy bitch and she done got herself a nine and I know she gone pop a cap in me if I shows my face cause I ain't give her no money and she been askin fo' three monfs. My oldest girl, Dexatrina, her mama still be in love wif me. I could go hit it once, but gettin out, man it like gettin coke outta milk. I decide I'm gone go see my boy Rexall. He got Down Sinder, but he okay. In dis fuckin world, he don't need no brain no way. Better not to have one. He be three now and he was always knocking shit over. I smack him once and his mama say fo me not to, say he cain't help it. I told her to go fuck herself, little big-head nigger got juice on my good pants. Yeah, I'm gone smack him. I'm gone go see Rexall, cause I'm his daddy. I takes care of my babies.

My name is Van Go Jenkins and I'm nineteen years old and I don't give a fuck about nobody, not you, not my Mama, not the man. The world don't give a fuck about nobody, so why should I? And what I'm gone do instead of going to work over at that Jew muthafacka's warehouse over on Central is go over to the high school and wait for Rexall's mama. Her name be Cleona. She's a dreamer, always talkin bout graduatin and goin to the communy college and bein a nurse or some shit. Her dreamin don't bother me none. I hope she do make herself some real money some day. But she be actin funny a lot, like she think I ain't good enough fo' her ass. Fuck her. All I know is I can go over her house when her mama gone and cut me out a piece. She ain't too good then.

I'm standing outside the school lookin up at the second floor and I see that bastard who got me kicked out way back when. I was just sittin in the back of the class, mindin my own business when the fucka come back talkin shit.

"Is there a problem, Mr. Jenkins?" he ax.

I'm just kicked back, chillin, talkin to Yellow. I look at Yellow like what this fool think he is and what he be sayin, like what language he be talkin and we bust out laughin. Then that muthafucka laugh too, like he makin fun of me. I get real quiet and cut a stare at him.

"What you laughin at, cracker?" I say.

"You, my man," he say. "I'm laughin at you. You want to be tough, fine, but don't drag all these other kids down the toilet with you. Right now, you feel good, strong, full of it, but when you get out there in that world, a world that doesn't know you from a speck of dirt, when you're twenty-eight, say, and you can't read a job application and somebody else gets the job, then you won't be so full of it. You'll be just another loser with a dick that's too small."

He throwin all them words out and then he gets to the part about my dick and I hear a couple of people laugh and I just lose it. Shit. My dick be twice as big as his. I jump up and knee the fucka in his balls. He slump over and I wanna make him suck me off in front of everybody, but I just hit him again, wif my fist this time, across his pasty white face. I cut my knuckle on his tooth and then I gets madder. The police come and pull my ass off him. The ambulance come and get him, sorry son of a bitch, fuck wif me like that, talk bout my dick. He the reason I didn't graduate. I coulda been out there wif a good job, makin some good money in a office or sumpin, instead of liftin furniture for the man over at that warehouse.

I got another coupla minutes before that lunch bell ring and that Willy the Wonker nigger come walkin down the street my way. He be singin that song what ain't no song that always be gettin on people's nerves. He swayin like the junkie he is, all fucked up and about to fall down and I laugh thinkin that if you gets really fucked up then you fall down, up, down, up down. He singin and swayin and preachin to the air, to the sidewalk, to the bus passin by.

"Lawd Gawd," he say, "let these niggers on these streets leave me alone today. Please, Jesus. Don't let no drive-by gang punk-ass muthafucka put a hole in me. Don't let no junkie kill me fo' my junk. Don't let no white man throw me in his dungeon. Don't let yo son, who died fo my sorry ass, come back down here just yet, not until I gets my shit ironed out." Then Willy see me. "Hey, I know you, young nigger."

"Just keep yo junkie ass away from me," I say.

"Junkie? Who you callin junkie? Sorry ass muthafucka. I'll dust yo junkie ass off."

"Step bad if you wanna, bitch," I say and look in his red and yellow eyes.

"I know you," he say. "I know you. You be Clareece Jenkins' boy. I knew I knowed you. How old you now? Eighteen? Twenty?" He laughs and points at me. "I hit that shit back in the sebenties. Nigger, I might even be yo daddy."

A chill run through me and I feel my lip shakin. "I'm gone kick you in the ass, you don't shut up."

"Fuck you," he say.

"Fuck you," I say.

"Fuck you," he say.

"Fuck you," I say.

"Yo mama still fat?" He smile big. "She was fat back then, not real fat, not too fat, but fat, you know, fat enough to make it fun." And then he grab an invisible woman and fucked the air. "Clareece," he croon out. "Clareeeeece."

I was about to punch him in his face, but the lunch bell ring. I step on away from him. "You better watch yo ass, old nigger."

But the junkie won't let me alone. "You do looks a lil' like me, you know that?"

"Shut the fuck up!"

"Round the eyes and mouf."

"I'm gone slam you, I swear to fuckin Gawd."

He back up then. "Okay. We cool. We cool." And he give me a knowin look. "We cool."

Finally, Cleona come out the door and she be talkin to some pretty nigger. I walk up to her and I says, "Hey, baby."

She look at me and laugh, then turn to the pretty boy and say, "I'll talk to you later, Tyrell."

"Yeah, she talk to you later, *Ty-rell*," I say.

The nigger just smile at me and then he walk on down the street where he climbs into a bright red Jeep. Rich-ass nigger muthafucka.

"Ain't that a blip," I say.

"What you mean callin me yo baby," Cleona say. "I ain't nothin to you, boy."

"You my baby's mama," I say.

"So?"

"Chill out, baby. Let's go over to yo house so I can see Rexall."

"Fool, where I be right now?" she ax.

"School," I say.

"And where my mama be right now?"

"Work," I say.

"What you think, I'm gone leave a little retarded boy in a house by hisself?"

"Let's just go to yo house then," I say.

"Don't even go there," she say, gettin her head to movin.

"Come on. I wanna give you some money for the retard."

"Don't call him that," she snap.

"Okay, okay. I wanna give you a coupla bucks and talk to you bout him a lil' bit."

She laugh, throwin her head back on her fat neck, then she look at me. "You talk like you think I'm the retarded one."

"You the one had a retard for a baby."

"Don't start wif me, nigger," she say. "Just give me the damn money right here."

"Cain't do that."

"Why not?"

"Just cain't," I tells her.

"I gotta be back to school in an hour," she say.

"You be back. Don't sweat it. I make sure you be back," I say. "I'll give you the money and you can tell me how Rexall doin and if you need sumpin and that be it." I look up and down the street. I sees a girl checkin me out and I smiles at her.

"What you smilin at?" Cleona ax.

"You done said I ain't nuffin to you," I say.

"C'mon, let's go."

"Yo mama comin home?"

"You know she ain't gone be home till late," she say.

I love Cleona and I hate Cleona. There be two lil' niggers in my head. Nigger A and Nigger B. Nigger A say, Be cool, bro, you know you ain't gots no money, so just let this girl go on back to school and through maf class and English class and socle studies so she can get out and be sumpin. Just let her have a chance, one chance to be that nurse she always talkin bout bein. But Nigger B be laughin, say, Shit, take this bitch home to her house and hit it one times, two times. She got the nerve to be talkin to Jeep-nigger in front of you. Fuck that shit. If she gone dis you like that, nail her ass. Later you can go out and find that Jeep-muthafucka and fuck him up. Right now, take this pussy home and get a taste. You remember how good that shit was, the way she whimpered, like she be crying, like it hurt. Nigger be hurtin a pussy. Fuck school. She ain't gone be no nurse. She ain't gone be nuffin.

When we walk to her house I see some guys playin ball. I ain't played no ball in a long long time, I thinks to myself. At one time I was real good. I could dunk from the top of the key and all like that. I had me a nice jumper too, but shit, how you gone get into college and get all that big money when you ain't nuffin to begin wif and when the muthafuckas make it so you cain't stay in school. And I wasn't bout to suck no coach's dick for a chance to play. I shoulda gone over there when I was good and tried out for the Lakers. I woulda fit right in. Showtime. Me and Magic. I didn't even need no practice, that how good I was.

Cleona unlocks the door and we goes inside and she turn to me and say, "Now give me the money."

"Slow down, baby," I say in my smooth voice. "Why don't you show me where the baby sleep."

"You know where the baby sleep. The baby sleep in my room and we ain't goin in there. Now, give me the money."

"Well, could you get me some ice water?" I ax.

She sigh real heavy and stomp them big feet off in the direction of the kitchen.

I sits down on the sofa and I see that the thing be new. I run my hand along the cushion beside me and I'm thinkin, shit, where this mutha come from. Brand new.

Cleona come back into the room with the glass of water and hand it to me and then just stand there.

"You got a new couch," I say.

"So?"

"Where you and yo mama get the money for this here?"

"That ain't none o' yo business," she say.

"I think it is," I say. "If my baby's mama gone out sellin her ass fo money to buy furniture, that be my business. Maybe you don't need no money."

"You s'posed to give me money every monf for Rexall."

"S'posed to ain't the same as got to," I say. I looks around the room. "Shit, y'all got a lot of nice shit." I sips my water and it be warm. "I said ice, bitch."

She just stare at me.

"I'm sorry, baby," I say. "That just come out all wrong. C'mon here and sit down beside me."

She still just lookin at me.

"Sit down," I say again.

She plop her big ass down heavy next to me and I put my arm round her and she get all stiff.

"C'mon, Cleona, loosen up some. Ain't nobody home." I touch one of them big titties with my finger and say, "That's where my baby be havin dinner."

Cleona don't want to but she let out a giggle.

I touch her titties some more. "That's a big ol' tittie," I say. "I wanna taste what my baby be drinkin. You want me to taste what my baby taste?"

Her eyelids be flutterin closed now and I think she say yes and I pull her shirt and look at that big-ass bra she be wearin. I try to undo the muthafucka in the back, but shit, I cain't get it loose and I say, "Hep me out, damnit."

Cleona reach her hands back, one from over her head and through her collar and the other up the back of her shirt and she open it up. Those giant jugs just flop there like big pillows, like bags of sand. I grabs on to them and sucks 'em real hard till she moans and I whispers a lil' sumpin, I don't even know what the fuck I be sayin, but I squeeze and suck and squeeze and suck. The clock cross the room says one o'clock and I remember that I'm s'posed to meet Yellow and Tito over at the pool hall, so I gotta pop it quick. I push her back and undoes her pants, all the while I'm suckin on them titties and she's moanin. It's hard to get her pants over her big ass, but I do it and then I puts it in her, all of it. Wham! Just like that and she cry out and man I feel so powerful. I bang it, man, I bang it and she start cryin, openin her eyes and seein me and she be cryin, sayin for me to get off her. But I be hittin it now and I smile at her.

"I said, get off me," she say. "Get off me, you nuffin nigger."

That shit makes me mad and I pull out and shoot my juice all over that fuckin new couch. She don't know what to do now. Her mouf just fall open like she stupid. Then she run cross the room and look back at me.

"Mama gone kill me," she say.

"Shoulda thought of that shit before you started to fuckin on her new couch," I say.

"I hate you!" she shout. "I hate you! Get the fuck out my house!"

I take my time pullin on my pants and doin up my belt. I look at her naked body. "You fat," I say.

"Get out!"

"You cain't tell me what to do, girl," I say to her and get my shoes on.

"You rape me, nigger," she say.

I laugh at her ass. "I ain't raped shit. How I'm gone rape my baby's mama? You gone always be my woman."

"I ain't yo woman!"

"You my baby's mama," I say.

"Rexall ain't yo baby," she say.

I just stare at her.

"You hurd me," she say. "Rexall ain't none of yo baby."

"What the fuck you be talkin bout? If I ain't the waterhead's daddy, then who is?"

"That don't matter," she say.

"It matter when I be givin you money for that big-head retard."

"You ain't never give me no money!" she scream. "You talk about it and that be all."

"I was gone to, but I ain't givin you shit now," I say.

"Get the fuck out!"

I laughs and walk over to the door real slow. "You a fat ho," I say. "Rexall ain't yo baby, but he sho look like you."

"He mine awright," I say. I was at the door now. "I hit and I don't miss. If I hits it, you be pregnant. It be like that."

"You rape me!" she scream.

I laughs and walk out.

Too

From Cleona's I goes over to the pool hall where I'se s'posed to hook up wif Yellow and Tito. Yellow is called Yellow cause he light-skindid and got that kind of red hair. Girls always be making a fuss over that nigger's hair. But Yellow awright. He my partner, him and Tito. We calls Tito Tito cause he always want to Sing but he cain't say. He just like that Jackson brother with the big hair. I see Tito standing outside smokin a square.

"Hey, man," I say.

"What up?" Tito say.

"Whatchew doin standin out here?" I ax.

"Fatman say I gotta smoke out here. He say no mo' smokin inside."

"What the fuck? What kinda pool room you got to smoke outside?"

"His pool room. Sides, Fatman cool."

"Yeah, he cool," I say.

Tito throw his Kool down and step on it. Then we walk on inside. The room be dim like always and Fatman be sittin on his stool behind the counter. He nod to me and and I nod back.

"Over here," Yellow calls out from a far table. He be playin a game with a tall, slick-looking nigger in a hat. Another nigger be standin by watchin, filing his finger nails.

"What up?" I say to Yellow.

"Whippin this boy's ass, that what," Yellow say.

"Ain't over yet, youngblood," the smooth nigger say just as calm as anything.

"Look to be over to me," Yellow laugh.

"Wanna bet?" Smooth say.

Yellow hesitates and I can tell he ain't got no money.

Smooth be pullin out some bills. "How about twenty?"

"I don't wanna bet, man."

"You sure you gone win, right? Or was that just a pussyfart?" Smooth look over at the nail-filin muthafucka. And they laugh.

"Nigger call you a pussy," Tito whisper to Yellow.

"I ain't gots no money," Yellow whisper back.

"You got his ass whooped for sho?" Tito ax.

Yellow kinda nods his head.

"I got ten," Tito say and then he look at me.

"Shit," I say. "Fuck, Yellow, and you better for sho kick his ass." I hand him my ten dollars and look at the table.

"Okay," Yellow say to Smooth.

"Well, awright."

Yellow takes a shot and misses, but he say, "Don't worry, he cain't get to the six for shit."

I looks at the table and I see that the nine ball is smack in between the cue and the six and I think he right.

"You ain't gone make it, tight-ass nigger," I say to Smooth.

"You talk a lota shit for a lil' boy," he say.

Tito say, "Ohhh, nigger called you a little boy."

"He just mad cause I got a piece o' his mama," I say.

"I didn't want none of yo mama. She so fuckin fat and ugly," he say.

"Fuck you," I say.

Then the smooth nigger just laugh and he make the cue ball jump over the nine and knock the six just as pretty as shit into the side pocket. Then he run the table and pick up the money. I look at Tito and I gets to thinkin bout my ten dollars and I get pissed.

"Youse a hustler," I say.

"And youse a hustlee," he laugh. The nail-filer laugh too.

"You ain't taking that money, nigger," I say.

"Let him have it," Yellow say.

"Naw, man," I say.

"Listen to yo friend," Smooth say.

"I ain't listenin to shit," I say.

"Then listen to this," Smooth say and he pull a .380 out his pocket and stick the muthafucka in my face. "You want some of this?"

I back away a step.

"Just take the money, man," Tito say.

"There wasn't never no doubt bout that, youngblood," Smooth say and he and his partner just walk on out sweet as they want.

Fatman call over to us with his gravelly voice. "Ya'll okay over there?"

"Yeah, we okay," Yellow calls back.

Tito blows out a sigh. "Shit, man." Then he hits Yellow in the shoulder. "You cost me ten dollars."

I look at the door and then at Tito and Yellow. "I got to get me a gun."

"And whatchew gone do with a piece?" Tito ax.

"First thing we gone do is rob that K'rean muthafucka over in the plaza."

"Why you wanna fuck wit him?" Tito say.

"I don't like the way the bitch be lookin at me when I be in there. Like he think I gone steal from his ass."

"You is gone steal from his ass," Yellow say.

Tito laugh.

"So?" I say. "That ain't give him no right."

Yellow say, "Nigger, you crazy."

"Gots to be crazy to survive," I says.

"You think you in some damn movie, nigger?" Tito say. He pull out a Snickers bar and start tearin the paper.

"Crack me off some," Yellow say.

"See," I say. "Y'all niggers act like you ten or eleben. Talkin bout candy and shit. We can get us some real money."

"And get shot fo' the trouble," Yellow say.

"Pussy," I calls him.

"Yeah, and yo mama got her own zip code and area code," Yellow say.

"Well, your mama work as a roach terminator and don't need no sprays or no shit, just her breath."

"Yo mama look like J. Edgar Hoover," Yellow say.

"What he look like?" I ax.

"Yo mama," Yellow say.

"Fuck you," I say.

"Fuck you," Yellow say.

"Fuck you," I say.

"Fuck you," Yellow say.

"Fuck you," I say.

"Fuck you," Yellow say.

"Fuck you," I say.

"Fuck you," Yellow say.

"Fuck you," I say.

"Fuck you," Yellow say.

"Fuck you," I say.

"Fuck you," Yellow say.

"Fuck you," I say.

"Fuck you," Yellow say.

"Fuck you," I say.

"Fuck you," Yellow say.

"You ain't shit," I say.

"Well, you is shit," Yellow say.

"Nigger called you shit," Tito laugh.

"Pussy," I say and I'm bout to hit him.

"Where you gone get a gun?" Tito ax. "Wanna gun to get money. Need money to get a gun. Nigger in big bad circle."

I forget about Yellow and looks at Tito. "Oh, I'm gone get the money for my piece, awright," I says. I walk over and pick up a pool stick and tap the table with it. What I'm doin be makin Yellow nervous. "What wrong chew, nigger?"

"Ain't nuffin' wrong wid me," he say. "You the one."

I walk over to him. "I thought you and me was homeboys," I says. "Why you want be acting all pussy-like?"

"We homeboys," he say.

I'm all up in his face now, lookin at him wif my head cocked and I can see him sweatin and lookin over at Tito like for help. "What you lookin at him fo?" I say.

"Come on, Go," he say. "We cool, right?"

I smile and back away a step. "Yeah, we cool," I say. "We cool and you gone do that job wif me."

"What?"

"You," I say. "You gone wif to hit that K'rean muthafucka. I'm gone get my gun. Smooth nigger comin up in here pullin his piece and shit." I shakes my head, then I look at Yellow. "I thought you say you had the nigger beat." Then I let out a smile that makes Yellow relax. "Don't be worrin, Yellow. We cool."

Later on, me and Tito be leanin against the wall outside in the back alley smokin a joint.

"Where you get this shit?" I ax him.

"My brother scored it," Tito say. "Good shit." He look at me and hand me the J. "Lemme ax you sumpin. Why you fuckin wit Yellow like that?"

"Fuck, I didn't mean nuffin by it."

"You shook him up," Tito said.

"Then his ass ought to be shook up," I says. "Sometimes he act just like a punk. You think he a punk?"

"Naw man, he ain't no punk."

I takes a long drag off the joint and hand it back. Coupla guys pass by the alley on the street and I watches them. "How much you think a gun gone cost me?" I ax.

"Hell, I don't know. What chew want?"

"I wants me a nine, man," I say.

"I dunno, a hundred, maybe. I dunno," he say.

"Your brother get me a gun?" I ax.

Tito shrug his shoulders.

"Ax him."

"I'll ax him," he say.

"I wanna know how much it cost."

"I'll ax him," he say again.

When I be walkin home I stops and looks at this fine red Mustang convertible in the parkin lot of a Ralph's grocery stow. It be sharp and then I see this real fine sister come out and bleep bleep undo the alarm on the muthafucka and I thinks, Damn that bitch be fine as shit. She fumblin wid her keys, tryin to get in and so steps around so I can see her face and all that make up she be wearing. Then she see me and snap up like some kinda snake and she be holdin a can of pepper spray and pointin it at me. I jumps back.

"Chill out, baby doll," I say.

"I'm not your baby doll," she say.

"You ain't gots to be all uppity just cause a nigger wanna look you over," I says.

"You've seen enough. Now, kindly move along," she say.

I looks at this bitch. "Kindly move along?" I say. "Girl, where you from. College or some damn place? You ain't no better n' me."

"Fine," she say and got her car door open. "Now, just back off."

I back away some more. "Okay," I says.

I watch her drive off in her fine ride and think, "Fuck you, bitch."

I'm so mad I could scream. The whole world screamin. So, why not me.

Free

Mama just be gettin home when I walks in. She and Baby Girl been out grocery shoppin. I'm lookin in the bag what be on the table and she tell me to get out of there.

"I'm hongry," I say.

"Boy, I ain't got no time to be foolin wif you right now. I got to make dinner for you two and then go over to my sister's house."

"Why you goin over there?" I ax.

"That no good man o' hers been beatin on her again," she say.

"She ought to shoot him in the ass," I say.

"Boy, don't be using no language up in here," she tell me.

I laugh.

"I be serious, Van," she say. "And I don't want you hangin round wif that Tito none either. Boy be bad news." She shake her head that way that make me mad right away.

"Tito cool," I say.

"Tito stink," Baby Girl say.

"Shut the fuck up," I say.

Mama slam the cabinet where she be standin and stare at me with fire in her eyes. "What did you say?" she ax. "I know I didn't hear you right. Don't make me have to whip yo ass."

"Yeah, well. You can shut the fuck up too," I say and I stare right at her eyes. Cause I hate my mama and I love my mama. I'm starin right in her eyes and she can see I a man now. "You heard me, old lady," I say. "You heard what the fuck I said. And don't be thinkin you can tell me what to do."

"Lawd, have mercy," she say. She hot and I can tell she wanna grab a pan and knock me in the head. But she just shake her head there for a while. "I cain't believe it," she say.

"Believe it, bitch." I loves my mama. I hates my mama.

"Van," Baby Girl complain.

"I'm gone be in the other room," I says. "Call when they some shit to eat." And I walk on into the living room. From there I can hear Mama cryin and Baby Girl tryin to comfort her some.

I turns on the television and lean back into the sofa and I think that it be one uncomfortable muthafucka. I want me a couch like that one Cleona and her mama got. Fuck Cleona, no good ho. Think she something, fuckin round wif that ol' rich nigger. Got her though, stuck her one and creamed on that couch. Fuck wif me.

I watches some cartoons and then I flip through the channels and I find the Power Rangers and watch that shit for a while. Then I finds the Snookie Cane Show, that fat bitch be talkin a mile a minute. Got all them losers on there and I think, shit, I could be on there too. They shoot the fucka over there in Burbank and they pay them bastards to be on. I know they be payin 'em. And them people in the audience, always got sumpin to say, always giving advice.

Mama call me into the kitchen and I go on in there and sit down at the table. I look at my plate and I say, "What this shit?"

"Hamburger Helper," Baby Girl say. "And I helped."

"Well, you ought to help throw this shit in the toilet," I say.

"That's it, you little smart-ass, smellin-yo-own-piss, little nigger," Mama say and she pick up a big ass knife.

Baby Girl run to her, screaming, "Please! Please, don't cut on Van, Mama! Please, don't be cuttin on him!"

"Let her cut me," I say. "I got sumpin for her big ass."

"Move out the way, Tardreece!" Mama say.

"No, Mama! No, Mama!" Baby Girl be screamin.

"I'm outta here," I say, knockin over a chair. "Eat all this shit and get big as a house and see if I give a fuck." I slams the door as I leave.

I be standin outside in the night. A police chopper go by and shine some lights in some backyards and I think, shine that light on me muthafucka. Shine me some fuckin light so I can see where the fuck I be at. Then I thinks about my mama. I hate her. I loves her. And what bout my daddy, wherever the fuck he be. He might be in jail or running a string o' hoes. Shit, I dunno. But I hate him wherever the fuck he be. I walk on down the street and I start to pretend I'm that Forrest Gump muthafucka. I ain't seen the movie, but I seen all them TV ads and I feel like I seen the movie, the way he be running for that touch-down straight through everybody and the way he be sitting on that bench talkin bout them chocolates. I thinks, hey, I'm a chocolate. I be a chocolate in a box o' chocolates. "Here I be, America!" I scream up at the chopper whats leavin. "Open me up! Never know whatcha gone get!" I hates my daddy.

I'm crossin the street over by the playground and I see that Jeep-nigger sittin at the light. I walks over and stand right in front of his headlights. The nigger look at me like what the fuck be goin on, then he recognize me and he smile. I smile back at him and don't move. He rev his engine a coupla times.

"What you want, muthafucka?" he ax.

"I want chew, nigger," I say.

"What, you wanna suck my log, muthafucka?" He look over at the nigger sitting beside him and they both laugh.

"Yeah, whip it out so I can see it," I say.

"Get out the way, bitch," he say.

"Step out," I say.

"I ain't got time to be fuckin wid you," he say and rev his engine again.

I don't move. "I said I wanna bite me off a piece o' yo ass."

He try to drive around me and I stay in front of him. "Move, nigger!"

"Move me, muthafucka."

Another car come up behind the Jeep and blow his horn. Then Jeep-nigger blow his horn. The car behind him whips out and speeds by. Then he gets and out and his friend do too.

"What the fuck yo problem, nigger?" Jeep ax.

I walks up to him and stand all up in his face. "You my fuckin problem."

He look over at his friend who be walkin round the back of the Jeep. The fellas what been playin ball on the playground come over to the fence and watch. Then I hit him in the stomach, quick and make him double up. His friend come runnin now and I kick that muthafucka in the nuts and he fall down on his knees and I leave him there cause he ain't nuffin' to me. I goes back to Jeep and I punch his face so hard he fall on his knees too. Bam! Bam! I hit twice mo' and his nose just blow up. Red be all over his face. I look at them pretty eyes now and bam bam, I bruise 'em up. Niggers over on the court be shoutin out sumpin' I cain't hear. I walk round that nigger now. He stretch out on the ground, gettin the street all bloody.

"How you like it, muthafucka," I say. "You won't be sniffin' round my shit no mo' now, will you? You gone leave Cleona alone?"

He don't say nuffin'.

So I kicks him in the side and he spit blood. "I ax you a question, nigger. You gone leave the bitch alone?"

He say something through all the blood in his mouth, but I don't know what. Then I hear the police chopper blades and I run.

I go home and I get in bed wif my clothes on and my knuckles be sore as shit. I look up at the peeling paint on the ceilin and think about my babies. I hate my babies. I loves my babies. I hates my babies. I loves my babies. I hates . . .

I dreams when I'm sleepin and it be on an island somewhere in them islands down there. There be all these beautiful, fine-ass bitches walkin round wearin nuffin but strings over they nipples and shit. I think, damn, these some fine bitches here and I know they gone give me some and I start countin the babies I'm gone make and I start thinkin up names for them babies. Their names gone be Avaricia, Baniqua, Clitoria, Dashone, Equisha, Fantasy, Galinique, Hobitcha, I'youme, Jamika, Klauss, Latishanique, Mystery, Niggerina, Oprah, Pastischa, Quiquisha, R'nee'nee, Suckina, Titfunny, Uniqua, Vaselino, Wuzziness, Yolandinique and Zookie. I gone hit that many of them bitches, I think. I'm just sittin in one of them beach chairs watchin 'em go by. Big butts on all of 'em. But then in the dream I looks down and I see that my dick ain't nuffin but a bump. I yell, "Shit, my dick ain't nuffin but a bump." What I'm gone do with a little bump fo a dick? Then them bitches see it and they starts pointing at my bump and I'm there tryin to cover myself. One of them bitches say, "That nigger got a real lil' dick, look like a baby dick." And she and all the rest of them bitches starts laughin at me, pointin and laughin, and I go runnin off into the water. My hands coverin up my bump, what used to be my dick. And in the cold water, this ho come swimmin over to me and she reach between my legs and move my hand and she say, "I don't care if you ain't got no dick." I look at her face and it start to melt and she get real ugly and she become my mama, so I stab her. I stab her over and over and over and over until the ocean be fulla blood.

Then I wakes up in a sweat.

Next mornin at breakfast, Mama done forgot bout our fight and she singin some damn gospel song. Baby Girl be hummin along and then she say, "Mama, what that song you singin?"

"It's What a Friend We Have in Jesus," she say. Then she look at me. "I heard bout a job you might want." She put some bacon on my plate. "Over in West Hollywood."

"Doin what?" I ax.

"This and that. I dunno," she say. "I think drivin a car for a man."

I think about drivin a car and I kinda like the idea of drivin. "A driver for some white man."

"It a job," she say.

"Well, I gots a job," I say.

"You never go to it," she say.

I eat the bacon. "What's the address?" I ax.

She walk over to the counter then and dig round on it. "I wrote it down. Here it is." She come back and hand it to me.

I shoves the paper in my pocket.

"So, you gone go over there?" she ax.

"Dunno yet," I say. "And don't be ridin me."

"I ain't ridin you," she say.

"You is too," I say.

"I is not," she say.

"Is too."

"Is not, you good-for-nuffin," she say.

"That be me," I say and laugh. "Just like my daddy."

"Hush up, boy."

"Who is my daddy, Mama?" I ax.

She turn her back and wash some damn dish in the sink.

"What his name, Mama? You know his name? I know Baby Girl's daddy's name. I seen him. He in jail now, right?"

"Hush up, nigger," Mama say.

"Is my daddy in jail?" I ax. "Did you ever know his name?"

"Van," Baby Girl complain.

"I'm gone," I say and walk on out.

Fo

I goes over to the warehouse and old Freddie be sittin out on the dock smokin and he just start shakin his head when he see me comin. He look back into the buildin and then at me.

"What?" I ax.

"Don't even bother," he say.

"Don't even bother what?" I ax.

"Don't bother takin you ass on in there," he say. "Reynolds say about an hour ago, 'Where that good fo' nuffin Jenkins?' Then he say, 'If you see 'em, tell 'em he can slap his ol' lazy feet down the road.' That's what he say."

"What? I be fired?"

"You quicker than they gives you credit fo'," he say.

"Cracka cain't be firin me," I say.

"Cracka done did it," Freddie say.

"I'm gone talk to him," I say and start into the buildin.

"Suit yo'self," he say.

"Just cause I be late," I say.

Freddie laugh loud. "Three fuckin days late, nigger."

I go on into the buildin and that fuckin radio be playin that country-ass shit. Reynolds be standin over by a forklift talkin to that great big nigger who always be kissin his ass. Reynolds always be callin him. "Big Jim, come here. Big Jim, do that. Big Jim, suck my dick." Reynolds look up and see me comin.

"Freddie say you done fired me," I say.

"Freddie told you right," he say.

"But why?"

"Because I ain't seen you in three days, that's fucking why," he say.

"I been busy," I say.

"Well, you ain't busy no more," he say. "Not around here anyway."

I looks at him and I really want to hit him but that big nigger climb off that forklift and stands beside him. I look at Big Jim and say, "What you got to do with this, *House Nigger*?"

Big Jim make like he want to hit me, but Reynolds stop him. "Don't hurt the boy now, Big Jim." Then he say to me, "Now, you take your skinny ass away from here before I let Big Jim have his way with you."

I looks at Big Jim's giant hands all balled up into fists like that and I don't say nuffin else. I just turns and walks away from the sorry muthafuckas.

So, I makes my way over to the address what Mama done give me, to that man's house, the one who have the job. I figger I can work fo' a coupla days, get some money so I can buy my gun, then score real big. Maybe go down to Mexico and get some of that senorita pussy.

The house be on a hill and got one of them circlin driveways. I mean, man, it be huge and there is a coupla fancy cars parked in front. One of them is this fine red BMW convertible with a white roof. It's like it ain't got a speck of dust on the fucker. The license plate say *COOL*. I walk on up to the front door but before I can find the bell to ring it, the door opens and there's this brother in a pink shirt and khakis.

"May I help you," he say.

"Yeah, I'm lookin fo' Mr. Dalton," I say.

"I'm Mr. Dalton," he say.

I'm kinda shocked, you know. I been expectin this muthafucka to be white and here he is darker than me. I don't know what to say.

"What can I do for you son?" he ax.

"I'm here about a job," I says.

Then this kinda fat woman come up behind him. She black too, but she dressed like a maid in them movies. "You be Sadie Jenkins' boy?" she ax.

"Yessum," I say.

"Mr. Dalton," she say, "this here is the son of my friend Sadie. I told you bout him. You said I could hire somebody to clean up the pool area and trim the grass when Felipe don't come."

"I remember, Lois," he say. He look at me and reach out to shake my hand. He give it a squeeze and say, "Lois, will take care of you. I've got to go. I'll be back late, Lois, so don't wait dinner."

"Yessir, Mr. Dalton," Lois say.

Lois and I watch as Dalton drive off in his fine Mercedes. Then Lois turn to me, her face all changed into sumpin' hard. "Sadie told me bout you," she say. "Now, you got a chance here, boy. Mr. Dalton can help you. Yo mama is my friend. That's why you got this chance. You understand?"

I still be stunned by the house and the fact that Dalton be black.

"You hear me, boy? Yo name Van, right?"

"They calls me Go," I say.

"Come on in the house, Van." She let me inside and close the door. "Fuck up once and you out the door, boy," she say.

"Why we gots to start out like this?" I say.

She stop and nod her head. "Okay," she say. "Yo mama my friend. You want this job?"

"I don't know what it is," I say.

"Sweepin, cuttin bushes and grass and washin cars," she say. "Can you do that?"

I looks around the house at the fine-ass furniture and the paintins and the vases and I think about the gun I'm gone buy with the money I make. Then I can come back and steal this shit. "I can do it," I say.

"Don't you be sayin you gone work when you ain't," she say. "I ain't gone take no mess. You mess up once and you gone. You study on that fo' awhile."

"Don't sweat it, old girl," I say, tryin to flirt with her.

"And don't think I got this old by bein stupid," she say. "You show me some respect or you can slap them dogs on down that hill."

"Okay," I say.

"Now you gots to bathe fo' you come to work," she say, turnin her head away from me.

"I'm just gone get sweaty and funky while I'm workin," I tells her.

"But you shows up clean," she say. "Got it?"

I nod. "Want me to go home and wash up?"

"Don't get funny," she say. "Now c'mon with me out back and I'll show what you can do first."

We walks through that fine house and I just cain't believe it. We pass on through this party kinda room with a bar and I'm thinkin I'm gone be sneakin back in there. We go on out these glass doors to outside. The pool is giant, man. And the bottom is all painted up in a design and the water look so clean and blue. There be benches and chairs everywhere and it look like a fancy park.

Lois hand me a broom. "Sweep everythin that ain't ground," she say. "And pick it with that dustpan over there and put in a plastic bag. The bags be in that shed."

"You want me to put dirt from outside in a bag?" I ax.

She just look at me.

"That's stupid," I say. "I can just sweep it over on the ground."

"Do what I say, boy," she say.

"Okay."

I sweeps everthin. Then I rakes part of the big yard. Then the bitch got me moppin the floor of the pool house. Man, if I wasn't funky befo', I'm sho 'nuff funky now. Lois look at what I done and nods, but she don't smile. She just tell me she see me tomorrow and then walk on back in the house with her big fat ass.

I decide I'm gone go on down to the pool hall and check out Tito and Yellow, see what they be doin, get Tito to buy me a taco or sumpin'. When I gets there Yellow and Tito already be in the middle of a game.

"Where you been, nigger?" Tito ax.

"I been workin, man."

"Naw, you ain't been workin," Tito say.

Yellow laugh.

Tito take a shot and stand up straight. "I know you ain't been workin cause I went lookin fo' yo ass over to the warehouse and they told me yo ass been fired."

"Yeah, but I been workin anyway," I say.

"Where?" Yellow ax.

"Over in West Holly," I say. I pick up a stick from the rack and walk round the table. I takes a shot.

"Hey, we was in the middle of a game," Yellow say.

"You was going to lose anyway," I tell him.

"What you doin way the fuck over there?" Tito ax.

"Don't even ax," I say.

"Nigger shamed of what he do," Yellow laughs.

"I workin at this rich dude's house, okay," I say.

"Doin what?" Tito ax.

"Sweepin," I says under my breath.

"Say what?" Tito say.

"Sweepin," I say and both of them bust out laughin. "Fuck botha y'all."

"Sweepin what?" Yellow want to know.

"Round the pool area," I say. "Happy now?"

"What, you some whitey's houseboy now?" Tito ax. He puts a cigarette between his lips.

Fatman yell over, "No smokin in here!"

"Is the muthafucka lit?" Tito yell back.

"Make sho it stay that way," Fatman say. Then more to himself, "I don't give a shit what you do outside, but I be damned you gone smoke in my 'tablishment."

"Shut the fuck up, old man," Tito say.

"I ain't no houseboy," I say. "And he ain't no whitey." I shake my head. "I gets fired, right? So, I go to check out this job my mama told me 'bout. I just want to make a coupla dollars to buy me a piece. Anyway, I get there and the dude's blacker than me. And this house, man oh man, this house is a son of a bitch. Paintins on the walls, a Benz, a Beamer. I couldn't believe the shit."

"What the nigger do?" Tito ax.

I looks at him.

"How he get rich?" he ax.

"I don't know. But he a rich muthafucka. The swimmin pool bigger than yo fuckin house," I say.

"Drug dealer," Yellow say.

"I don't think," I say. "He didn't look like no drug dealer."

"I bet he be a lawyer then," Yellow say.

"Shut the fuck up, Yellow," Tito snap. "I want you to make me a list," he say to me. "I wanna know what he got in the house."

"I ain't makin no fuckin list," I say.

"I thought you and me was tight," he say.

"That ain't got nuffin to do with shit," I say. "I'm gone make my money and buy me a gun and then I'm outta here."

"See, there you go, nigger," Tito say. "You make yo money and buy yo gun and then you and me go back wif the list you gone make and we rob the muthafucka and split."

I laughs at him. "How you gone run anyway with a big ass paintin under your arm?" I ax. "I'm robbin that K'rean mutha and a bank. I can run with money. I can spend money. I cain't spend no paintin."

"We sell the paintin, buckwheat," Tito say. He frown at Yellow for lettin out a laugh. "We fence the shit."

"Where you gone fence a paintin in a fuckin ghetto, nigger?" I ax.

"Nigger got a point," Yellow say.

"Shut up, Yellow," Tito say. "What it gone hurt, you makin me the list?" he ax me.

"Okay, shit," I say. "I'll think about the fuckin list."

"See, I told you we was tight," Tito say.

I takes another shot. "Since we so tight, you can buy me some food cross the street," I say.

"Okay," he say.

Tito buy me a burrito across the street at Sammy the vendor's wagon. Sammy be blind, but he can tell the dif'rence between a one and a five. Nobody know how he do it, but he do it all the time. We be standin there eatin when this bitch come walkin by. She be wearin some little shorts and her butt meat be hangin out a little bit.

Yellow whisper to me, "Girl got some junk in the trunk."

I don't pay him no mind. I'm just lookin at the bitch and I see she lookin at me and so I walks over and catches up wif her at the corner.

"Hey, baby," I say.

"Hey, baby, yo'self," she say back.

"I ain't seen you round here befo'," I say.

"I ain't been round here before," she say.

"Dangerous neighborhood," I says.

She look me up and down and say, "I see."

"Oh, you gone be like that," I says.

"I ain't bein no way," she say.

I realize how funky I am and I say, "I just got off work. I don't always stink."

She laugh and I laugh wif her.

"What yo name, girl?" I ax.

"My name be Kesrah," she say.

I nod, thinkin bout her name. "I be Go," I say. "Where you goin,
Kesrah?"

"Home," she say.

"How old you?" I ax.

"What you care?" she say.

"Yo mama home?"

She shake her head.

"Like I said, this be a bad neighborhood. I better walk you home.
That be awright wif you?"

"Awright wif me."

Tito call out to me. "Nigger, you be careful! That shit must be
fourteen."

Me and Kesrah halfway cross the street now. "You fourteen, girl?"

"I might be," she say. "What you care?"

"I don't care," I say.

I lookin at Kesrah while we walkin to her house. She be little, but
she got some big titties. She short and kinda fat, but I'm gone get behind her in her house ride her dog-style, gone make the bitch bark like
a dog. That's what I'm gone do. And I gone make baby number five.

"You got any babies?" I ax her.

"No," she say.

"You ever been wif a man befo'?" I ax

"Sho I have."

"Then you ain't been doin it right," I says. "You wants a baby?"

"Yeah, I wants a baby. Everybody want a baby."

"I'm gone give you a baby," I tell her.

Fibe

So, I gets to the girl's house and her big fat uncle be asleep on the couch, stinkin of Colt 45. She giggle as we sneak past him to the back of the house. I tells her to shut up. Man, her uncle is big so I sho don't want his ugly ass waking up.

"Don't worry none," she say. "He ain't gone do nuffin' even if he do wake up." And then we in her bedroom and she push her tongue down my throat. I gab her sweater and pull it off and she almost ain't got no titties.

I laugh, "Shit, girl you be almost flat-chested."

She get mad then. "I a woman, though."

I kiss her. "Oh yeah, you a woman though."

We gets our clothes off and I get on top her and ride her real good for a long time and she be crying and shit and saying it hurt, but she like it. I know she like it, the way she moanin like that. I fucks her good. Then I get up and pull on my pants.

"You gonna come back tomorrow?" she ax.

"Naw, baby, I can't be comin round here seein you."

"But," she say.

I shake my head. "You too young, girl. I cain't be runnin round havin people see us together."

She don't know what to say, then she walk to the window. "So, you doggin me," she say.

I shrug.

"Nigger," she say.

"You ain't no woman neither," I says. "You call that shit you was doin fuckin?"

She startin to cry. Then she commence to screamin for her big ass uncle. That muthafucka be drunk as shit, but he haul his big butt off that couch and start talkin trash.

"Who the fuck you?" he say.

"Yo daddy," I say and try to get through the room to the front door.

That big sonofabitch steps in front of me and I see the nigger be wearin these funny-ass pajamas with clowns on 'em. I says, "Nigger, look at yoself."

"What you talkin bout?" he ax.

"That shit you be wearin. You looks like some kinda circus fool."

Then that bitch come standin in the doorway lookin all pitiful and cryin and shit with a blanket pulled up over her.

"What goin on?" that big nigger say.

"He rape me," she say.

"What the fuck?" Then he try to jump at me, saying he gone kill my ass, but I jump over the couch and get to the door. Old fat ass fall down and knock over his forty what been on the floor. "I'm gone get you," he say.

"You ain't gone get nothin," I say. Then I looks over at the girl and I say, "But a nephew, cause I don't miss."

"I hate you," she scream.

"And I hate you too," I says. "What that got to do wif anythin?"

I run on out the house and into the street and I be laughin. I run through a coupla backyards in case the uncle got a gun or some shit and I come out on the next street.

I be on my way to the pool hall where I'm gone tell Tito and Yellow about the young pussy and that fat uncle muthafucka. They gone laugh, I just know it. I round the corner near the school when it just gettin to be dusk and I see a coupla headlights comin down the street real slow. I think, who the fuck is this? And then I see it's a Jeep and a buncha niggers jump out and start runnin at me. I run, man. These is some fast niggers too. I try to climb the fence at the basketball courts. One of them catches my leg and I kick him off and then I get over. I run into the shadows and slip through a hole in the wall and down an alley. Then I kick into this abandon buildin and hide, be real quiet. I don't hear 'em. Then I realize somebody in there wif me.

"Who dat?" I say.

"Who dat?" he ax. Then he start laughin. He strike a match and light a candle. It's that Willy wino muthafucka.

"Put that candle out, nigger," I say.

"Shit, they gone, boy," he say. "What they want you fo'?"

"Some rich boy. I kick his ass and now he comin back wif his posse. Muthafucka. I bet not catch his ass alone."

"You bad, huh?"

I look at his red eyes behind that candle. "Yeah, I'm bad."

"I used to be bad my ownself," he say.

"You sho ain't bad now," I say. "No, man, you worst." I laughs at my joke.

"You a funny nigger too, huh?" he say. "How yo mama?"

"Don't be bringin up my mama," I tell him.

"She still got that mole just under her tittie?" he say.

I get up and I'm bout to kick his ass.

"Sit down, boy," he say with this hard voice that don't sound like it could come out his head.

I sit back down.

"Listen, boy, I'm gone tell you somethin. I done fucked up my life."

"No shit," I says.

"Shut up and listen," he say. "I don't want you fuckin up the way I did."

"Who the fuck you be to me," I say. "I don't know you from shit."

"That don't matter none," he say. "I don't want you messin up and hurtin your mama. She been through enuff."

"What the fuck you talkin bout?" I ax. "I'm gettin the fuck outta here." I move to the door.

"Yo mama is a good woman," he say.

"Yeah and you a wino," I say. "So, what your point?"

"Don't fuck up," he say.

"Yeah, well, you too," I say. "And Merry Christmas and Happy Easter."

At the pool hall Tito in the back gettin his dick suck by that fat ho who come around sometime. That what Yellow tells me. I halfway wants to go back there and watch, but I don't. The ho might get after me and I don't want none of that shit. Tito let anything suck his dick. Yellow be lookin at me.

"What you lookin at?" I say.

"Why you sweatin?" he ax.

I thinks about tellin him about that Jeep muthafucka, but I don't like the way runnin sound in my head. "I took a coupla shots over at the hoops," I say.

"You was shootin baskets," he laugh.

"What so funny?" I ax.

"You out there shootin baskets," he say. "What really happen?"

"That's what happen," I say. "Now, shut the fuck up."

Tito in back and he hear us. "What's goin on?" he say.

"Nothin," I say. "Nigger just gettin on my nerves."

"Yeah, well I ain't the only one be gettin on nerves," Yellow say.

"Watch where you steppin, funky ass muthafucka," I say and I gives him a hard look.

"Fuck you," he say.

"Fuck you," I say.

"Fuck you," he say.

"Fuck you," I say.

"Fuck you," he say.

"Fuck you," I say.

"Fuck you," he say.

"Why don't you two niggers just go outside and fuck each other," Tito say.

That fat ho come from out the back and walk past. She wave her fingers at Tito.

I shakes my head. "How can you let that ugly bitch put her mouth on yo thang?" I ax.

"She better lookin than yo babies' mama," he say. "At least she know what she doin."

"Don't be talkin bout my babies' mamas," I say.

"Like you give a shit, nigger," he say. He pull out a cigarette and strike a match.

Fatman yell over to him. "No smokin!"

"It too cold to be outside, Fatman. Let a nigger have his fix."

Fatman must be tired cause he don't say nothing else.

Yellow chalk up a stick and smile at me. "So, what happen with that jailbait," he ax.

"I knocked it out big time," I say.

"What could that little girl do for a man?" Tito say.

I just look at him.

"Fuckin children and havin babies don't make you no man," he say.

"What yo' problem," I ax. "Why you comin down on me?"

"Let's play pool," he say.

Now, I'm really upset. We shoot a game without sayin nothin. Tito be smokin his fourth cigarette and be puttin 'em out on the floor. Fatman come over and look at Tito.

"See, that another reason I don't want you niggers smokin in here. Look at this shit."

"Shut up, Fatman," Tito say. "You gots to sweeps the fucka anyway."

"Yeah," Yellow says.

Fatman grumbles and walk on back to his stool behind the counter.

"You guys ever look at the Willy the Wonker muthafucka?" I ax.

Tito sink the five and look at me. "You mean the wino over near the courts?" he ax.

"Yeah," I say.

"I seen him," Tito say. "Why? What he to you?"

"He ain't nuffin to me."

"Why you be askin bout him then?" Yellow ax.

"You shut the fuck up," I say.

"Suck my dick," he say.

"Whip it out, muthafucka," I say.

"I would but I don't wanna make you cry," he say.

"Listen to you two niggers," Tito say. "Sound like you be twelf years old. Talkin shit like that."

"Fuck both you," I say and I walk out.

Sex

Next mornin I gets up and I wash my pits cause they real funky from workin and gettin on that gash. I puts on some clean drawers too, then I sit on the bed and look at the Mickey Mouse clock I got during the riots. Niggers was laughin at me left and right, pointin at the clock. They had TV's and stereos, but, shit, I liked the fuckin clock. Made me think of Dissyland. I was there once and all I can remember is that Main Street and me thinkin "this is what it s'posed to be like." Fuck 'em for laughin at my clock. The shit work. Time just keep movin, them hands keep sweepin and that make me think about work. I work there two weeks and I'm gone have enough for my gun. And then, watch out Van Go gone be gone and went.

I go out to the table and Baby Girl already be sitting there workin on a bowl of Life cereal. "You like that shit, don't you, Baby Girl," I say.

Mama turn around at the stove and say, "Don't be swearin' in fron' o her like that, boy."

I don't pay her no 'tention. I sit down and eat the eggs she slide in front of me. "Ain't you got no meat?" I say.

"No, that's it," she say.

I think about gettin up and walkin out. No meat? What kind of shit? But I be hongry, so I eat.

"How you like yo job?" Mama ax.

"It a job."

"Lois say they house is like a mansion," Mama say.

"It is a mansion, Mama," I say. "That nigger is loaded."

"Don't be callin Mr. Dalton that," she say.

"You call me that," I say. "'Cause he gots bucks he ain't no nigger? 'Cause I ain't got nuffin, I am?"

"Shut up, nigger," she say.

She look at me and I look at her and we bust out laughin. It feel good to laugh with Mama again. We laugh for a few minutes and then I tells her I gots to get to work.

"Okay, nigger," she say.

We laugh again.

I get on the bus and start my trip over to the hills. I'm still laughin in my head about what Mama say. She give me three dollars 'fore I left. So, I be sittin on the bus and this white girl get on and sit cross from me. She look like she goin to work.

"Goin to work?" I ax.

She nod and look away.

"Where you work at?" I ax.

"I work at a store," she say, still not lookin at me.

"What sto?"

She don't say nuffin.

"What sto?"

Nuffin.

I leans forward and put my elbows on my knees. "You 'fraid I'm gone walk into the place you work at and say hello?"

She shake her head.

"I come in there and say hello and yo' boss take you aside and say, 'Who that nigger?' That what you 'fraid of?"

She get up and walk on to the back of the bus. An old black woman who been listenin be starin at me.

"What you lookin at?" I ax.

She look away.

I walks another six blocks after I get off the bus. I guess rich folk don't like buses comin too close to they houses. Maybe it the fumes they don't like. Maybe it's guys like me. Shit, I don't know. I just walks up the hill past the big driveways and I sees the gardeners starin at me. Most of 'em is oriental and they givin me the evil eye and I thinks about the gun I'm gone buy and how I'm gone rob that K'rean mutha.

I walk up the driveway and Dalton honk his horn at me as he drive out. I wave and I feel stupid doin it. I put my hands in my pockets.

When I gets to the door, Lois is standin there and she be lookin at her watch.

"Well, you ain't too late," she say.

"I ain't got no watch," I say.

"That ain't my problem," she say. "You make yo'self some money, maybe you kin buy you a watch."

"I ain't got no need fo' no watch," I say. "Time is the white man's. Time ain't mine."

"Nigger, you crazy," she say.

I laugh, cause I 'member Mama callin me a nigger at the house that mornin. I laugh and Lois laugh too, but she don't know why I be laughin.

"Come on in and gets to work," she say. "First thing you gots to do is wash the cars." She lead the way into the room off the kitchen. "All the keys be in this here cabinet. They is four cars in the big garage. You takes 'em out one at a time and washes 'em."

"How I s'posed to get 'em out?" I ax.

"I told you, simple, the keys in this here cabinet," she say.

"You mean, I drives the cars out?" I say.

"I swear, you *is* as stupid as you look," she say.

I think about gettin mad cause she call me stupid, but I'm too excited about drivin them cars, even if it is just out the garage. I takes all the keys and go outside. The doors be open and there's them cars. I wonder why they needs to be washed. They already be so shiny that they 'bout to blind my ass. They's this one little red car, real low down to the ground, one of them F'raris. I gets in behind the wheel and it be like a glove and I wish Tito and Yellow could see my ass now, lookin all fine up in there with the leather. I turn the mutha fuckin key and the sound damn near make me shit my pants. Va-roooom! That engine sound like the army coming through, but smooth as sick shit. I thinks that one day I gots to have me one of them. 'Cept I wants a black one. Black on black with a red stripe run straight down through the middle of the muthafucker. I put it in gear and roll it out into the yard and my heart be beatin like nobody's goddamn bizness. Kabamada kabamada kabamada, my heart be poundin. I turn off the engine and get out. I close the door and step away and look at it, tryin to wonder what I look like when I was sittin behind that wheel.

"Nigger, you better get to washin that car and stop yo dreamin," Lois call at me from the glass door.

I gets the hose and the bucket from the shed and I'm rinsin this muthafucker off when this fine ass bitch come out the house with this bikini on and I think I'm gone die for damn sho. The bitch put her towel on one of the lounge chairs and then she dive into the water. It don't even look like she make a splash. I'm watchin her, but I can't see for shit from where I am wif the car. I walk over to the hedge so I can look over at her. She sees me lookin at her and I turn away. I be a long way from the car and I feel kinda stupid. I think shit I better git back on over there and wash that damn car. I go back and I start sloppin suds on the muthafucka and I hear somebody callin to me. I turns around and there that bitch in the bikini, standin at the hedge.

"Yeah you," she say. "Come over here."

I walk over to her and I'm feelin kinda scared and then I feels kinda mad cause I hates feelin scared.

"What's your name?" she ax. Her eyes is bright.

"My name be Van Go," I says. "Van Go Jenkins. But my friends, they calls me Go."

"Go," she says. "I like that."

"I'm Penelope," she say. "Penelope Dalton. When did Daddy hire you?"

"Other day," I say. And I find I cain't look right at her.

"Well, I hope he's paying you okay," she say. "Daddy can be pretty tight."

"He payin okay," I say.

"How old are you?" she ax.

"Why you wanna know that?" I say.

"Just a question," she say.

"Twenty," I tells her.

"I'm twenty-two," she say. "I just finished school. Stanford. What about you? You go to school?"

"No."

"Did you finish high school?" she ax.

"Listen, I gotta get back to washin that car," I says. I feels sick.

"I didn't mean to hurt your feelings," she say. "Maybe we can talk again soon."

"Sure," I says.

"Hey, can you drive?" she ax.

"Sho, I can drive," I say.

"Good," she say. "I'll be right back."

So, I be finishin up wif the car and wonderin what this bitch got in mind fo' me. I'm gettin all nervous, waitin and wonderin. I gets the car all rinsed off and sits down on the bumper.

Lois yell out at me from the house. "What you doin'? Ain't nobody payin you to sit round."

"Mr. Dalton's daughter told me to wait here," I say.

Lois come out the house. "Why she tell you that?"

"I don't know."

"Boy, you bet be careful now," she say.

"What you talkin bout, ol' lady," I say to her. "I ain't studyin you."

"You bet be studyin sumpin," she say.

Penelope Dalton come back out the house then. She wearin this tight, short dress what look mo' like a slip than anythin else.

"Where you think you goin'," Lois bark at her.

Penelope laugh it off just as cool as shit. "I'm going to have young Mister—." She stop and look at me. "What's your name?"

"Van Go."

"That's right," she say. "I'm going to have Van here drive me down the hill for a little shopping."

"Lawd, have mercy," Lois say.

"I'm sure he will," Penelope say.

Lois give me the evil eye and say, "You mind now."

And I'm thinkin, shit, I ain't no dog. I gives her the evil eye back and gets into the car. Penelope surprise me and be gettin in the front seat wif me. Shit if I ain't sweatin now.

"Drive," she say.

"Just like that," I says.

"Just like that," she say. "Let's go, Van."

Ain't nobody call me Van. Everybody call me Go all the time. But I don't say nuffin. I kinda like the way it sound when she call me Van. "Where you want me to take you?"

"Take me to Rose's," she say. "That's in Santa Monica. Just drive. I'll tell you when to turn and which way." She say that last part real slow and it make me nervous, wondering what she be meanin, cause I know she be signifyin.

We gets to this fancy ass restrant and it just covered wif people. Blond bitches with shades and white dudes with they shirts open showin stomack muscles. But Penelope dont wanna go in, she just wanna pick up this candyass nigger who be waitin outside. She get out the car and hug the guy then they gets in the backseat.

"Okay, Van, let's go," she say.

"Where to?" I ax.

"Let's go to your neighborhood," she say.

I just look at her in the mirror. Then I looks at the dude in the silk shirt and the shades hangin round his neck.

"We want to see where you live," she say.

"Yeah, brother," the guy say.

"Van, this is Roger. Roger, this is Van. He's working for my father."

"Cool, brother," Roger say. "Take us to the hood and we can shoot some hoops and then maybe score some weed and eat some chicken." They laughs.

"Let's go, Van," Penelope say.

"I don't know. This is your father's car," I say.

"This is my car, Van," she say. "Now, let's roll." Penelope lean back into the seat and look at my eyes in the mirror. "You like my daddy?" she ask.

"I guess so," I say. "He hired me."

"You know he puts a lot of money into the 'hood," she say.

"I don't get it," I say.

"He makes loans and gives some cheap legal help," she say.

Roger laugh out loud, then say, "You mean he's a loan shark and an ambulance chaser."

They giggles together and Penelope say, "You watch what you say now. Van might run home and tell daddy."

I be filled up with heat now. They be laughin at me? The mutha-fuckas laughin at me? Shit, I wanted to stop the car and kick they asses. That Roger muthafucka, think he all cool and shit and that he look good. He ain't shit. He ain't nuffin but a sorry-ass muthafucka and I oughta slit his sorry-ass throat.

"You live around here, Van?" Roger asked. "What is this? Compton?"

I don't say nothin. I just glance at them in the mirror. They starin out the windows like we in Jungleland or some shit. Like we at Dissy-land in that fuckin submarine. Niggers on the street be lookin at me drivin this fine car and I feels cool till I remember that I'm in the front by myself and them two bitches be in the back and I be lookin like some flunky-ass chauffeur.

Penelope lean forward and put her hand on my shoulder. "Take us someplace colorful to eat," she say.

The feelin of her hand on my shoulder makes me less mad. "What you wanna eat?" I ax.

"Something funky," she say. "Ribs. Something like that."

"Hey, Van," Roger say. "You finish high school?"

I don't say nothin.

"It's okay if you didn't. No jobs out there anyway." Roger look back out the window. "I didn't expect the houses to have yards here."

"Whatchew 'pect?" I ax.

"You know, like slums and stuff."

"They're people just like you and me," Penelope say.

"You ought to think about going back to school," Penelope say, loo-kin at my eyes in the mirror. "I bet daddy could help you get a schol-arship to college."

"What kinda schola ship I'm gone get?" I ax.

"I don't know. You're underprivileged, you've that going for you."

Roger laugh. "Can you run fast?" he ax. "If you can run fast then you can run track. Can you play basketball?"

"Yeah, I can play ball," I say.

"There you are then. A basketball scholarship." Roger got this smar-tass look on his face. I stared at him in the mirror, but he don't look at me.

I starts worryin and hopin that Yellow and Tito don't see me. I de-cide to take them to this rib joint a couple blocks away. I know Tito and Yellow won't be in there, cause Tito got throwed out for feelin the waitress. But once we parked in front, I don't wanna go in. I don't want nobody I know seein me out with these fuckas.

Penelope and Roger gets out, but I stay behind the wheel.

"Aren't you hungry?" Penelope ax.

"Naw, I ain't hungry," I say.

"We're paying," that Roger muthafucka say.

"Somebody better watch the car," I says.

"Come on," Penelope say. "Don't worry about the car. I've got insurance. It's just a car. Come on."

I be trapped. I be feelin like a little animal they found on the road some damn place. I'm pissed as hell now, but they gots money and I realize how important that be. Mr. Dalton got all the money in the world. And I ain't got shit. I don't wanna go in, but I do. I'm wonderin why they so interested in me and be actin so nice to me like this. The sun be bright and I feels like I be caught up in a web of light. I follow them into the place called Ernie's Kitchen.

This one dude I know wave at me from cross the room, but he be starin at Penelope and Roger. Then I see Cleona starin at me from the far wall. She still mad, but she interested. She wave.

"You know her?" Penelope say as we sit at a table.

"Of course he knows her," Roger say. "He probably knows everybody in here. Right, Van?"

I don't say nothing.

"Invite her over," Penelope say.

"She all the way over there," I say.

The waitress bring us some chicken and beer and we start eatin.

"This stuff be jammin," Roger say. He look at me. "Did I say it right?" he ax.

"Yeah, that's how they says it," I say.

They keeps eatin, but I can't.

"Eat," Penelope say.

"I ain't hungry," I tell her.

"Want some more beer?" Roger ax.

"Yeah," I say and I watches him fill my glass.

"What's your father do?" Penelope ax me.

"I ain't got no father," I say.

"Did he die?" she ax.

"He was born dead," I say.

"What about your mother?" Roger ax. "Is she alive?"

"Yeah, she alive," I tell them. "She a slave."

Penelope and Roger look at each other and then they laughs loud. Eveybody in the place looks over at us. "You're a riot," Penelope say to me. "A slave," she repeat. "That's rich."

"Tell me, Van," Roger say, "you got a girlfriend?"

I looks at him and laughs. "Shit, man, I gots me fo' babies."

Penelope look at Roger and he look at her and they bust up laughin.

"You're kidding me," Penelope say. "Four babies? Are you married?"

"Hell no," I say.

"You're not married and some woman has had four babies by you?" Roger ax.

"No," I says. "Fo' different womens."

They look at each other and Roger make like he whistlin but don't no sound come out. Then they be starin at me.

"What the fuck you lookin at," I say.

"Oh, nothing," Penelope say. "Four babies. Do you see them?"

"I sees my babies," I say and I starts to eat some of that chicken. I be rippin into a thigh like it the last food on earf. Grease be all on my mouth and shit. I drink some beer and I see they ready to go. I wipes my mouth on my sleeve.

"That was good, Van," Penelope say. "Thanks for bringing us here."

They sits in the back seat and I be drivin them around like some kinda natral-born fool. I takes them out of my hood anyways and they don't even notice cause they in the backseat drinkin booze out a flask. Roger offer me some but I say no and he takes a big swig and laugh at me.

I wanna pull over and drag his skinny ass out the car and kick the shit outta him. But I don't do it and I realize they money scare me and then I feels sick.

They makes me drive them over to downtown and Roger say he know a corner where he can score some weed and Penelope say, "Oh goody." And I just drives the car. There we is on Union and I'm leanin against the car watchin Richie Rich and Veronica buy they little bag when I see a jeep comin up. Damn, if it ain't Jeep Man and he got one of his partners with him. He parks behind me and they hops out and I'm thinkin oh shit and here they comes.

"Looky, looky," Jeep Man say.

"Fuck you," I say and since I know why he stop, I just drives on his face with my fist. Bam! Blood fly out his eye like a bug and the punch feel real good to me. Real good. So good I don't hardly feel it when Jeep Man's partner hit me in the chest. I comes up with my knee in his fuckin balls and he double over. But I don't want him. I want Jeep Man and so I drives on his face again and I feel it soften under my knuckles, like bread or sumpin. Bam! I gots blood on my fist and he gone. He ain't gone be trouble to nobody for awhile. I hears a scream and I turn to see Penelope standin there. She turn and Roger catch her in his arms.

"They try to jump me," I says.

"Let's go," Roger say.

We gets into the car and I tear off. My fist is bloody and my heart be beating fast and I feel good. I feel real good. "So, you get some smoke?" I ax.

"Yeah," Roger say.

"Well, light it up, nigger," I say. I look at Roger in the mirror and I see in his face that he ain't never been called nigger before. "I don't mean nothin by it. I'm a nigger, too."

He rolls a joint while Penelope kill off the flask. She drunk as shit. We smoke and I drives.

"You ever been in a fight?" I ax Roger.

"Not really," he say.

"Whatchew mean, not really?" I ax.

"I've got a black belt in Kung Fu, but I've never actually been in a fight."

I hold up my fist and show him the dried blood on my knuckles. "That there be my black belt."

Penelope lets out a high and drunk giggle.

"You get fucked up like this every day?" I ax.

But they don't answer me. Penelope is almost passed out and Roger is feelin on her titties.

"Hey, Roger," I say.

"What?"

"I gots to get back. I'm gone let you out here," I say. I pull over and turn to look him in the eyes. He too fucked up to argue. He look at Penelope. "I'll take her on home," I says.

"Okay," Roger say. He gets out and lets Penelope fall over on the seat. He watch as I drives off.

It be almost dark by the time I gets Penelope back to her house. There some lights on but otherwise it be quiet. Penelope is in and out, talkin shit and babblin and shit and I can't make out what the fuck she be sayin. I gets her out of the car, but she can't stand up by her own self. I starts to take her to the front door and my heart be beatin a mile a minute. Bam Bam Bam Bam Bam, in my chest like that, like it bout to bust out my body. Bam Bam Bam Bam Bam. Then the bitch start to singin and I tells her ass to shut up. She look at me like who the fuck I be tellin her to shut up.

"Celebrate, celebrate, dance to the music," she sing louder.

I begs her, "Please, Penelope, please don't make no fuss. You don't wanna gets into no trouble, do you?"

She looks at me and then she put her finger to her lips and say, "Shhhhh." She look at the house. "Don't take me in there," she say. "Take me around back to the pool house."

"Okay," I says. I do like she tells me and I damn near have to carry her round the side of the house and past the pool. The lights from inside the house be shinin off the water in the pool. A pump or some shit somewhere is makin a hummin noise. I open the door of the pool house and put Penelope on one of them lounge chairs. I watches her body sink down into the cushion. I'm lookin at her and my feelings is all tied up in knots. I want to be like her. I hate her. I hate her money. I hate her daddy. I hate the way she look at me me like I don't know shit bout the world. But, damn she fine. Sumpin bout her almost white though and I hates her. Damn, she be fine as shit. Her shirt be open just a little bit and I can see her tittie almost. She look good, awright. I put my hand down there and touch that tittie. Just like fuckin silk. I squeezes her little nipple and she moan and I don't think she know it me. Then I hear this tappin sound. I looks up and I see somebody comin.

"Penelope?" the woman call out. "Penelope? Is that you?"

A woman is standin by the pool. Shit, I thinks. I'm in here with this drunk bitch. They gone throw my ass in the jail for damn sho. Penelope make a noise. The woman hear her and come to the door of the pool house.

"Penelope?" she say.

But I put my mouth over Penelope's so she can't say nuffin. I'm in the shadow with Penelope and then I see the woman got this white cane. Shit, the bitch be blind. I almost laughs out loud. But my mouth is still on Penelope's mouth and she be kissin me now. She don't know who the fuck I is. The blind bitch walk on away and back into the house. And I be into it now. Penelope call me Roger and I think I don't care who the fuck she think I is, I'm gone knock it out. Damn straight. And that's what I does. Her bony ass ain't for shit, but I knocks it out anyway. I spreads her open and stabs her. I stab her again. I wanna wake her up and say the pussy ain't no good. But she asleep. Sleepin like in that story. But my kiss dint wake her ass up.

Seben

Next mornin, Baby Girl come runnin into my room. She be yellin for me to get up and come to the phone. I tells her I be tryin to sleep, but she keep pullin on me.

"What the fuck is it?" I ax.

"They on the phone," she say.

"Who on the phone?" I be wakin up and my mind be racin like crazy. The cops? Mr. Dalton? Who be on the phone. I awake now.

"From the telebision," Baby Girl say.

"What?" I ax.

"Snookie Cane," she say. "From that Snookie Cane Show."

"Leave me the hell alone," I say. "You ain't funny."

"I'se for real," she say.

I gets up and walks out in my underwear to the phone. There's some bitch on the other end and she wants to know if I'm me. I tell her, "Fuck yeah, I'm me! What you want?"

I hears her laugh away from the phone. Then she says, "We want you to be our guest on Snookie Cane."

I'm thinkin this a joke. "Yeah, right," I say. "And why you want me on the show?"

"Well actually we have a guest who wants to surprise you with something. Someone who has a crush on you." She take a breath, then say, "We're taping the show today at one. We're at Oplie While Studios in Burbank. Stage F."

"You fo' real?" I say.

"Yes, I am," she say. "Can you make it?"

"Somebody got a crush on me?" I ax.

"Yes, indeed."

"The Snookie Cane Show?"

"Yes," she say.

"Snookie Cane gone be there?" I ax.

"Yes."

"I'm gone be on TV?" I ax.

"Yes."

"Okay, I be there," I say.

"Be here by twelve-thirty," she say.

"Awright," I say.

She hang up. I hang up. I looks down and sees Baby Girl lookin up at me. I says, "I'm gone be on Snookie Cane."

Baby Girl start screamin. "Mama! Mama! Go gone be on Snookie Cane!" She go runnin in the kitchen. I follows. She tell Mama again.

Mama look at me. "What you done, boy?"

"I ain't done nuffin. Somebody gots a crush on me," I say.

Mama just starin at me.

"That what she say on the phone. Say they doin the show today."

Baby Girl look like she gone bust wide open. "Mama, we gone go watch Go on telebision?"

Mama look worried. She smile at Baby Girl and say, "I guess so."

"Boy, that what you wearin to be on nashnal TV?" Mama ax.

"Yeah and don't fuck wif me," I say.

"Don't talk to me like that," she say. "And you cain't be talkin like that on the telebision."

"They can't tell me how to talk," I say. "Come on, let's go."

Our neighbor-lady, Quanita-Mack drive us in her car. I be sittin in the back wif Baby Girl and them big gals be sittin all over the front seat. They talkin and maybe they even talkin bout me or to me, but I don't be hearin them cause I'm thinkin bout last night and what I done to Penelope.

I feels big. Then I'm thinkin bout who it be that gots a crush on me. I feels real big.

When we gets to the studio there's this nigger in a uniform tellin us we gots to park all the way the fuck across the street. I lean up and out of Quanita-Mack's window and yells at the muthafucka. "I'm supposed to be on the telebision, nigger," I say.

"Listen, I don't care if you're s'posed to be on the moon," he say. "You gotta park over there in lot C."

"You think you the man cause you wearin that uniform," I say.

He just looks at me.

"Sit back, now," Mama say to me.

Quanita-Mack park the car and we walks across the street and into the studio and we find a line at Stage F. I walks up to the front and tells the guy at the door that I'm s'posed to be on the show.

"What's your name?" he ax.

"Van Go Jenkins," I say.

"Okay," he say. "Go on in to door three. They'll take care of you in there."

"What about my Mama and sister," I say.

"And Quanita-Mack," Mama say.

"Yeah," I say. "They gotta get in."

"Okay, okay," he say. "I'll see to it that they get in."

I walk on in and I see the way them people in the line be lookin at me. They know I'm gone be on telebision by now. I find door 3. I knocks on it and it opens. There's a fine lookin white girl standin there, but she lookin at me hard and mean.

"My name be Van Go Jenkins," I says.

"Good, get in here," she say and she grab me by the arm and pull me in. "Gloria!"

A skinny blond headed girl come runnin up. "Yes, Pam?"

"Take this gentleman over to makeup and get him shined up a little bit," Pam say. She look at her clipboard. "Then take him to booth one and put the headset on him."

"Got it," Gloria say. Then she look at me. "Come on."

"So, what the show bout today?" I ax.

"Can't talk about it," Gloria say.

I follow her down a long hallway. "Somebody gots a crush on me," I say.

"How about that," she say.

We gets to this room and there's this fag nigger standin there in purple pants and a pink shirt tied in a knot above his navel and he say, "Come on in, baby, and have a seat. Queenie gonna do you good."

"Fuck that," I says. I turns to Gloria. "That eye ain't gonna touch my ass."

Queenie say, "I don't want to touch yo' ass. Yet."

Gloria put her hand on my arm. "You want to be on TV, right?"

"Yeah," I say.

"You want all those people out there to see you on the stage, right?" she say and she straightens up the front of my shirt.

"Yeah," I say.

"Then let Queenie shine you up just a little bit," she say. "I promise it won't hurt."

"Now, come on, boy and get in this chair," the faggot say to me. "Are you afraid of me?"

"Naw, I ain't scareda you or nobody," I say.

"Then sit down," he say.

I sit down and the nigger take to spread vaseline on my face.

"What that shit fo'?" I ax.

"This will make you shine like a proper TV nigger," he say. Then he laugh real loud and I can see in the back of his mouth. He got gold fillins. He calm down. "So, somebody's got a crush on you, eh, baby?"

"So I hear," I say.

"I can see it," he say. "You think you know who it is?" he ax.

"I don't know who it be," I say. "Could be a lotta peoples."

"Ohhh," he squeal. "I likes that. Confidence. Could it be a man?"

"Bet' not be," I say. "I don't wanna have to kick nobody's ass on nashnal telebision."

"Well, well," he say. "All done."

"That it?" I ax.

"That's it," he say. Then he call out, "Gloria! Gloria!"

Gloria come in and look at me. "All shined up," she say.

"You can take little-Mister-afraid-for-his-ass away now," Queenie say.

"Don't make me have to jump on yo' ass," I say.

"Promises, promises," he say, laughin. "You couldn't handle it."

"Come on," Gloria say and pull me out the room and back into the hallway. "It's almost show time. I've got to get you into the booth and put the headset on you. What kinda music do you like?"

"I likes rap," I says.

"Got lots of rap," she say. "Now you just stand here and put on these headphones. You see that camera?"

"Yeah."

"Well, when that red light comes on, you're on televsion," she say.

"No shit," I say.

"No shit. But don't say anything," she say. "After a while I'll stop the music and tell you to come on out. You just follow the red line on the floor to the stage. Got it?"

I nods.

"Okay, then," she say. "I'll call you in a while."

"Okay."

She leave and pretty soon some lame-ass rap wanna-be shit start comin through the headphones. Just like she say, bout ten minutes later the light on top of that camera come on. I smiles at it and kinda dance to the music. It happen a couple mo' times. Then, just like she say, the music stop and Gloria tell me to walk on out to the stage.

I be struttin cool as shit along that red line, round the corner, through the door and down the stairs to the stage and there they be. My fo' babies sittin on they fo' mamas' laps. Aspireene be sittin on Sharinda's lap. Tylenola be sittin on Reynisha's lap. Dexatrina be sittin on Robertarina's lap. And Rexall sittin there on Cleona's lap. The empty chair be next to Cleona and that big waterhead retard be grabbin at my shirt when I sits down. The audience be booin me and I look up and I can kinda see they ugly ass faces, but the lights in my eyes and I gives them the finger. Booin me? Shit, I kick all they asses.

Snookie Cane, that fat bitch, he standin in the middle of the audience and she say, "What a tough audience. Welcome to the show, Van Go. Look at the expression on his face," she say. "We told Van Go that he was coming here to meet someone who had a crush on him. Are you surprised, Van Go."

I look at the camera. "Yeah, I surprised," I say.

"Today's show is called, You gave me the baby, Now where's the money," she say. "So, where is the money, Van Go? These four ladies say you have never given them any cash for their children."

"I takes care of my babies," I say.

"Well, that's a different story from the one we've been hearing," she say.

"I don't know what you been hearin, but I takes care of my babies."

"Youse a damn liar," Reynisha shout. "You ain't gave me a damn penny, you dog."

The audience laugh.

"Sit down and shut the fuck up," I say.

"You can't use that kind of language on the television," Snookie Cane say. "And I can't believe you would talk that way in front of your children."

"But the ho be lying," I say.

"Who you callin a ho?" Reynisha say.

"You, bitch."

The audience makes a big noise all together. Snookie Cane steps down closer to the cage. "Check the language, Van Go."

"He ain't bout nuffin," Cleona say.

I give her a hard look since she sittin right next to me.

"Have you given Cleona any money, Van Go?" Snookie Cane ax me.

"What?"

The audience laugh.

"Yes or no, have you given Cleona any money for Rexall?" she ax.

"You see, I ain't had a job," I say.

"But you have a job now, right?" Snookie Cane say.

"Yeah, but I ain't got paid yet," I say.

"So, when you get paid, are you going to give money to each of these ladies?" she ax.

"Hell, no," Sharinda say. "He don't care bout nobody but hisself."

"Yeah, I'm gone give them some money," I says.

Robertarina laughs loud. "I'll believe that shit when I see it."

"Your language, Robertarina," Snookie Cane say.

"Sorry," say Robertarina.

"Some surprise, huh," Snookie Cane say to me. Then to the camera. "When we come back we'll see if we can get to the bottom of this and we'll hear what our audience has to say."

The lights on the cameras goes off and Snookie Cane is surrounded by people makin up her face. She ain't payin no attention to me. Cleona give me a look.

"What yo' problem?" I ax.

"Shut up," she say.

"Who the fuck you tellin to shut up?" I say.

A big muthafucka wearin sumpin' on his head come trailin a wire over to me. "You're goin have to watch yo' language," he say.

"You bet' get yo' big-lipped ass away from me," I say.

"One more fuck and you're off the show," he say. He poke a finger in my chest and look at me hard. "Got it?"

"I got it," I say.

Reynisha is lookin at me and laughin. "Keep laughin, bitch," I say.

"And whatchew gone do?" she say. I got sumpin' fo' you if you come to my house." She talkin bout that nine she got. "Come on ova."

The camera come back on.

"Welcome back," Snookie Cane say. "Our show today is You gave me the baby, Now where's the money? And on our stage we have Van Go Jenkins, father of four children by four different women. Van Go, so you admit you haven't contributed any money to the care of your children."

"I ain't admittin nuffin," I say.

"He ain't bout nuffin," Cleona say it this time.

"Shut up, bitch," I say.

The audience makes a noise.

Snookie Cane put the microphone in front of a fat woman with corn rows on her head. "His problem is he don't respect himself," the fat woman say. "So, how he gone respect anybody else."

"I respect myself," I say.

"You ain't showin it, boy," the fat woman say.

"Who you callin boy?" I say. "Sit yo' big butt down."

A tall, skinny dude stand up and say, "I think Mr. Jenkins here gots a problem wif his self-confidence, you know wif his manhood."

"I'll show you mine if you keep yo's to yo'self," I say.

The audience laugh and that feel kinda good.

"You have an answer for everybody, don't you," Snookie Cane say.

"Damn straight," I say. "Somebuddy wanna answer, I gots one."

Snookie Cane say, "We hear from Sharinda that you ain't all that in bed."

The audience laugh.

"Sharinda be lyin," I say. "Sharinda be screamin."

The audience make a noise.

"I be screamin to keep from laughin," Sharinda say.

The audience laugh.

I feels blood in my face and my leg is shakin and my mouth feel like it movin but ain't no words comin out.

"She got you, Van Go," Snookie Cane say.

"You the one ain't nuffin," I say.

Sharinda lean back and snap her fingers and say, "All I know is I gots me a real man now and I be screamin fo' sho."

"Let's meet that man," Snookie Cane say. "Want to, audience?"

The audience say yeah.

Snookie Cane say, "Come on out, Mad Dog!"

The audience laugh at his name and I laughs too and this itty bitty lil' nigger come struttin out. I bust up laughin. That be Mad Dog? I'm sho 'nuff beside myself now.

"A real man," I say to the audience.

Mad Dog just look at me like he don't care what I say. For a second I feels kinda like a fool. But I cuts a look at him. I oughta fuck him up.

"Mad Dog," Snookie Cane say, "what do you know about all this."

Mad Dog lean back like Sharinda and say, "I don't know much, but I know this nigger ain't shit."

The audience scream.

"You have to watch your language, Mad Dog," Snookie Cane say.

"I'm sorry," Mad Dog say.

"Damn right, you sorry," I say.

Mad Dog laugh. "Listen, boy, I takes care of yo' baby everyday like she my own. Where yo' money?"

The audience howl.

"Same place yo' business be," Mad Dog say. "Nowhere."

I jumps up, but that little muthfucka don't move, just look at me like I ain't bout shit. That big dude with the headset on come and sit me back down.

"Bet sit yo' butt down," Mad Dog say, cool as shit.

Mad Dog talk to Snookie Cane and the audience. "I tell you what his problem is. He wanna knock boots wit Sharinda, but he ain't even got shoes."

The audience howl again.

"Aspireene is a sweet lil' girl," Mad Dog say. "I love Aspireene like my own."

The audience say, "Awwwww."

"That's beautiful, Mad Dog," Snookie Cane said.

Mad Dog smile at Sharinda and touch Aspireene's face.

I look at the first row and I see Mama's face and she look like she bout to cry. I hates Mama. I loves Mama. I hates Mama. I loves Mama.

Snookie Cane put the microphone in front of this white dude and he put his hand on his hip and say, "I think loverboy up there needth to get on away away from the girlth."

"Shut up, faggot," I say.

"Come thhut me up," the faggot say. "But you probably ain't got nothin that can thhut me up."

The audience laugh.

The faggot say, "The female in the red top."

"Cleona," Snookie Cane say.

"Cleona," the faggot say. "Cleona, you need to jutht cut him loothe and find you a man."

"What you know bout men?" I say and try to laugh.

"Honey, I know all about men," he say.

The audience laugh.

"Shit," I say under my breath. I looks back at Mama and she sho 'nough cryin now.

Snookie Cane see my mama cryin and walk down to her, put the mike in her face. "Who are you, ma'am?" she ax.

"I'm his mother," Mama say.

"Why are you cryin Mrs. Jenkins?" Snookie Cane ax.

"I didn't raise him up to be like this," Mama say.

"You made your mother cry," Snookie Cane say.

"She always be cryin," I says. "Ain't nuffin new."

The audience yell at me.

Snookie Cane put the microphone in front of a fat white dude. "He can't respect these here women cause he don't even respect his own mother."

"Good point," Snookie Cane say.

"But wait," Snookie Cane say to the audience, then to me, "Van Go Jenkins, we have another surprise for you."

"Yeah, what that be?"

"Where do you work now?" Snookie Cane ax.

"I'm in between jobs," I say.

"Don't you work for a family named Dalton?" she ax.

I don't say nuffin.

"Do you know the Daltons?" she ax.

"Yeah, I know 'em," I says.

"What about Penelope Dalton?" Snookie Cane ax.

I looks at the door on the stage and then behind me. What Penelope gone be on this show for? "Is she here?" I ax.

"No, Van Go, she's not here, but these gentlemen are," Snookie Cane say.

And two policemans come through the door to my right.

"It seems you stepped over the line last night, Van Go," Snookie Cane say, steppin down to beside my mama. "I'm sorry, Mrs. Jenkins," she say.

The cops is walkin at me.

Snookie Cane say, "It seems our guest raped a woman last night. At least that's the allegation."

I jump up out the chair and run for the other door. There be two cops there too. Fuck! I run for the back of the stage and I see Mad Dog's face and he just as cool as shit. He don't even get up. He say, "They ain't after me."

I run through the audience. That faggot try to stop me, but I runs right through him, kick him with my knee and he go down. People be tryin to grab me and I get thrown back to the front. I'm next to Mama. Mama be cryin. I'm right next to Snookie Cane. She don't look real. The policemans are about to grab me. I drop down on my knees and start crawlin through legs. I'm trippin people and knockin 'em over. I gets to the door in back and punch a security guard. I run. I gets out that building and I run out the studio and past the parkin lot and down a steep bank and across the highway and some railroad tracks. My heart is beatin, beatin, beatin.

Ate

So I gets away from the police and hangs around some alleys for a while. I gots a coupla dollars my mama give me before the telebision show, but I dont wanna spend it yet. But I be hongry as shit. I think it aint a good idea to go back to my hood, but that where I gotta be. I knows the streets and places to hide. I go to the grade school and kicks up in the shadows by the door and looks at the basketball courts. I hears some footprints comin my way, but there aint noplace for me to run, so I stay sunk down in the dark.

"Go, nigger, you here?" the voice call out. I recognizes it as Reynisha.

"That you, Reynisha?" I ax.

"Yeah, it me," she say. "Come on out from dem shadows."

"You by yo'self?" I ax.

"Yeah," she say. "I dint think you was gonna get away from there. Them police still lookin through the studio."

"Take mo' than twenty police to catch me," I say. "You come lookin fo' me?"

"Yeah," she say. "Come on down."

I step out the shadows and down the steps and stand in front of her. "What you want?" I look at the street and down the block. "You got any money or food?"

"No, nigger, but I gots this fo' yo' ass," she say and she pull out that nine and point it at me.

"Shit, Reynisha," I say. "Is that muthafucka loaded?"

"Dame straight it loaded, you sorry son of a bitch," she say. "I'm gone shoot yo' ass dead and get you out my baby's life fo' good."

"Chill out, baby doll," I say.

She laugh. "Baby Doll?" she say and shake her head. "You got some fuckin nerve."

"What you talkin bout, baby?" I say. "You know you aint wanna shoot me now, do you?"

"Oh, I wanna shoot you. There aint no question bout that," she say. "I wanna shoot you and let somebody else clean up the blood."

"Give me the gun, Reynisha," I says and I take a step her way.

"One mo' step and it will be yo' last," she say.

"What you want?" I ax.

"I wanna shoot you, stupid," she say.

"You want money?" I ax.

"You know you aint got no money," she say.

"Who that?" I say, lookin at the street. When she look, I takes the pistol from her. "Woooo. I'm glad I a smart muthafucka. So, you was gonna shoot my ass?"

"Damn straight," she say, mad even though I got the gun.

"You lucky you my baby's mama," I say. "If you wasn't I be puttin a bullet right tween yo' eyes." I put the barrel of the pistol on her forehead.

"You aint got the balls," she say.

I dont pay her no attention. I pull the gun back and look at it. "I been wantin and needin me one of these."

"Gimme my gun back," she say.

"Fuck you," I say.

"You a big man, right?" she say.

I feels the weight of the pistol in my hand. "I is now," I say. "I is now."

"I'm gone tell 'em you got a gun," she say.

"Tell 'em," I say. I be lookin at the gun, the way it look in my hand, feelin the weight of it. "You go 'head and tell 'em."

"What you gone do?" she ax.

"What that mean to you?" I say. "I got what I want from you and you kick them Hush Puppies on down the road."

"I hope they kill yo' ass," she say.

"Yeah," I say. "Me, too. They kills everybody else. So, why not me?"

I'm walkin downtown now. Just in case Reynisha go runnin to the cops and tellin 'em she seen me in the hood. I be feelin the nine in my pocket and my head feel light. Then I see this cop cruiser comin toward me on the street. I ducks into a store. The store be full of stereos and telebisions and I think it would be cool as hell to actually have me one of them fine stereos. I wanna use my gun and take one. But the stereo be heavy and the cops be outside. I aint stupid. And there on the screen, on screen after screen down the row, is me, me on the Snookie Cane Show. Me in front of everybody. Me on telebision. I be lookin good and then the police come in. Then they rolls the tape back and show it again. Over and over. On screen beside screen beside screen. And there be this fat bitch standin down in front of a big screen and she look at me and I looks away. I walks on out back to the street where that cruiser been. But the cops aint there when I gets out. I heads down this alley and that, this street and that until I be back at the hood.

I sits under a tree in the park across from the licker sto' and looks at my pistol. It be so black and shiny. It like a black diamond. It like money that aint money yet.

I walks on down out the park and down the street. I'm goin to the K'rean muthafucka's sto'. He owe me. He owe me all he got for tellin me to get outta his fuckin' sto' and then callin the police. Just cause I wasn't buyin nuffin. K'rean muthafucka. I just know that register of his be fulla money.

I stand cross the street and I watch people goin in and comin out the lil' grocery sto'. Finally aint nobody in there but that K'rean. I crosses the street, give another look up and down the street and I go in.

That K'rean recognize me when I walk in. I can tell by the way he look at me. But he dont say nuffin. I look at the chips on the rack and he step real slow round the counter. He be runnin his hand through his hair like he nervous, shootin glances at me wif them little squinty eyes. Then he behind the counter, facin me and I see he's reachin down for sumpin.

I pulls my piece and point at his yellow face. "Put yo' hands on the counter," I say.

He put 'em flat on the counter. He lookin at my eyes. "What you wan?" he ax. "Take what you wan and go way."

"Gimme the money in the register," I say. I watch him while he do it. It look to be bout round a hundred. "Okay, where the safe."

"No got safe," he say.

"Fuck you, man," I say. "Where the safe." I push the gun closer to his face.

"Safe in back," he say. "Don't shoot."

"Come round from there real slow," I tells him.

But he don't come round real slow. He duck down behind the counter and try to come back up with a shotgun. I pop him. The pistol jump in my hand and I almost drop it. I hit him in the head, in the side of the head. The hole look neat and there aint much blood at first. I shoots him three mo' times until he in a lake of blood. Muthafucka. Shit, fuckin K'rean made me kill his ass. I dint tell him to grab no gun. I grab the money up off the counter and run out.

My head be throbbin. I dont know what to think or where to go. I run and run and run but I aint gettin nowhere. I be hongry as hell and I go into a Popeye chicken place. I eat some chicken and drink me a Sprite while sittin in the back booth near the bafrooms. I just be hopin I dont see nobody I knows. But the food be good.

I walk past the high school and down a wide alley and somebody call out to me. I pull the gun real fast and turn round and there is Willy the wino.

"Whoa," he say. "Dont shoot me, pardner." He drunk as shit and swayin in the light from a window above him. "That you, Van Go."

"Yeah, it me, you drunk muthafucka," I say.

"Where you runnin to and why you got that gun?" he ax.

"Just leave me alone," I say.

"How yo' mama?" he ax.

"What?"

"I say, how yo' mama?" he say. "I think bout it, Van Go. Look at my face. Look at my coal black skin and then look at yown. Look at my black eyes and then look at yown. Look at my big black lips and look at yown. I be your daddy whether you likes it or not."

"Shut up," I say.

"It true," he say.

"Then where you been?" I ax.

"I been doin what I do, survivin," he say. "You aint worth a piss. Yo' mama aint worth a piss. So, here I is."

I can feel the rage swell up inside me. I hates this man. I hates my mama. I hates myself. I'm seein my face in his. I see the ape that stupid girls say they be fraid of. I see my long arms hangin down. I see eyes that dont care what happen tomorrow. I see myself rockin on my heels, waitin, waitin, waitin for sumpin I won't recognize when it come. My only cure gone be death. I heard it all my life. I be hearin it now. I see Mama bleedin in my dream. I see my babies. I see Rexall, wifout a brain, growin up and axing "Why not me?" I see my daddy. I see myself. I shoot the muthafucka. Pop! In the gut.

Willy double over and he look at me like to say, "Why?" I yell at him. I be standin over him yellin at the back of his head. "Cause you aint shit!" I say. "Cause you made me, muthafucka! Cause I aint shit!" I be cryin now and I think I hear sumpin out at the street. I run again.

I falls asleep in the basement of an empty buildin.

I has a dream. In the dream this big white man tryin me out for a basketball team. He makin me run laps round the court. Lap after lap after lap. And everytime I comes by him he laughin harder. So, finally I stops and looks at him and I ax, "What you laughin at?"

"You runnin the wrong way, nigger," he say.

"Why dint you say sumpin," I say. Then I turn around and start runnin the opposite direction. And everytime I pass by him he laughin harder again. So, I stops and stares at him. "What the fuck so funny now?" I ax.

"You're running with your left foot first," he say.

"What you talkin bout?" I ax. I dont understand. "I s'posed to start on my right foot?"

"No, but it's supposed to fall first every time," he say. "It don't matter which one you start with."

"I don't get it," I say.

"Okay, forget that," he say. "Try running backwards."

I run twenty laps backward and my legs be achin and I realize that I aint got on no shoes and my feet be bleedin. And then Willy is runnin backwards beside me, keepin up with me. The coach nods at me everytime I come by. I look over at Willy and he's smilin.

"See, it aint so bad," he say.

"What you doin here?" I say.

"I come to tell you that you was wrong," he say.

"Bout what?" I ax.

"You say you aint shit," he say. "You say I aint shit. Well, I is shit and so is you." He laughs loud and stops runnin. I pass by the coach and he be laughin too.

Nine

I wakes up the next mornin sweatin like a fuckin pig and I be stank. I crawls outta that hole and the light hurts my eyes. I duck through the alleys until I come up to the back of the pool hall. I climb up the fire escape and gets in through the bafroom window. I splash water on my face and then I just sits there for a while, restin, wonderin where I'm gone go. I falls asleep again in one of the stalls.

When I wakes up I hear balls breakin on a table outside. I opens the door and takes a peek and I see Yellow and Tito playin a game. I walk out there but I stay in the shadows. Yellow see me.

"Nigger, what you doin here?" he say, tryin to keep his voice down.

Tito come over. "Man, you hotta than a Swisher Sweet."

"You been on the TV non-stop," Yellow say. "They gone gas yo' ass."

"Shit," I say. "They don't gas you for rape and runnin."

"They does fo' murder," Yellow say. "They caught yo' butt on the security cam shootin that K'rean."

"Oh shit," I say.

"Oh shit is right," Tito say.

"Who dat back there?" the fat man call to Tito and Yellow.

"Aint nobody but us, Pops," Tito say.

I ducks down in the hallway.

"What you gone do?" Yellow ax.

"I guess I'll go down to Mexico," I say.

"Nigger, you dont eben speak Spanish," Yellow say.

"So what," I say. "Them muthafuckas come up here and they dont speak no American."

"Police been here lookin for you," Tito say. "Fat Man look at yo' picture and took they card. There's a reward. He'll drop a dime on yo' ass in second."

"Buncha niggers would," I say. "I need a car."

"We aint got a car," Tito say.

"Get me one," I say.

"And why should we get yo' stupid ass a car?" Yellow ax.

"Cause I'm a brother," I says.

"Fuck that shit," Tito say. "You just lucky we aint turnin yo' ass in."

"That how you treat a brother?" I say.

"Who dat?" that fat bastard say again.

"Nobody, Pops," Tito say.

"Is it that Snookie Cane Show nigger?" Fat Man say. "Where my phone."

I jumps up and run to the desk. I be pointin my pistol at him, but he keep dialin. "Hang up, Fatso!" I yell. But he keep pushin in the number. I rip the phone out the wall. I stick the gun in his face. "You still drive that piece-a-shit Ford?" I ax.

"It aint no piece-a-shit," he say.

"Give me the keys," I say.

"You bet give him the keys, Pops," Tito say.

The fat man reach into his pocket and give me the keys.

"Awright," I say. "Awright. Now, dont go runnin to the cops. You hear me?"

"I hear you," the fat man say.

Then I point the gun at Yellow and Tito. "You, too!"

"Okay," Tito say.

Tin

I be in that fuckin Ford Torino belong to Fat Man. It from the seben-ties and it be dirty as shit. Beer cans and burger wrappers be all on the floor. The thing put smoke out the back and the engine be soundin like a jar full of pins. I can see a piece of the vinyl roof flappin in the wind on the passenger side. I member how smooth that Dalton car drove. It was like a cloud and I was floatin somewhere above all this shit. Everybody else floatin, so why not me?

Then I hears the choppin of blades and I sees people on the street lookin up and I just knows there be a helicopter spotted me. I look in the mirror and I see a cruiser way off. But he comin. They always be comin. I turns onto the 101 and the traffic be thick but I speeds on through them cars, blowin my horn and usin the shoulder. People be gettin out the way. There is a couple of cruisers behind me now. They lights be on, but they hangin back. I see a sign for Union Station and I think SHIT, cause I'm goin the wrong muthafuckin direction. I swings off and head down some side streets. Maybe the chopper cain't see me for the trees, I thinks. The cruisers still back there and now I be passin some at the intersections. I gets back on the 101. I know it go south. They be behind me and above me and be drivin a hole in the highway.

Somehow I end up goin the wrong way again. I be on that 60 hea-din to Riverside. I know cause I gots a cousin who live there. He used to live out there. Nigger got shot for pokin round a speed lab. Niggers always wanna be gettin sumpin fo' free.

I turns on the radio and hear they be talkin bout me. I can see a news helicopter off to the side, but it be from the telebision. I can see the cameraman hangin out and pointin it at me. Hey, I be on the tele-bision three times in two days. My heart feel all big. I press harder on the gas. There aint much gas in this fucker and there bout six cruisers behind me now. Sheriff cars be back there now.

I drives past Ontario and Chino and I miss the 15 headin souf to Mexico. I drives through Riverside and I'm sho'nuff bout to run outta gas and I turns onto the 215 headin souf, but I know I gotta get off the freeways. I gets off and I'm drivin through someplace call Moreno Valley and the car startin to knock and shake and them cruisers still back there and them helicopters still choppin up the air. I wave to the camera.

I pull into the post office, jumps out the car and runs in. I shoot my gun into the ceilin and people start screamin. I yells for them to shut up. "Shut up!" I says. "Everybody get down on the flo'!" I screams. They gets down but one old lady is goin slow. "I say DOWN!" I yells at her and she start cryin.

The police be outside. Must be twenty cars. I can see them through the big window.

A black cop call to me on one them horns. "Van Go Jenkins!" he say. "It's all over, son! Time to call it quits!"

"I aint quittin nuffin!" I yell back through the glass. But he aint hear me. I points to a skinny blond girl. "Come here!" She crawl to me. "Get up!" She stand up and I grab her round her neck and put the gun to her head. I walk to the door and lean out with her in fronta me. "I'll shoot her!" I shout. The girl be cryin. "I swear to God I'll shoot her."

"Let's talk, Van Go," the nigger with the bullhorn say.

"Fuck talk!" I say.

"What do you want?" he ax.

I see a telebision news crew settin up. The camera be pointin at me. "I want some money and another car," I says.

"We can't do that," he say.

"You bet do it," I say. I go back in and throw the girl on the flo'. This old black woman be starin at me. "What you lookin at, old bitch."

She shake her head. "What happen to you in yo' life?" she say.

"I aint had no life is what happen to me," I say. "Now shut the fuck up."

"Just give up, boy," the old lady say.

"You aint my mama," I say.

"Thank the Lord for that," she say.

"You think you funny," I say.

She dont say nuffin.

I counts the people in the room. Then I realize that them workers been behind the counter. I run over there and they all gone. I got seben hostages. All I want is a car. I yell at the window, "Just get me a fuckin car!"

The cameras are starin at me. Three of 'em now. I see someone I recognize from the news. I waves at her. The phone ring. I go and answer it. It be somebody wantin to know bout a package.

"I aint got yo' fuckin package!" I say and hang up.

The phone ring again. This time it the police. "You're going to have to give it up, Van Go," he say. It the same nigger that was on that horn.

"I aint givin up shit, man. Now you get me that car!" I say.

"The car is coming. Why don't you give us a couple of those people in there?" he say.

"Old lady," I say and point at her. "Go on out there. If you say a muthafuckin word I shoot you."

She get up and walk to the door real slow. Then she out and she run cross that parkin lot like nobody bizness.

"Okay," I say into the phone. "You got one."

"The car is comin, Van Go."

I hang up and I be sweatin like a pig. I shoulda killed that rich bitch. It be all her fault. Callin the cops and makin me run. And it be Reynisha fault too for comin after me wif that gun and lettin me take it from her. It be my mama fault for sho', gettin pregnant wif me and havin me. It be that basketball coach fault. It be that white teacher fault. It be everybody fault.

After bout ten fifteen minutes, the phone ring again. It that cop. "Your car is here," he say.

"Bout time," I say. I watch as it pull up in the lot. It be a little red sport car. It look fine as shit. Awright, I says to myself.

"Okay?" the cop say on the phone.

"Okay," I say. "I'm comin out wif this girl in here. I takin her wif me."

"Okay," he say. "Be cool and don't hurt anybody."

"I cool, fool," I say. "You the one be cool." I hang up. "You!" I points at the white girl again. "How old you?"

"Sixteen," she say.

"Just be cool," I say.

The light outside is brighter than I member. The cameras is pointin at me. All them cops be pointin they guns at me. I tell the girl not to move again. We walk to the car. I yell out at the cops, "Try sumpin! Try sumpin and this girl get it in the head."

That car be little as shit and it hard for the girl crawl over the brake to the passenger side. I tells the girl to be cool again. I smile at the cameras. I turn the key and BAM! I dont know what happen. I think maybe I been shot. I cain't see nuffin for a second and then I be covered with this powder shit. Then I be yanked by my hair out the car to the ground. I don't know what goin on. Somebody kick me in my side. Somebody grab my arm and I think it be broken.

"What happen?" I say.

The cops be laughin. "Air bag, you dumb fuck," one says to me.

I looks up and see the cameras. I get kicked again while I'm bein pulled to my feet. But I dont care. The cameras is pointin at me. I be on the TV. The cameras be full of me. I on TV. I say, "Hey, Mama." I say, "Hey, Baby Girl. Look at me. I on TV."

It was the middle of July and Washington was a big bowl of soup. I was parked in the study, counting time to the air-conditioning unit in the window. I picked up the heavy black telephone and called my agent, who recognized my voice and said, without much pause, "Are you crazy?"

"No, not quite," I said. "Why do you ask?"

"This thing you sent me. Are you serious?"

"Yeah, why not? You'll notice I didn't put my name to it."

"I did notice that. But I'm the one who has to try to sell it, with my name. I have to work in this town."

"Look at the shit that's published. I'm sick of it. This is an expression of my being sick of it."

"I understand that, Monk. And I appreciate your position and I even admire the parody, but who's going to publish this? The people who publish the stuff you hate are going to be offended, so they won't take it. Hell, everybody's going to be offended."

"The idiots ought to be offended." I looked over at a cluttered secretary desk across the room. On the lowered surface, below the encased medical books was a gray box.

"So, what do you want me do?"

"Send it out."

"Straight or with some kind of qualification? Do you want me to tell them it's a parody?"

"Send it straight," I said. "If they can't see it's a parody, fuck them."

"Okay, I'll send it out. A couple of times, anyway." Yul sighed. "But no more than that. This thing scares me."

"I understand," I told him.

My tools were in storage in LA and I found myself missing the smells of wood, glue and varnish. I missed the splinters and the blisters, the sawdust and the red eyes. More than a few times I found myself standing in the garage, imagining Mother's Benz parked elsewhere and the space filled with table saws and planers and jigsaws and stacks of wood. I bought some basic hand tools and built a birdhouse, painted it and gave it to Lorraine for the garden. Then I began visiting antique shops in Northern Virginia, in Falls Church and Maclean and as far away as Manassas, picking up a rabbet plane here and a block plane there, hammers, chisels, mallets, until I was a collector. I didn't want to be a collector and decided I had to build something and that something became a nightstand for Mother. While I was using the rabbet plane to make the sloping edge of the table's top, I considered Foucault and how he begins by making assumptions about notions concerning language that he claims are misguided. But he does not argue the point, but assumes his notions, rightly or wrongly, to be the case. As I recalled his discussion of discursive formations, I stepped away and looked at myself. To watch shavings fall away from a fine piece of ash wood and have such thoughts. I could feel my sister watching me.

I was just tall enough to dunk the basketball, but not quite big enough to get close enough to the basket in a half-court game to do so. I enjoyed the exercise and the game, but not so much playing the game. I wasn't very good at it. I would catch the ball, look to make a reasonably safe pass while dribbling, then make that reasonably safe pass and move to another spot on the perimeter. One day, a sunny May Saturday, I was playing on a court near my house. I was seventeen and feeling more awkward than I ever had or would feel again. I had been playing for about thirty minutes, making safe pass after safe pass when I found myself considering the racist comments of Hegel concerning Oriental peoples and their attitude toward freedom of the self when I was bumped into the lane and so appeared to be cutting to the basket and the ball was thrown back to me. I threw up a wild and desperate shot which had no prayer of going in; it was ugly. A member of my team asked me what I was thinking about and I said, "Hegel."

"What?"

"He was a German philosopher." I watched the expression on his face and perhaps reflected the same degree of amazement. "I was thinking about his theory of history."

The order of the following comments escapes me now, but they were essentially these:

"Get him."

"Philosophy boy."

"That's why he threw up that brick?"

"Where the hell did you come from?"

"What are you thinking about right now?"

"You'd better Hegel on home."

Novel idea: The Satyricon

Let us put this affrontery behind us. This from Fabricus Veiento, and he laughed in the middle of his lecture on the follies of what we took generally to be religious belief, though he couched it in terms of particular mania for revelation and prophecy. Indeed, all lofty themes, religious, political or otherwise, were equal in their being subjects of ridicule or simple askance-looking. Indeed (again), I learned from him and agreed that the seductiveness of the verbal engagement which Veiento so disparaged was the reason why so many pupils, namely young men like myself, grow up to be idiots. That the young would rather be entertained by tales of the extreme rather than the mundane is not arguable. Pirates defeat accountants. Beheadings outweigh slivers of wood in buttocks.

Academic training catering to such vulgar taste can only promise vulgarity. Rhetoricians are at the root of the decline of Oratory—empty speech for empty heads, pretending eloquence and so redefining the very thing it has killed.

While paying Mother's and my own bills in mid-August, I found myself nearly ready to accept the poorly salaried lecturer position at American University. I put in a call to my brother to see if he might be able to help.

"I have no money," he said.

"She's your mother, too," I said.

"I can't even see my kids," Bill said. "I have my own problems."

"Do you have a car?" I asked.

"Yes."

"What kind of car is it?" I asked.

"What are you asking?"

"Is it expensive?"

There was a long pause and he said, finally, "I don't actually own the car. It's a corporate lease. I'm incorporated. I get paid a salary and that's just enough for me to live."

"Can you take a less expensive apartment?" I asked. "Listen, Bill, I've left my job to come here and live with Mother. You could do a little something."

"Sell the house and move her to a cheaper place."

"The house is paid for. There is no cheaper place."

"But selling it would give you some cash. You could get three-four hundred thousand for that house."

"Actually, Monk." His pause was a fat one if not terribly long and I could imagine his habit of looking at the ceiling before speaking. "I've taken a lover." Taken a lover was how he put it. Removed one from the closet? Conned one out of his savings? Taken a lover.

"So?" I said.

"His name is Claude."

"I don't care what his name is," I told him. "What is he? French?"

"I want you to meet him." And suddenly Bill's voice was different, but it was more than just the sound of a man in love. His pronunciation changed. It was not quite that he developed a stereotypical lisp, but it was close.

"Why are you talking like that?"

His voice went back to normal. "Like what?"

I collected myself and tried to make my way back to important matters. "What about Lorraine?"

"What about her? We don't owe anything to Lorraine."

"So, you're telling me to sell Mother's house, move her into a home and kick Lorraine out into the street."

"Basically."

I hung up.

X X X

The phone rang the next morning while I sat at what had been my father's desk staring at the gray box across the room. It was my agent.

credo quia absurdum est

"Sit down," Yul said.

"I'm sitting," I said, though I was standing and looking out the window at the street.

"I sent it over to Random House."

"Yes?"

"I didn't offer any qualifiers or anything."

"Yes?"

"Six hundred thousand dollars."

"You're kidding me," I said, sitting now.

"Paula Baderman, a senior editor over there, wants to meet Mr. Leigh."

"Tell them he's shy." I was elated and ready to be angry. "Tell me what she said."

"She called it true to life. Called it an important book."

"What did she say about the writing?"

"She said it was magnificently raw and honest. She said it's the kind of book that they will be reading in high schools thirty years from now."

I said nothing.

"Monk?"

I looked out the window.

"Monk? This is what you wanted, right?"

"Random House."

"Yep."

"This is really fucked up, you know that."

"You don't want the deal."

"Of course I want the deal," I said. "Just tell them that Stagg Leigh is painfully, pathologically shy and that he'll communicate with them through you."

"I don't know if that will cut it."

"It'll cut it."

I never before felt so stranded. Alone in that house with Mother and Lorraine. But with the new bit of change I would be collecting for that awful little book, I could hire someone to come in and care for both of them. Perhaps for dramatic effect, I should have had to wait longer for my windfall, given my brother's newfound flakiness and my sister's debt (both what she owed and what I owed her), but it didn't happen that way. The news of the money came and I breathed an ironic and bitter sigh of relief. Maybe I felt a bit of vindication somewhere inside me. Certainly, I felt a great deal of hostility toward an industry so eager to seek out and sell such demeaning and soul-destroying drivel.

"Monk?"

"Bill? What time is it? Jesus, Bill, it's three in the morning."

"Sorry, it's only one here."

"Is something wrong? Are you okay?"

"How long have you known I was gay?"

"Come on, Bill, it's too early to talk about this. I mean, it's too late. Too late in a couple of ways. You're gay. Deal with it."

"How long have you known?"

I sat up and switched on my bedside lamp. "I don't know. For a while, I guess."

"Did you know when I was in high school?"

"I don't know, maybe."

"I didn't know then, but I must have been, right?"

"I don't know how these things work. Are you all right?"

"Have you ever had any gay feelings?"

"I don't think so."

"You know that I love my children."

"I know you do, Bill. Is there anything I can do?"

"Can you imagine if Father knew I was gay?"

"He wouldn't take it well, that's for sure."

"How do you think Mother will take it?"

"I don't know. Why tell her?"

"Why not tell her? Do you think I should be ashamed of what I am?"

"That's not what I'm saying."

"Then what are you saying?"

"Tell her if you want to. But first, she's not going to understand what you are telling her and second, she's going to forget two seconds after you're done. So, tell her if you want to. It's not going to make much difference to anybody but you."

"So, you think I'm only concerned with myself."

"I didn't say that either. But, basically, that's true of all of us."

"I don't need your platitudes."

"Did you call looking for a fight?"

"No, I didn't. I just thought I'd get a little more support from my little brother."

"Support. You don't need me to be gay. How's your new—"

"Partner, it's called a partner. Or boyfriend. You can say boyfriend. His name is Tad and he's fine. I don't know where he is right now, but he's fine. Are you seeing anyone?"

"No."

"Sell any books lately?"

"No. Listen, I've got to get some sleep."

Click.

Often humans will seek to improve the habitat of trout in a stream by providing some kind of structure under the water. People will sometimes dump anything in the stream, think that the fish will want to take shelter in it. Car bumpers, shopping carts, dog houses. Generally fish prefer the smooth curves of nature to the hard edges of humans. But more importantly, if the structure is not proper and is not put in the right place in the stream, the flow of the current might find an erodible bank and so cause more harm than good.

I walked in the morning, all the way to McPherson Square where I took the Metro to the mall. I walked around the National Gallery for a couple of hours, ate lunch alone in the cafeteria and imagined that I had a life. I contemplated also that suddenly I was slightly well off and that I really didn't have to teach for a while. This was good, as I couldn't bring myself to accept the slave wages over at American to teach a survey course to kids who didn't care a hill of beans about Melville, Twain or Hurston.

Having come into what I considered a lot of money, I decided to go see something worth more than money. Granted, not all of it was worth more than money, in fact much of it was not worth the canvas or linen it was slathered upon, but some was and that was enough to put my new gain, rightly and sadly, into place. I thought of Cocteau and his saying that everything can be solved except being, this while staring at a Motherwell that both seduced and offended me. I stopped at a late Rothko, the feathery working of the brush, the dark colors, the white edges and I thought of death, my own death, my making my own death. I could not think like Antoine de Saint-Exupéry that death was a thing of grandeur. Death was frighteningly as simple as life, instead of waking everyday and just doing it, one didn't wake everyday and just did it. In the painting, whether the colors were there or not, I saw the cream of my mother's skin and the brown of mine. My self-murder would not be an act of rage and despair, but of only despair and my artistic sensibility could not stand that. Throughout my teens and twenties I had killed myself many times, even made some of the preparations, stopping always at the writing of the note. I knew that I could manage nothing more that a perfunctory scribble and I didn't want to see that, have my silly romantic notions shattered by a lack of imagination.

I tried to distance myself from the position where the newly sold piece-of-shit novel had placed me vis-à-vis my art. It was not exactly the case that I had sold out, but I was not, apparently, going to turn away the check. I considered my woodworking and why I did it. In my writing my instinct was to defy form, but I very much sought in defying it to affirm it, an irony that was difficult enough to articulate, much less defend. But the wood, the feel of it, the smell of it, the weight of it. It was so much more real than words. The wood was so simple. Damnit, a table was a table was a table.

The stream of humanity pouring down the tunnel into the Red Line was too much for me. I walked for a while, watching the sky darken, then a light rain began to fall. At first it was a pleasant relief to the heat, then it fell harder. I had walked as far as New York Avenue and decided to hail a taxi. Three or four empty ones passed me and I thought of the old joke: What do you call two black men trying to get a cab in Washington, D.C.? Pedestrians. I raised my arm again and this time a car stopped, no doubt because the Ethiopian driver had a male companion with him and he felt safe enough. They looked back at me after I gave them my address, one saying, "Are you Ethiopian?" and the other, "You look Ethiopian." I said, "No, I'm just Washingtonian." I closed my eyes and drifted.

Mother's bridge club was meeting at our house. Mrs. Johnson, widow of the mortuary owner Lionel Johnson, greeted me as she entered as if I were ten. "Oh, little Monksie, you're looking so fit." She was with her daughter, about my age, who carried her bag and wore on her face an expression of fatigue like the one I imagined I wore. "This is my daughter, Eloise," Mrs. Johnson said. Then she saw my mother and told us to run on and play.

The others arrived. And soon there were eight old ladies seated at two card tables, all of them too arthritic to shuffle and too senile to remember to whom the last card was dealt. While in the living room, eight children, around the age of forty, sat holding purses, stoles and umbrellas. We looked at each other and all regarded that as adequate and eloquent enough commiseration, then closed our eyes for naps.

"Hey, Washingtonian," the cab driver said. "This your house?"

I paid and made my groggy way up the walk to find Lorraine sitting on the porch. "Enjoying the rain?" I asked.

She shook her head and looked at the door.

"What's wrong?"

"It's the Mrs."

"Is Mother all right?" At that moment I heard a noise at the narrow window by the door and turned to see Mother holding aside the curtain and staring out, somewhat wild-eyed, then she disappeared. "What's going on?"

"She's locked and bolted the doors," Lorraine said.

If it was true, that the doors were bolted from the inside, then my keys wouldn't help. "Why won't she let you in?" I asked.

"She doesn't recognize me."

I went to the window and knocked. Mother's face, at least it resembled her face, flashed wild again behind the glass. I spoke to her. "Mother, it's me, Monk."

"Go away," she hissed. "We don't want any."

I looked back at the shrugging Lorraine.

"Mother," I said. "Please, unlock the door."

She dropped the curtain and was gone again.

I stepped out into the yard into the rain, away from the house, and looked up at the roof covering the porch and the windows of the second floor. I recalled the window behind the desk in Father's study had a broken latch.

I climbed while Lorraine watched from the porch, having never moved from her seat. The bark of the crepe myrtle was slick and I felt my age as I hauled my weight onto the roof. I got the window open and crawled in, knocking over a stack of books on the sill. Then I looked up to see Mother.

She said, "Monksie, there's a man at the door who won't go away." In her hand was the thirty-two-calibre pistol Father had kept in his nightstand. She pointed the gun at me and said, "You might need this."

I walked slowly to her, watching her shaking hands on the dry metal of the gun. I pushed the muzzle away from me as I took it from her. "I'll take care of the man, Mother. You just go to your bedroom and take your nap."

I watched her turn the corner into her room, then checked the pistol to find it loaded.

X X X

I took Mother to the doctor. He x-rayed her chest and told me that she did not have any kind of lung infection. He did a CAT scan and told me that she had not had a stroke and that he could see no brain shrinkage. She did not have a vitamin B-12 deficiency. He did say there was a presence of tangled nerve fibers. He talked to her, waited and then had the same conversation with her a second time, to which she responded, "Why are we going over this again?"

When we were alone, the doctor stared at me.

"Yes?"

"You're probably seeing the early stages of Alzheimer's disease. It could be due to a hardening of her arteries, poor circulation, any number of things. We just don't know. But all that is really beside the point, because there's nothing anyone can do to stop it if that's what it is."

"What about slowing it down?"

He shook his head.

"So, what do you recommend?"

"Right now things are not so bad. But everything could change overnight. The fact that she didn't recognize you suggests that the disease is progressing somewhat rapidly. Finally, you'll have to institutionalize her."

"I can't care for her at home?"

"It's going to be awfully difficult. She really shouldn't be left alone. She might wander away. She could hurt herself. Falls or other accidents. She could hurt somebody else. Fires, unlocked doors."

The memory of her holding the pistol flashed in my mind.

"In the later stages, moving will be difficult for her. Her personality will disappear. She'll lose her abilities to think, perceive and speak. At the very least you'll have to hire a full-time nurse then." He stared at me again, then said, "I'm telling you what will eventually come. This might be several years away. I can't say."

"Or it might be next week?"

"Unlikely, but possible." I thanked the doctor, collected Mother and left.

Lorraine was putting Mother to bed. I was in the garage, staring at the nearly finished bedside stand. I looked at the edges and imagined Mother's thigh bruising upon walking into one. I began to take off the point of one of the corners, finding that as I sawed the wood away I was making two points. I shaved and cut and tore away wood until the top of the table was nearly round and now too small to be practical. The rectangular, tapered legs were not only wrong for the round top but were stuck out beyond the area of the surface. I haphazardly fastened three of the legs to the top, then sat on it. It wobbled a bit, but I didn't care. It was something to feel in my hollow stupor.

X X X

I was about twelve. Father was down to the beach for the weekend as usual. We had gone as a family in the boat to the city dock in Annapolis and bought sandwiches at the open air market. I had my favorite, soft-shelled crab on a hard roll. The day was not too hot. There was a breeze. Everything felt perfect.

Bill waved to a couple of buddies near the shops and seemed to want to go with them, but stayed. Father became cool when he saw the wave.

Lisa was sitting on the long seat in the back of the boat, reading, and I was sitting on the dock, my feet on our boat, eating my sandwich and telling her how I was going to be a writer some day.

"But I'm not going to write stuff like that," I said. "I'm going to write serious things."

Lisa laughed. "Yeah, like what?"

"I don't know yet, but it won't be crap like that," I said.

"Monksie, your language," Mother said.

"All I said was *crap*," I said.

"That's enough, Monk," from Father.

"This is not crap," my sister said.

Mother sighed.

"Is too. I want to write books like *Crime and Punishment*."

Lisa laughed. "He reads one book and he thinks he's literary."

"If Monk says he'll do it, he'll do it," Father said. Then he made one of his pronouncements, the one that did come true. "Lisa, you and Bill will be doctors. But Monk will be an artist. He's not like us."

I felt both celebrated and ostracized at the same time. The looks from my siblings were both resentful and mocking. But Lisa loved hearing that she would be a doctor and she turned the attention to herself.

"What kind of doctor will I be, Father?"

"A good one," he said, as he had every other time she'd asked and it satisfied her.

"And what about Bill?" I asked.

To which Father replied, "I don't know."

We ate on in silence.

I was sitting in the study, contemplating the notion of a public and its relationship to the health of art when I looked across the room at the gray box. The box, the contents of which my father deemed so private he'd asked my mother to burn it. But also the contents must have been important enough to him that he failed to burn it all the years he had the chance. My father's private papers. Somehow I had never imagined any existing beyond deeds and contracts and standard legal documents, but I knew that box contained none of those.

"Father?" I was ten. I had walked into my father's study on a cold night near Christmas.

"Yes, Monk?" He turned to face me in his swiveling chair, the one he had requested that I not spin around on "like a top." "It's late."

"Sorry."

"Say, I'm sorry, not sorry."

"I'm sorry."

"You're sorry about what?"

"About it being so late," I said.

"You can't change what time it is."

Then I realized he was having fun with me and I laughed.

"What is it, Monk?"

"I have a question. If somebody tells you something and they tell you it's a secret, can you ever tell?"

"You can, but I take it your question is *should* one tell." He turned his head and looked briefly out the window. "No, you should not betray a confidence."

"But what if it's—"

He stopped me. "Never betray a confidence." When I tried again to speak, he said, "I can tell you're troubled, but I can also tell that soon you're going to tell me the secret you're carrying. If you don't want a secret, don't accept it."

"Okay." I started out of the room.

"Monk?" When I turned to him, he asked without looking at me, "Does this have anything to do with Bill?"

"No, Father," I said, telling the truth, but also realizing with him that no could be my only answer to his question. Years later I would wonder if I had unknowingly and accidentally shaded my father's perception of my older brother.

The box was not large, not terribly deep, and not very full, but these were in it:

2 February 1955

Dr. Benjamin Ellison
1329 T Street NW
Washington, D.C., USA

Dear Benjamin,

I cannot begin to tell you how surprised and of course thrilled I was to find your letter, however brief, in the box this morning. When you told me that you would write, I had my doubts. Not about the sincerity of your feelings certainly, but about your being able to collect time in the midst of your busy professional and family lives.

I have just now returned from Southampton. My mother is very ill. It seems she has suffered a stroke. The doctors say it was a minor stroke and that we should see little or no physical manifestation of it. To my perception she appears greatly altered, however subtly. Perhaps it is merely age. She is of course less sharp as we must all become less sharp.

What has it been, darling? Six months since we said goodbye? I hope you returned to find your family well and in good shape. I say again, to assure you, that I harbor no ill will toward your wife. She must be a wonderful woman to have you. Are your boy and girl big and rambunctious?

I do have some rather good news. I'll be visiting America in September. I'll be spending a week of holiday with my sister and her husband in New York. Wouldn't it be wonderful if we could somehow manage a sighting of each other? I am a dreamer, I know.

Well, darling, I must sign off now. It's late and thinking of you is, frankly, a bittersweet exercise. Remember that I love you.

Yours forever,
Fiona

25 February

Dear Benjamin,

Rain. Rain. Rain. That's all our skies have to offer lately. And so sight of your letter was a bit of sunshine. Then of course I opened it and discovered that you are expecting a third child. Certainly I am happy for you, but the sting is considerable.

My mother is again in the hospital. I've not made the trip to see her because of my new job. Finally, I am again a nurse. I'm afraid I must have romanticized our time in Korea, because now the work feels so much like work. I've been rethinking my suggestion that we get together in New York. With your family obligations, I'm sure you're too busy anyway. And the whole matter is just too painful for me to consider.

Please know that I love you dearly and miss you, but I am afraid I cannot keep up this letter writing.

With love, forever,
Fiona

20 April

Dearest Ben,

I've not received a letter from you for a couple weeks now. I hope all is well. I have this fear with each letter posted that you might be suffering with a cold or flu and that another member of your family might collect the mail from your office. It fills me with such dread to imagine causing you such an embarrassment and problem.

My mother is doing worse I am afraid. She's had a string of small strokes and she seems hardly herself. I'm quite sure she doesn't recognize me. Writing this now seems to help me detach myself from the grief and so I thank you for this. My brother, who has been seeing to most of the business concerning my mother, is wearing away to nothing. He is running himself ragged and I feel I've done little to really help him. I wish you could meet Bobby, whom we affectionately call Booby. His heart is an impressive one. He has encouraged me to make the trip to the States in the fall. I believe he thinks mother will be dead by then. I cry a lot thinking about her death, and then I cry because I feel guilty for thinking death might be the best thing for her.

I've rattled on about myself for too long here. I hope that you and your family are well. Last night, I don't know if it was a dream or a thought, but I saw the way we used to have to sneak around in Seoul. It was only when we had to sneak, when someone looked at us crossly, that I ever considered our difference.

Anyway, I love you.

Yours forever,
Fiona

A very small, leather-bound book. *Silas Marner* by George Eliot. An odd book to find, but pressed in its pages was a small flower, pink and white. The pages between which the little flower was pressed seemed to have no significance or bearing on anything.

Three more letters, the contents of which were not unlike previous letters, except that the mother died.

One round trip train ticket from Washington to Penn Station, dated 15 September 1955.

One receipt from the Algonquin Hotel, showing two nights' stay and three room service visits.

A book of matches from the Vanguard.

18 September

Dearest Benjamin,

I never believed that I would really see you again. And who could have known how wonderfully thrilling such an impossibility could turn out to be. Do I sound giddy? Well, perhaps I am. Seeing you was so lovely, my darling. To be held by you once more would make life too much for me.

I am sorry for the reaction of my brother-in-law. I did not know—how could I—what a bigot he is. But it seems your country has no paucity of bigots. I had deluded myself into thinking that the stares and comments, mumbled and not, were the domain of those awful soldiers during the war, the territory of the uneducated and the uncultured, but I was wrong. I can only imagine how awful it is for you daily.

I can still clearly see your smile in the morning. And your dark hands on my near translucent breasts. You were so kind not to tease me. The contrast is striking and wonderful. I did so love being with you, my beautiful lover. Think of me at night, please.

With love undying,
Fiona

1 October

Dearest Benjamin,

I arrived at home to find your card waiting. Sadly, I also learned from my brother that my mother had died. I wonder how it is that knowing what is coming never abates the anguish. But still I feel, deep down, that my grief is somewhat artificial, that I believe her death is for the best, especially hers. I suppose it is normal to think such a thing, but still it is difficult to express it outwardly. I guess this then is further evidence to the closeness of spirit I feel with you.

I must run now. I miss and love you.

Yours through eternity,
Fiona

12 November

Dear Ben,

You mean more to me than you can ever know. I'm sorry I have not written for a while now. And in an odd way, I'm thankful that you haven't either. What I have to tell you is both wonderful and terribly anxiety-making. Ben, darling, I am pregnant. I don't want anything from you and I want you to know that I will not seek to complicate your life. I am moving from this address and my mail will not be forwarded. Please, let this be our last communication. I love you far too much to hurt the family you love so dearly. And I do not wish to hurt you, though I know that this does. So, do not write for your letter might reach someone other than myself.

Love forever,
Fiona

A postcard mailed from Chicago, dated 2 July 1956.

It is a girl. Her name is Gretchen.
[unsigned]

Dear Gretchen,

Your mother is a kind, sweet, dear woman, but she was wrong to remove you and herself from my life. You must know that she did so believing it was the right and moral thing to do. She has strength which I can only pretend to fathom.

I want you to have this letter, but I do not know where you are. Your mother's sister in New York will not take my calls and so there is no help there. The card notifying me of your birth was postmarked Chicago, but tells me nothing.

Wherever you are, I love you and wish I could be a father to you. You have two brothers and a sister. They know nothing of you, but I dare say that you would love them. They are fine people. Your mother is so fine that you have no choice but to be the same. I wish that I could hear your voice, see your face, a photograph, a sketch. I hope that you have your mother's eyes. How I love those eyes.

I suppose I could be ashamed of the relationship between your mother and myself, but I am not. It pains me that I could not be with her, that it all remained so secret and, therefore, dismissed. I was married with two children when I met her and, truth be told, I should have left with her then, but I did not. But because I didn't, I have your nearest-in-age brother, my son, Thelonious. I dare say of the three I love him best.

I wish that I had someplace to send this letter. So that you could know how much your father loves you, how much he misses you and how sorry he is that he does not know whether you are left or right handed, what color your hair is, or whether you can forgive him.

The letter was unsigned. That was all that was in the box. I had read a voice of my father's that I had not heard directly in life, a tender voice, an open voice. I couldn't imagine the man who had run off to New York to have an affair. I knew my mother had read the letters, but I didn't know when. I knew she wanted me to read the letters. Knowledge of the affair gave me, oddly, more compassion for my father, more interest in him. Even when I considered my mother and her feelings I did not find myself angry with him, though I worried about her pain.

I had another sister.

I grew up an Ellison. I had Ellison looks. I had an Ellison way of speaking, showed Ellison promise, would have Ellison success. People I met on the street when I was a child would tell me that they had been delivered by my grandfather, that I looked like my father and his brother. Father's older brother had also been a physician until he died at fifty. When very young I enjoyed being an Ellison, liked belonging to something larger than myself. As a teenager, I resented my family name and identification. Then I didn't care. Then the world didn't care. Washington got bigger and all the people my grandfather had delivered died. I knew Father's father only through stories, but there were many. His nickname, one of them, was Superdoc, as he apparently had been able to start his battery-less car and drive it home from a house call.

My mother's maiden name was Parker and they lived on the Chesapeake Bay, south of where we summered. A couple of Parkers were farmers, others worked in plants of one sort or another. Mother's brothers and sisters were considerably older and were all dead before I was an adult, leaving me with a herd of cousins that I never saw, never heard anything about, but kind of knew existed out there somewhere with names like Janelle and Tyrell. Mother had become an Ellison. As a child, I saw some Parkers only once, visiting a farm house near the bay. They frightened me. Big-seeming people with big smells and big laughs. Had I known more of life then, I would have liked them, found them thriving and interesting, but as it was, I found them only startlingly different. Lisa, Bill and I stood around the house, which smelled of coal fire and stale quilts, like frozen carrots.

Mother seemed apologetic for her family. She seldom spoke of them, though I am sure that they did not summarily write her off. She was the only Parker to go to college and, as so often happens, education functioned as a wedge between them. Perhaps my mother understood better than I gave her credit my feelings of alienation and isolation. I believe that much of her life she felt self-conscious and somewhat inadequate. There was no particular event I recall that substantiates that belief, no habit or anything I heard her say that might serve as evidence. But maybe there was a look here or there, a physical attitude just this side of cowering that I noticed without knowing what I was noticing.

Mother and Father never seemed terribly close to me. They formed a unified front against which we kids collided and bounced off. They were not outwardly affectionate, though the three of us were evidence of some touching. Indeed, I thought they were decidedly distant, cool to one another. An attitude that would seriously impair my attempts at relationships later. I of course would be taking a convenient turn to have that alone cut as any kind of excuse for my interpersonal failures. My mother saw her life as a wife and mother as a service, a loving service, but a service nonetheless. My father saw his station rather as one defined by duty, and discharged said duty with military efficiency.

In the garage, I looked at my table that was now a stool, and not a very good stool, and considered my mother's discovery that all those years of somehow feeling she was not quite enough were in a few minutes made valid. The wood of the piece of furniture I had mutilated to make safe was still beautiful, the touch of it, even the smell of it, but it was inadequate. I imagined that my mother discovered the letters just after Father's death, when he'd asked her to burn and not read them. But he of course knew that she would read them. I found myself angry with him, a stupid enough feeling with a live person. Then I wondered which was more confidence-killing: believing that you should not have felt inadequate when in fact you were, or discovering that, all along, you were actually smart enough to see things clearly, that you were correct in your fears. This suddenly explained the newfound serenity and composure of Mother after Father's death. Perhaps he knew that was what she needed. Now what she needed was to have her nerve fibers unlooped and her newly detected brain shrinkage stopped.

Yul was doing his level best to contain his glee, but doing a piss-poor job. He was paying lip service to my vexation and indignation at the completely nonironic acceptance of that so-called novel as literature, but I could hear him counting the money. I could also hear him telling me, without saying as much, to grow up. What he said was, "We're talking about a lot of money here."

"I appreciate that, Yul," I said.

"The editor wants to discuss the manuscript with Mr. Leigh. What do I tell her?"

"Tell her I'll call her." After he said nothing, I went on. "Tell her Stagg R. Leigh lives alone in the nation's capital. Tell her he's just two years out of prison, say he said 'joint,' and that he still hasn't adjusted to the outside. Tell her he's afraid he might *go off.* Tell her that he will only talk about the book, that if she asks any personal questions, he'll hang up."

"You're sure about this?"

"I'm sure."

"Okay then. I don't mind telling you this is weird."

"Well, Mister Bossman, I'se so sorry dis seem so weird to ya'll."

"You're a sick man, Monk."

"Tell me about it."

I was seven.

The drive to the beach took us along Route 50 which was the slowest straight shot on the planet. We would take two cars, my brother always riding with Father. My Mother drove slowly, Lorraine in the front seat with her, staring at the map, and so we always arrived twenty minutes later. Still, Father would wait for us all to be there before opening the house for the summer. He and Bill would have pulled the bags out of the Willys wagon my father loved so much and have them arranged neatly, ready to be taken inside.

It was June 16, a Saturday morning. I remember that so clearly. It was sunny, but not terribly hot. I was wearing long khaki trousers and a striped shirt that I always hated. It seemed no one had come to the beach yet. The only car parked in a drive was Professor Tilman's. As soon as Howard let out, he was at the beach. He had no children and his wife had died years earlier, but still he seemed to be able to take or leave company. I couldn't understand why he came at all since he never left his house except for groceries. Sometimes I would see him sitting at the corner of his porch taking in his sliver of a view of the bay.

"Get that box," Father said, pointing.

I picked it up and carried it into the kitchen. Lorraine was already sweeping, Mother was putting away dishes and Bill was wiping dust and leaves from the sills of the breakfast porch.

"How do the leaves get in here?" Bill asked, as he always asked.

Father could be *sudden*. I thought of him as generally a kind man, perhaps because of the way his patients adored him, but living with him was like living on the crater of Vesuvius. Perhaps the comparison would be better made to some dormant or rather sleeping volcano. He wouldn't exactly erupt, but rumble or hiss, and sometimes you'd miss the event altogether and find yourself detecting a burnt smell, sulfur or just seeing some vapor in the air. To Bill, upon his asking the question, he said, "No house is tight."

It was not until Father had gone out the front door, to collect the last of the boxes, that we all exchanged fearful glances.

But, in part, that quality of my father's was one reason I felt so close to him. I admired his intelligence, his sagacity and his convoluted message delivery system. Bill kept his secret that was no secret, Mother kept no secrets at all, Lisa kept secrets that remained with her and Father kept secrets and talked about them all the time. I am convinced of this. I am certain that he told all of us any number of times that he was married to the wrong woman and probably that he had another child someplace.

Later, after a meal of sandwiches, Father and I walked down to the beach. I had to skip every few steps to keep his pace. We waved to Professor Tilman.

"Why doesn't Professor Tilman go anywhere?" I asked.

"Perhaps because he doesn't want to," Father said.

I thought about that and I suppose my silence was a bit loud.

"Is that hard to imagine?" Father asked. "Not wanting to go out?"

I said I guessed so.

We walked out the long pier and looked down at the water. A jellyfish swam by. A small boat motored by well away from us, a crabber checking his traps. I slapped a mosquito and flicked it from my arm.

Father laughed. "They take the blood and leave the itch. It's a trade-off. She gets to feed her eggs and you get to remember how good it feels to scratch an itch, how good it felt to not itch."

"All I know is I hate them," I said.

"The bluefish will be running in a few weeks," he said. "That will be fun. Do you think you and your brother can get the boat into the water by yourselves?"

"No."

He laughed. "I'll help you in the morning before I go back."

Rothko: I'm an old man.

Motherwell: You're not so old.

Rothko: And I'm a sour old man. I've taken to this house painter's brush I found. It makes the edges almost feathery. Funny, eh? A house painter's brush. I'll bet that devil Hitler used the very same thing when he was a nasty youth. And here I am with one. I have all these powdered paints and I mix and mix, but are my colors really so different? Are people sick of my panels? I like my early work. This stuff I'm doing now has me depressed.

Motherwell: Work depressed us all.

Rothko: A nice homily from a nice young man.

Motherwell: Not so young myself.

Rothko: And steady. I've noticed that about you. I'm planning to take my own life, but you've no doubt surmised this. And you fathom that you understand the feeling in some way. Yes, you're a steady one. Of course, your paintings stink.

In considering my novels, not including the one frightening effort that brought in some money, I find myself sadly a stereotype of the radical, railing against something, calling it tradition perhaps, claiming to seek out new narrative territory, to knock at the boundaries of the very form that calls me and allows my artistic existence. It is the case, however, that not all radicalism is forward looking, and maybe I have misunderstood my experiments all along, propping up, as if propping up is needed, the artistic traditions that I have pretended to challenge. I reread the paper I claimed to dismiss summarily and realized that epiphanies are like spicy foods: coming back, coming back.

Paula Baderman had a smoker's voice, but she sounded young and spirited enough. She came to the phone quickly when I called.

"Mr. Leigh," she said.

"Yes."

"I'm glad we could get together, even if it is over the phone. I just wanted to touch bases with you. You know of course that I love the book."

"So I understand," I said.

She paused, leaving a blank between us, then said, "How long did it take you to write it?"

"It took me just a little over a week."

The quality of her next silence was clear to me. She was surprised, if not put off by my diction, being not at all what she expected. I was not going to put on an act for her.

"A week. Imagine that."

"Are there any changes you'd like me to make?"

"Not really. In fact, I think it's about as perfect a book as I've seen in a long while. But I just want to get to know you right now. If you don't mind my asking, what were you in prison for?"

"I mind your asking."

My abruptness was apparently pleasing to her, if not downright exciting. I detected a change in her breathing. "Certainly, I don't mean to pry."

"Did you read a lot in prison?"

I didn't say anything.

"Well," she said. "We're hoping for a spring pub date. I think this is just perfect for summer reading."

"Yes, white people on the beach will get a big kick out of it."

That sent walking fingers up her spine and if I had been in her office (looking the part), she would have been tearing off her blouse and crawling across her desk toward me, perhaps not literally, but at least literarily.

"Do you think I might take your number in case I have any further questions?" she asked.

"No, I don't think so. You just tell Yul that you'd like to speak with me and I'll call you. Everything will work better like that."

"Well, okay. Oh, and Stagg? May I call you Stagg?"

"You may."

"Stagg, thank you."

"You're welcome, Ms. Baderman." I hung up before she insisted that I call her by her first name.

X X X

The first half of the advance arrived. I found Mother sitting in the living room listening to Mahler. My father had always loved Mahler, but even as a child I found it heavy and overwrought. She was listening to the *Kindertotenlieder* and looking near tears. I was smiling.

"Why are you so happy, Monksie?"

"Just got paid for a new book."

"A new book? I can't wait to read it."

"Yes, you can," I said. "But anyway. I'm taking you on a trip. Anywhere you'd like to go." I wanted to take her on a vacation while she could still enjoy it, while she could still remember who I was and who she was and what a fork was for. "Where would you like me to take you?"

"Oh, Monksie, you know how I've always been about traveling. You decide. I'll be happy with wherever you pick."

"Detroit," I said.

The expression that crawled over and sat on her face was precious and let me know that she was no vegetable yet.

"Just joking," I said.

"I should say."

"Well, it's summer, so what do you say we head north. How does Martha's Vineyard sound?"

"Why don't we go open the beach house," she said.

It wasn't what I'd had in mind, but the idea was perfect. The house had sat empty now for three years. Lisa had used it with her ex-husband, but never returned after the divorce. "That sounds good," I said. "We'll take Lorraine and we'll leave tomorrow. How's tomorrow?"

"Fine, Monksie."

Yul: What did you say to her?

Me: What do you mean?

Yul: She's more gung-ho than ever.

Me: I don't know why that would be.

Yul: They're going to take out a full page ad in the New York Times *and the* Washington Post.

Me: You're kidding me.

Yul: She wanted me to ask if Stagg will do a couple of talk shows. Morning network stuff.

Me: Laugh laugh.

I called the number Bill gave me and a man answered. He seemed cool until I identified myself as the brother, and then he, Adam, was quite pleasant and told me more about Bill's problems than I believe Bill would have wanted me to know.

"William tried to see his children the other day, but it became a big scene. His ex is seeing some homophobic highway trooper or something and they nearly came to blows. The kids aren't taking the truth very well, I'm afraid. I believe he told me that he's picked up a few new patients. That's a good thing." Then Bill came home. "It's your brother," Adam said away from the receiver.

"What have you been telling him?" Bill's voice was stern.

"We were just chatting."

Bill took the phone. "Monk?"

"Hi, Bill."

"How's it going?"

"Fine. What about with you?"

"Things could be better," he said. He sounded near crying.

"Bill, I'm calling because I'm planning to take Mother out to the beach tomorrow. We're going to stay there for a few weeks. I was wondering if you could make a trip out. I'll pick you up at BWI."

There was a long silence.

"Bill?"

"I'd really like to, but things are pretty hectic around here these days. I'm having to go to court about visitation and all that stuff."

"I'm sorry."

"Thanks."

"Well, I just thought I'd ask. Hey, what if you brought Adam with you?" Before he could respond, I said, "I'll buy your tickets. Mother's not doing well, Bill."

"Okay, Monk. I'll talk to Adam. Are you going to turn the phone on down there?"

"I guess so."

"Okay, well, I'll call in the next couple of days."

"Okay."

I hung up and stared at the phone on my desk. It was black and heavy and had been used by my father and sometimes I imagined I could still hear his deep voice humming through the wires. Bill sounded so remarkably sad, so lost. When we were kids I had often felt, however vaguely, his sadness, but this hopelessness, if it was in fact that, this lostness, misplacedness, was new and not easy to take. For the first time I sat back and watched the destruction of my family, not a weird or unnatural thing, indeed it was more natural than most things, but it was a large portion to swallow. My father was dead for several years. My sister was recently murdered. My mother was slipping away on her kite of senility. And my brother was finally finding himself, I suppose, but seemingly losing everything else in the process. I wouldn't use the cliché that I was the captain of a sinking ship, that implying some kind of authority, but rather I was a diesel mechanic on a steamship, an obstetrician in a monastery.

"Would you rather lose your sight or your hearing?" Lisa asked one evening while we all sat at the picnic table behind the house. The mosquitoes were just starting to come out and the crabs were almost gone.

"Hearing," Bill answered quickly. "There's too much in this world to see. Paintings, landscapes, faces. You can get around if you don't hear and you can learn to read lips."

"What about you, Monksie?" Mother asked. She saw these sorts of things as good conversation and good for us.

"I don't know. I'd miss hearing music and crickets. I'd miss seeing things like paintings like Bill said. I guess it would be hearing. I'd rather lose my hearing."

"Me, too," Mother said.

"What about you, Father?" Bill asked.

Father had been chewing and listening to us in that absent way of his. He looked at Lisa, then me, studying us, it seemed. He looked down the table to Mother, nodding his head. Then he looked longest at Bill. He then took us in as a group, and said, "Sight" with a smile that was not quite a smile, but enough for us to laugh as if we had been teased rather than insulted.

In my head, as I drove along Route 50, Mother by my side, disapproving Lorraine directly behind me, I considered everything that was not good about the novel I was about to publish, that I submitted for the very reason it was not good, but now that fact was killing me. It was a parody, certainly, but so easy had it been to construct that I found it difficult to take it seriously even as that. The work bored and had as its only virtue brevity. There was no playing with compositional or even paginal space. In fact, the work inhabited no space artistically that I could find intelligible. For all the surface concern with the spatial and otherwise dislocation of Van Go, there was nothing in the writing that self-consciously threw it back at me. Then I caught the way I was thinking and realized the saddest thing of all, that I was thinking myself into a funk about idiotic and pretentious bullshit to avoid the real accusation staring me in the face. I was a sell-out.

Mother touched my arm as if she recognized my torture. "Are you okay, dear?" she asked.

"Fine, Mother." I looked into the rearview mirror. "Okay back there, Lorraine?"

"Yes." Lorraine had not really wanted to come, but I needed her help in taking care of Mother and, frankly, I couldn't see leaving her alone. "I could use a ladies' room."

We had been on the road for thirty minutes and had perhaps another twenty to go to Annapolis. "Do you think you can wait until we get to Annapolis?" I asked.

"I suppose if I have to."

"Lorraine needs to stop," Mother said.

I nodded and pulled off at the next exit which turned out not to be conveniently located for anything people in cars might want. I drove along the two lane highway until thirty minutes later we'd come to a gas station. I parked in front of the restroom doors and killed the engine. "Okay, Lorraine." I got out and opened her door for her. A greasy-looking, lanky white teenager watched us through the window.

Lorraine went to the door, opened it, then came back, got into the car. "I can wait," she said.

"What's wrong?" I asked.

"I can't go in there," she said.

"There's no place else."

"Lorraine said she can't use that one, Monksie," Mother said.

"I'll just wait until we get there," Lorraine said.

An hour later we were in Annapolis and Lorraine was asleep in the back. Mother was asleep beside me. I drove through town to the beach. The guard at the gate actually recognized me. He was as old as my mother, but I couldn't recall him. "Monk Ellison," he said. "My, my. You don't even remember me, do you? Maynard Boatwright."

I did recall the name, but I remembered a big, heavily muscled ex-marine with an iron jaw, instead of the sweet old man saying *my my* in front of me.

"I remember you," I said. "How's life treating you?"

"Finer than frog's hair." He looked over at my mother, then at Lorraine. I remembered that Lisa suspected he had a thing for Lorraine. "Is that?"

"Lorraine," I said.

"Well, I'll be."

I turned to wake Lorraine, but Maynard stopped me.

"You must be a good driver," Maynard said. "For everybody to fall asleep like that."

"I guess so."

"Well, I'll see you later." Then he waved to the sleeping Lorraine.

The naps must have had a restorative effect on the old ladies. Once at the house and awake, they set to the task of getting the place in order with single-mindedness. I was only a little tired from the short drive, but they wouldn't let me close enough to help with the cleaning. I went out to the side of the house, turned on the water and threw the main breaker. I poked my head back in to reaffirm my uselessness and stepped out the back to the little dock on the tidal pond. I looked east out to the bay. The old aluminum canoe was still upturned on blocks and covered with a tarp the way it always was. Later, I would take it out and just float on the water with a cigar. The rim of the pond was crowded with houses, nothing like it had been when I was a kid. I could hear the noises of families, music, dogs, a distant car alarm. I walked between our house and the neighboring one and to the road, where I walked toward the bay beach.

I wondered how far I should take my Stagg Leigh performance. I might in fact become a Rhinehart, walking down the street and finding myself in store windows. I yam what I yam. I could throw on a fake beard and a wig and do the talk shows, play the game, walk the walk, shoot the jive. No, I couldn't.

I would let Mr. Leigh continue his reclusive, just-out-of-the-big-house ways. He would talk to the editor a few more times, then disappear, like down a hole.

I walked along the beach, then turned to look back at the Douglass house. It had been owned first by the grandson of Frederick Douglass and had fallen into several hands since. When I was a child it was unoccupied and we would walk into it, climb the stairs and stare at the water from its tower. My father told me that James Weldon Johnson had written in that lookout. The thought of it scared me a little, but also made my mind race, searching for lines of poems of my own that would never come. Now the house was fresh looking and somewhat unfamiliar. The tower top was no longer screened in, but surrounded by glass. The house looked tight and air-conditioned. There was a Mercedes Benz station wagon parked by the front walk.

I walked back up the street. I stopped to look at the old Tilman house. A woman whom I had not seen was sitting on the porch and she asked if she could help me, in that way which really asked what the hell I was looking at.

"I'm sorry," I said. "I was just remembering a former owner."

"Oh, really?" Meaning of course, *yeah, right.*

"No, really. His name was Professor Tilman. I never knew his first name. Maybe it was Professor."

The woman laughed. She was tall, as tall as me, and she stepped off the porch and looked at the house with me. Her square face was framed by near blonde dreadlocks. "Professor Tilman was my uncle," she said. "We called him Uncle Professor."

She was funny. I smiled at her. "I didn't mean to be rude, but I didn't see you."

"That's okay."

"How is the Professor?" I asked.

"He died three years ago."

"I'm sorry."

"I inherited the house. Some of the house. My brother and I own it, but he lives in Las Vegas and never comes east." She said *Las Vegas* as if it were not to be believed.

"I've driven through there," I said. "My name is Thelonious Ellison. Everybody calls me Monk."

"Dr. Ellison's family?" I nodded and she said, "My uncle mentioned your father often."

"How about that."

"Marilyn Tilman." She shook my hand. "Are you down for the summer? What's left of it?"

"Just a couple of weeks. I'm here with my mother and her housekeeper. Speaking of which, I'd better get back there. I know they'll have a shopping list waiting for me. I'll talk to you later, okay?" I took a couple steps away. "Would you like me to pick up anything for you?"

"Why don't I ride with you?" she asked.

"It's the two story with the green shutters."

"I'll be over in a couple," she said.

"Good." I watched her take the porch steps two at a time and enter the house.

Back at the house, I discovered that Mother and Lorraine had gotten on each other's nerves. The outward manifestation of this nerve-pinching was an awkward silence. Mother told me she felt the need for a nap and Lorraine told me, aside, that Mother needed a nap. Lorraine had compiled the shopping list, at the end of which were a couple of things added by my mother's shaking hand. This was no doubt the source of trouble between them, especially as one of the items had already been listed by Lorraine.

"She's tired," Lorraine said again, this time loud enough for Mother to hear.

"It's no wonder," Mother said softly, looking around as if for a place to lie down.

"Lorraine," I said, "take Mother up and get her to bed, will you? I'll be back in an hour or so. And I'll pick up some food so no one cooks tonight."

"Yes, Mr. Monk."

Lorraine followed Mother up the stairs.

"I don't need your help," Mother snapped.

"I have to make up your bed," Lorraine said.

"Well, get to it, Lorraine. You're such a slow girl sometimes."

I stepped outside to find Marilyn approaching. She was wearing a straw hat that shaded her face, but still her youthfulness shone on her cheeks and in her eyes. It was a glow that I believed I recalled, but was faded from me. My eyes felt tired as I watched her confident gait, her cloth knapsack swinging by her side.

"Ready?" she asked.

"Oh yeah," I said.

We sat in the car and I fumbled a bit with the keys. The scene was strikingly and alarmingly unfamiliar to me. A woman less than seventy was seated beside me, a woman whom I found attractive, a woman whose short-term memory was at least as good as mine. I felt like a spinster and fought appearing too self-conscious.

Ten days drifted by. I walked alone, walked with Marilyn, once walked with mother. Marilyn met Mother and Lorraine. Maynard, the gate guard, paid a call on Lorraine. Mother told me she liked Marilyn. I told Marilyn I liked Marilyn. Marilyn told me she liked me. The four of us ate together. I ate with Marilyn. I rowed out onto the pond and smoked cigars. Mother and Lorraine got on each other's nerves. Lorraine muttered under her breath. Mother took naps. Mother spoke alone with Marilyn while I was at the market.

"Your mother tells me you have a new book coming out soon," Marilyn said.

My first thought was to say that Mother was mistaken and I nearly followed that thought, but considered how unfair it was to attribute a delusion to someone who was frequently suffering from real ones. I said, "Well, the book's not done yet, but I hope to have it out by the spring."

"What's the title?"

"I don't really have one yet. It's a retelling of *The Satyricon*." I laughed. "Another highly commercial venture for me."

"I'd love to read some of it."

"So would I." I said.

She offered a puzzled look.

"I'd love to see it too when done."

"I actually read *The Second Failure* when it came out. I liked it."

I nodded. "Thank you. I don't have many readers, I'm afraid."

We were sitting on the dock looking at the pond. We had a bottle of merlot, but the flavor had been badly affected by the citronella candles we were forced to burn. I had learned much about Marilyn and I guess she about me, but other people's information always seems more important or interesting or simply more like information. She had grown up outside Boston with her brother and physician parents, gone to Vassar, then Columbia and now worked as a federal defender for the Sentencing Guidelines Group. She traveled through the states explaining sentencing legislation to public defenders. She took her work seriously, thought of it as important, and so did I, and, in that way, Marilyn was very much like my sister. She liked some of her co-workers, but not the workplace, cared passionately about the rights of those she represented, but disliked them as people.

The mosquitoes were busy around our ankles. "Do you mind if I light this?" I asked, pulling a cigar from my shirt pocket.

"No, go ahead."

I lit it and blew smoke down over her legs. "This will help keep the mosquitoes away," I said.

"That's sexy."

I leaned back and looked at her eyes. She was not beautiful in that stupid movie kind of way, but her face was interesting, full of experience, full of thought and so, she was beautiful. I hoped that my face carried enough of that stuff to make me attractive. Our heads drifted toward a common point in space the way heads do when a first kiss is anticipated. And we kissed, softly, but resolutely, decisively. We came away from the kiss without anything to say. I was terrified, wondering if I would eventually alienate her and fuck up everything.

Then, on the pond we heard the dipping of oars, soft laughter. Under the moon, Lorraine and Maynard floated by in a little skiff. It was sweet. But as much as I wanted to be happy for Lorraine, I could only feel sad for my mother in the house with a loneliness that I was sure was killing her.

I could never talk the talk, so I didn't try and being myself has served me well enough. But when I was a teenager, I wanted badly to fit in. I watched my friends, who didn't sound so different from me, step into scenes and change completely.

"Yo, man, what it is?" they would say.

"You're what it is," someone would respond.

It didn't make sense to me, but it sounded casual, comfortable and, most importantly, cool. I remember the words, the expressions.

Solid
What's happenin'.
What's up?
Chillin'.
Dig.
Yo. (that should have been easy enough)
What it be like?
What it is?
You better step back.
That's some shit.
Say what?
It's hotter than a motherfucker out here.
Gots to be crazy.

I'd try, but it never sounded comfortable, never sounded real. In fact, to my ear, it never sounded real coming from anyone, but I could tell that other people talked the talk much better than I ever could. I never knew when to slap five or high five, which handshake to use. Of course, no one cared about my awkwardness but me, I came to learn later, but at the time I was convinced that it was the defining feature of my personality. "You know, Thelonious Ellison, he's the awkward one." *Talks like he's stuck up? Sounds white? Can't even play basketball.*

It was a cool morning and I was happy to have to reach for the blanket at the foot of my bed. Day was just breaking. From deep in those sweet half-waking minutes of sleep I heard Lorraine calling to me.

"Mr. Monk! Mr. Monk!"

I swung my legs around, pulled on my sweat pants and stepped into my slippers. "What is it?" I called down the stairs as I hit the doorway.

"It's your mother."

I hurried down the stairs and saw Lorraine in the kitchen. She was staring out the window. I looked around for Mother. "What's wrong? Lorraine, where's Mother?"

Lorraine said nothing, but pointed out the window at the pond. Out on the still, mirror-flat surface of the water, standing in the light blue skiff was Mother. Her arms were by her sides and she didn't seem the least bit excited.

"What's she doing out there?" I asked, realizing what a stupid question it was as it left my lips. To Lorraine's credit, she offered no response. "I guess I'd better go get her." But how? I wondered. Mother was in our boat. I looked at the neighbors' yards for something to commandeer. Nothing. "I guess I'm going for a swim."

The water was cold, very cold. Never a strong swimmer, I was at least confident I could reach the boat. I stopped halfway to get my bearings. I looked back to see not only Lorraine standing on the dock, but the neighbors, whom I didn't know, collecting in little clumps along the edge. I swam on. In an odd way, the exercise felt good. Mother hated the water, so I knew she was having an episode. It was always a huge deal when Father was able to talk her into a boat and now, here she was, having floated out on her own. I could have no idea just how far away she had drifted until I got there.

I stopped and looked, found I was just feet from the boat. I sidestroked to it and reached out of the water, then drew back my hand as Mother cracked it with an oar.

"Mother, it's me," I said, treading water and trying to find her eyes. The rising sun was slightly behind her and so I circled the boat. When I could see her eyes, there was nothing to see. She was not Mother, but of course she was my mother. I could tell her who I was for hours and it would mean nothing. I noticed the tie rope floating in the water and so I grabbed it, began sidestroking my way back to the dock. I could see her the whole time, standing, the oar raised to swing on me again if I approached. "It's okay, Mother," I kept saying. "It's okay, Mother." Finally, I said, in a stern voice, "Mrs. Ellison, there's no standing allowed in the boat." She sat. I could feel my movements in the water become immediately more relaxed.

Lorraine and now Maynard and Marilyn were on the landing to receive us. Lorraine and Maynard helped Mother out and up the ramp. Marilyn saw to me. I fell on my back, panting, staring at the by now bright sky.

"Good lord," I said.

"Are you okay?" Marilyn asked.

I looked at her, then sat up. People were standing all around the pond, even on the very far side, and they were all staring. I didn't mind the gawking so much. Had I been one of them I would have been standing dumbly about too. But their attention underscored what was already obvious, that Mother was in a very bad way and there was nothing I or anyone could do about it.

"Are you okay?" Marilyn asked again.

"I think so. I'd better go check on Mother."

She helped me to my feet and I think I actually coughed up some water. My sweatpants clung to my legs, feeling heavy and appropriate.

✗ ✗ ✗

Àpropos de bottes

"Welcome to *Virtute et Armis*."

"I'd like to be on the show," Tom said.

"Well, of course, you would," the blonde said. She handed a single-sheet form to Tom. "Fill this in and give it back to me and we'll go from there. You may sit over there at that table." She pointed across the room to a large wooden table at which sat three other black men.

Tom took the form and went to the table. He sat and picked up a pen that was tethered to the tabletop. He tried to see the faces of the other men, but they would not look up. The first question asked for his name and already he was stumped. He wanted to laugh out loud. Under the line, in parentheses, the form asked for last and first names. He wrote Tom in the appropriate place and then tried to come up with a last name. He thought to use Himes, but he was afraid that somehow he would get into trouble, more trouble. Finally he wrote, Wahzetepe. He didn't know why he wrote it, but it came out easily and so he said it softly to himself, "Wah-ze-te-pe." If asked, he would say it was an African name, but he knew that it was a Sioux Indian word, though he didn't know its meaning. He didn't know how he knew the word, but he was sure of it as his name. The form wanted his social security number and a number supplied itself, though he knew it was bogus. 451-69-1369. He stared at the number, wondering what it meant. He recognized the center cluster of two numbers as the zodiacal sign for Cancer. But the other two clusters, 451 and 1369, made no sense to him. He lied all the way down the page, about his address, about his place of birth, about his education, claiming that he had studied at the College of William and Mary, about his hobbies, in which he included making dulcimers and box kites out of garbage bags. He took the form back to the receptionist and she accepted it happily. She then handed him a stack of pages.

"If you would answer these questions to the best of your ability, we'll be able to make a decision about your candidacy for the show," she said. "You have fifteen minutes." She looked at her watch. "Starting now."

Tom went back to the table. The first question was: Can you describe the members of the insect family Haliplidae? After this Tom wrote simply "yes." Then he thought that he was being too literal and so went ahead and also supplied a description. He wrote, "The haliplids are the crawling water beetles. They are small, oval and convex and are usually yellow or brown with dark spots. They may be discerned from other aquatic beetles by their large and plate-like hind coxae." He knew that he could go on, but he felt he had to continue to the next question.

(2) Who was Ferdinand Albert Decombe? Tom did not hesitate, but answered. "Known simply as Albert, he was made maître de ballet of the Paris Opera in 1829. He produced a number of ballets, among them *Le Seducteur au Village, Cendrillon* and *La Jolie Fille de Gand*."

(3) Please state the Mean Value Theorem. "This theorem is a generalization of Rolle's Theorem. It states that if the function y = f(x) is continuous for a ≤ x ≤ b and has a derivative at each value of x for a < x < b, then there is at least one point c between a and b where the tangent to the curve will be parallel to the chord through the two points A[a, f(a)] and B[b, f(b)]."

Tom's brain felt like it was on fire. The answers came easily, though he didn't know why. But he understood it all and his brain was burning up. He was finally asked to and he did describe the single-point continuous fuel injection system that Chrysler Motor Company devised in 1977. He gave a detailed but boring response to a request for a description of the working of the concept in the Imperial automobile. But the boringness of the answer served to quiet the fire in his brain.

"Time's up," the woman called to Tom from her desk.

Tom took the test back to her.

"That's just fine," she said. "Now, you go on home and you'll be called if you're what we need."

"I don't have a phone, " Tom said.

"Oh, my," the woman said.

"I'll just wait here, " Tom said and went over to a sofa and sat. The receptionist was visibly troubled by his decision to remain in the office. She took what Tom thought was his test with her into another office. He picked up a popular science magazine and read an article about the army's new tank which traveled at a rate of more than 90 mph over rough terrain.

Tom was in the NBC building, in the outer offices of *Virtute et Armis*, waiting on a sofa for the receptionist to reappear at her desk. She did reappear and with her came a man in a gray suit with gray hair and a smile slathered across his face like an infection. The receptionist pointed to Tom and the gray-haired man nodded, then walked to him. Tom watched his confident stride as he approached.

"You did very well on the exam," the man said.

Tom nodded.

"It says on your sheet that you attended William and Mary. When did you graduate?"

"Actually, that's not true. I just wanted to put down something."

"My name is Damien Blanc," the man said. "I'm the producer of *Virtute et Armis*."

"I apologize about lying on the questionnaire."

"Don't concern yourself over that. This is television. Who really gives a fuck where you studied or what you studied or if you studied?" He sat down beside Tom on the sofa. "The fact of the matter, Mr. Wahzetepe—" He stopped. "May I call you Tom?"

Tom nodded.

"The fact of the matter, Tom, is that we've got a problem. You see, one of our contestants for tonight's show has taken ill. So, we need a quick replacement. And here you are."

"I'm going to be on the show?"

"That's right," Blanc said. "You're going to be live on national television. You know we're one of the few live shows left." He looked at his watch. "We go on in just a little more than six hours. So, I suggest you go get some rest, get something to eat, and take it easy. Our show can be pretty grueling."

"Yes, I know." Tom couldn't believe his quick and positive fortune. He was indeed going to appear on *Virtute et Armis*. But as he considered this, he also recalled the ugly ends met by his predecessors. They had been terribly bright people, but had fallen to nit-picking trick questions. Or had they simply been careless, finally not smart enough? Tom decided he would be smart enough. He would answer each question perfectly. He would succeed where the others had failed.

"Are you all right?" Blanc asked.

"Yes."

"Well, then, you report back here at seven. Meet me here and I'll take you up to the fifth floor."

"Thank you," Tom said. "Thank you so much."

"No, thank you, Tom."

Blanc had a large smile on his pasty face and kept running his long, bony fingers through his gray hair. "Good, you're here. If you hadn't made it I don't know what we were going to do. Come on, I'll take you upstairs and you can get made up and we'll even give you a brand new shirt and a tie. I'll bet you didn't expect that little bonus. You know, this is television, you've got to look good. *Virtute* is no low-class operation. We're the big time. I can't believe how well you did on that exam. Come on." Blanc grabbed Tom's shoulders, turned him around and got him walking toward the elevators. "Here we go. Are you excited?"

"No."

"Well, you should be. This is a golden opportunity for you. There's no telling where you'll go from here. The sky is the limit. Why you might even get a recording contract or a sit-com offer."

They took the elevator up to the fifth floor and got out. They walked down the hall toward some double doors, passing on the way a black man who was mopping the floor. As the man wrung out the mop over the bucket, Tom got a brief look at his face and thought he recognized him. As the doors closed he recognized him as a former contestant on the show.

Now, they were standing in front of a door marked Makeup. "They'll get you all ready in here," Blanc said, straightening his own tie. "I've got to go check on our other contestant, but you'll be just fine. You just relax and go with the flow. Just roll with it."

Tom nodded. He looked back at the double doors, wanting to go back out into the hallway and talk to Bob Jones, but Blanc ushered him into the makeup room. Two women took him from Blanc, spun him around and sat him in a chair in front of a large mirror.

One of the women had red hair and very fat cheeks, though Tom could not see the rest of her. "Just relax, honey," she said. "We haven't lost a patient yet."

The other woman was sick looking, she was so skinny. Her cheeks were hollowed out and looked as if they might meet inside her mouth. "What size shirt do you wear?" she asked.

"A large," Tom said

"Do you know your collar size?"

Tom shook his head.

The skinny woman sucked her teeth and said, "You are a big boy. You look like a sixteen-and-a-half to me."

"Let me see that face," the red-haired woman said, grabbing Tom's chin and turning his head this way and that. "You ain't half-bad-looking," she said, smoothing his forehead with her thumb. She reached over to the cart which was beside the chair and came back with her fingertips coated with a brown cream.

"What's that?" Tom asked.

"You ain't quite dark enough, darlin'," she said. She began to rub the compound into the skin of Tom's face. "This is TV stuff."

He watched in the mirror as his oak brown skin became chocolate brown.

"There now," the redhead said, "that's so much better."

The skinny woman came back with a white shirt. The garment had been heavily starched, but Tom struggled into it with the woman's help. The collar turned out to be just a tad tight. Tom tried without success to button the shirt at his throat.

"Here, let me help you," the skinny woman said. Her bony knuckles pressed into his adam's apple and he could not breathe. She fought with the button for several minutes and finally got it through the stiff hole. "There." She stood away.

Tom looked at the mirror and saw someone else. The contrast of the white shirt against the altered hue of his face was unsettling and confusing. He felt like a clown. "Do I have to wear this stuff on my face?" he asked.

"I'm afraid so, doll," the red-haired woman said. "I'm afraid so. Rules are rules. You wouldn't want to confuse the folks viewing at home, now would you?"

The skinny woman knotted a tie around Tom's neck, tightening it enough to squeeze his throat with the stiff collar.

"Are you ready?" This from Blanc who leaned suddenly into the room. "Hey, you look great, absolutely terrific. " He walked a circle around Tom. "Nice job, girls. Real nice. He looks just right. Tom, I almost didn't recognize you."

"Me, either."

Blanc laughed loudly. "You hear that, girls. 'Me either.' This Tom is a funny one." He stopped and put his hand on Tom's shoulder. "It's time, Tom. It's time to play *Virtute et Armis*."

Tom stood and followed Blanc out of the room and down the inner hallway to another door. A red light was on outside the door. They entered and there before them was the set of *Virtute et Armis*. Tom's breath caught in his throat. For the first time, he was nervous. He had to win this game. He just had to win. But he also knew how this game worked. It wasn't up to him. He had to be careful, not slip up anywhere. He was here in the studio, standing at the threshold of his future.

The studio lights were harsh. The cameras stood like hulking gorillas in front of the set. Tom had the feeling his makeup was melting and he wondered if his face was striped. There was Jack Spades, big as life, his slicked-back hair shining like it had batteries. He was wearing a plastic bib and looking over his note cards while the skinny woman from the makeup room powdered his brow. And there was the big circular board laid out on the floor, the squares of different colors appearing to Tom as his coming obstacles. His opponent was sitting in a recliner on the other side of the studio.

He was receiving a manicure from a woman with long brown hair. He was a handsome man, blond with chiseled features. Tom watched as Blanc and Spades chatted. The two men looked concerned about something, one shaking his head and then the other. At one point during their conversation, Blanc pointed over at the white contestant in his recliner. Tom felt a profound loneliness. He watched the audience file in and find seats. They were all white, all blond and all staring at Tom, an ocean of blue eyes.

Jack Spades left Blanc and walked over to Tom. "Jack Spades," he introduced himself. "Welcome to the show." His smile was somehow too bright, too clean, unreal. He shook Tom's hand. "I want to wish you luck. Just relax. I'm sure you'll do fine and be a credit to your race."

Spades walked away and was replaced by Blanc. "It's time for you to go over and take your place," Blanc said. "You're supposed to stand on the red mark. When in doubt, just look for the red mark on the floor. You've seen the show, so you'll know what to do. Just listen to Jack and watch the director. He's the one in the baseball cap. Look at the camera with the red light on when you give your answers. Now, go get 'em, Tom."

Tom walked onto the set and took his place, carefully toeing the red mark. The lights fell on him and he could no longer really see the faces in the audience, but he felt the eyes watching him, could hear their breathing. The theme music poured in and Jack's opponent was introduced. "From Elkhart, Indiana, a social worker and part-time blues musician in area night clubs, father of two and president of the PTA and his neighborhood association, Hal Dullard." Hal Dullard waved to the television audience. "And from Mississippi, Tom Wahzetepe." The camera stared at Tom and he stared back. "And now, your favorite gameshow host, the gamemaster of *Virtute et Armis*, Jack Spades."

Jack Spades came trotting out and greeted the audience. "Let's jump right into the game," he said. "Mr. Dullard, if you would, please name a primary color."

"Green," said Dullard.

The studio audience gasped collectively.

The stunned Spades cleared his throat and said, "I'm afraid that's not an acceptable answer."

"Tom," Spades said. "What is anaphase?"

"Anaphase is the phase of nuclear division characterized by the movement of chromosomes from the spindle equator to the spindle poles. It starts with the separation of the centromeres and ends with the termination of the poleward movement of the chromosomes."

"That's correct," Spades said. "One square forward for you."

"Mr. Dullard, in the Bible, who slew Goliath?"

"That would be Solomon."

Again the studio audience moaned. Tom looked over to see Blanc holding his face in his hands.

"Incorrect," Spades said. "The answer is David." He shuffled to the next card. "Tom, name the poem from which come the following lines, then name the poet and tell us something about him":

> *Weep for the tender and delicate ones*
> *Who barefoot now tread upon thorns,*
> *Drawing water for barbarians,*
> *Felling trees at their commands.*

Tom paused for a second and saw a brief smile flash across Blanc's face, then he said, "The lines are from the poem 'Lament on the Devastation of the Land of Israel.' The poet's name is Joseph Ibn Abithur. He was born in the middle of the tenth century. It is claimed that he gave an Arabic explanation of the Talmud to the Caliph al-Hakim II. He was known mainly for liturgical works, prayer books of Catalonian and North African Jews."

Blanc's face was blank.

Spades shook his head and said, "Correct. One square." He then announced a commercial break during which several makeup people ran to him and attended to his perspiring brow.

Blanc made quick, long strides over to Dullard and seemed to be yelling at him in a whisper. Though they were only two squares away, Tom could not hear what was being said. He sensed hostility in the studio audience.

The director counted backwards with his fingers from five and pointed at Jack Spades.

"Welcome back," Spades said. "Mr. Dullard, let's see if we can't get you moving here. Please name the first president of the United States of America."

"Thomas Jefferson."

"Wrong," Spades said, unable to completely hide his annoyance. "That's wrong."

"Tom, what is a serial distribution field?"

"It is a field that must be built when installing a septic system on sloping land. It possesses level trenches dug along the contours of the land, each lower than the next. Connections from trench to trench are set up to transfer the sewage to the lower trench only when the sewage in the trench above reaches the top of its gravel fill." Tom thought to stop, but added, "And so, the first trench of the system must operate to full capacity before the second trench receives any flow. Also, there is no need for a distribution box."

Blanc looked as if he might scream. He looked anxiously back at the unsettled audience.

"Correct, one square," Spades said.

Dullard did not know that a gorilla was a primate. He did not know the abbreviation for Avenue. He did not know what a male chicken was called. Soon, Tom had nearly made his way around the circle and was about to lap Mr. Dullard. The studio audience had stopped breathing. Blanc was chewing aspirin like candy. Spades was sweating so badly that no amount of attention from the puff-wielding staff could hide it.

"Tom, for the game and a purse of three-hundred thousand dollars in cash, with what lines does Ralph Waldo Emerson open his essay Self-Reliance?"

Tom was silent for a few seconds. The studio hushed. The red light on the camera facing him bothered his eyes. He said, "He begins with:

Ne te quæsiveris extra.

"And then lines from the epilogue to Beaumont and Fletcher's Honest Man's Fortune:

> *Man is his own star; and the soul that can*
> *Render an honest and perfect man,*
> *Commands all light, all influence, all fate;*
> *Nothing to him falls early or too late.*
> *Our acts our angels are, for good or ill,*
> *Our fatal shadows that walk by us still."*

Spades took a breath and was about to speak and Tom said, "And then four lines follow, which are:

> *Cast the bantling on the rocks,*
> *Suckle him with the she-wolf's teat,*
> *Wintered with the hawk and fox,*
> *Power and speed be hands and feet."*

Spades' disappointment was obvious as he formed the word, "Correct," but hardly said it out loud. "And so you, Tom Wahzetepe from somewhere in Mississippi, are our new champion."

The audience made no sounds. They were dead.

There seemed little point in maintaining the charade of a last and mean-ingful vacation for Mother. She again slipped through the perimeter the following morning and managed to lose herself one road over. Lorraine was concerned, but she was also consumed with what she had never, to my knowledge, had, which was a love relationship with a man. She seemed to feel some guilt over her sudden-found happiness, being extra nice to Mother and smiling more than normal at me. Marilyn was pre-dictably understanding and equally predictably space-giving. After put-ting Mother to bed early one evening, her frail body packed with enough sedatives to knock me out twice, I wandered down the lane to Marilyn's house. A man answered the door, Marilyn's face just behind him.

"I'm sorry for interrupting," I said.

"Monk," Marilyn said in a way to confirm my interruption. "Come on in. I'd like you to meet Clevon."

Clevon grabbed my extended hand about the thumb in a handshake I'd experienced, but still had never learned to expect, and said, "What's up, brother."

My mind raced. What was the proper response to a *what's up*? Should I say, *Nothing's up*, which would imply that I had no good reason for being there? I couldn't say *Several things are up*, because I would then be obliged to say what those things might be. And so I said, "Not much," which seemed right somehow, but also carried with it, I thought, a kind of insult to Mar-ilyn. "I live up the road," I said.

"Okay," Clevon said and walked a cool walk over to the sofa where he proceeded to thumb through a stack of compact discs.

"I didn't know you had company," I said to Marilyn.

"That's okay. Would you like something to drink?"

"Actually, I think Lorraine is going out. So, I'd better get home to Mother." The sound of it, *going home to Mother,* in front of Clevon, made me want to die. I felt like I was a teenager again. When I was gone, he would laugh and then ask her what kind of name was Monk?

Marilyn walked out onto the porch with me. She apologized and then said, softly, "I used to date Clevon."

"But not anymore?"

"We're kind of in the process of breaking up."

"That can be difficult," I said. "I'll see you tomorrow, okay?"

"Okay." She didn't lean forward to suggest that we might kiss and I, respectfully, followed her lead. I walked down the steps and away, turning back when she called to me.

"Tomorrow," she said.

I nodded.

Columbia, Maryland was noted as a planned city right up to the time that its population exceeded its plan. It then became simply a city and its original plan worked against it. The hospital, which was mercifully called a convalescence retreat, was just outside Columbia. The staff was dressed not in the usual hospital blue, green, or white, but in cheerfully patterned smocks and dresses. And they were all painfully young and fit. They smiled nonstop, leaning over drooling patients, conversing with faces that stared back at them blankly. My sadness was deep when I considered my mother as one of the patients and I just knew that when I brought her to this place to check in, she would be completely lucid.

"There is always at least one physician on the grounds at all times," the handsome blonde woman in the khaki business suit said. "We have seven recreation areas, all showing vintage and new release films. The food is exceptional. I encourage you to try it. You'd be hard pressed to identify it as the institutional fare it is."

"Do you have a decent library?"

"We have shelves of books in the recreation areas."

"Good books?"

"Mysteries. All sorts of things." Mrs. Tollison, that was her name, detected, but could not pin down my concern. "Of course, most of our guests' eyesight is so poor that reading is difficult at best."

As I drove home, I knew that I had seen my mother's future and final home, but I also knew that I could not yet commit her to the place. I needed one more episode to nudge me over the edge.

There are as many hammers as there are saws. A misplaced thumb knows no difference.

"Bill, I looked at a place for Mother to live this morning." Through the window I could see the backs of Lorraine's and Mother's heads as they sat on the porch.

"I think that's best," Bill said.

I was quickly furious. In spite of his being correct, in spite of his being a physician, in spite of his being a child of the woman, he had no business offering an opinion. I said, "I'm glad you agree."

After a short, but significant pause, he said, "I'll send what I can." To his credit, he did not quiz me on the suitability of the hospital, nor did he lecture me about what the place should offer. "I get to see the kids one weekend a month now."

The unfairness of his situation rang loudly and all my effort to be angry with Bill for his absence dissolved into pity. "Are they doing okay?"

"I think so. The only stipulation is that Rob can't be in the house when they visit."

"That's awful."

"Well, this is Arizona."

"This might not be the time to bring it up. In fact, there is no time to bring it up, but I'm going to do it anyway." Mother and Lorraine seemed

securely anchored on the porch. "We have another sister." Bill's silence
was predictable and, by rules, it was not his turn to speak yet. "Father had
an affair when he was in the army and it seems we have a sister."

"Did Mother tell you this?"

"Not exactly. She let me discover it in Father's papers."

"I can't deal with this right now," he said.

"What's there to deal with? Her name is Gretchen and I don't know
her last name. Her mother was a British nurse in Korea and I don't know
her last name."

"It's like him to spring this on us."

I laughed. "What are you talking about? He tried to cover it to the
end." As I said this, I wasn't sure it was true. "He asked Mother to burn
the papers."

"Listen to that," Bill said. "He asked *Mother* to *burn* the papers.
Mother's afraid to boil water too long, lest it combust." Bill was right. He
was as sharp as ever and, as ever, had a better read on Father than I ever
could. Enemies always understand each other better than friends.

"Anyway, there's nothing to do about it. There's nothing in the letters,
nothing else in the box."

"There's something in that box, believe me. Look again. But I don't
want to hear about it." A man's voice spoke to Bill and he answered, calling the man "darling." I couldn't deny that hearing it made me cringe a
bit and I felt badly for the reaction.

"Well, I'd better go check on Mother," I said, using Mother as an excuse to get off the phone, but I also immediately noted the possibly perceived implication that I was the one going to care for our mother.

I could tell Bill was angry. "Talk to you later. Maybe I'll make a trip
back this fall to check on the hospital and everything."

I allowed him that. "Okay."

I stayed about the house all day and there was no call from Marilyn. I
lied to myself, tried not to admit that I was in fact waiting for her to ring
me up or come by. Mother was down for one of the great battery of daily
naps on which she had come to rely for a semblance of stability. Her most
lucid moments seemed to occur when she first awoke and after that there

were any number of cracks in the surface of her world through which to fall. There was no steering her toward solid ground; she stepped where she stepped.

So, Mother was asleep. I stepped out the back and stood on the pier for a while, contemplating lighting a cigar. Then I went back into the house to find Lorraine and Maynard, as best I can describe it, rubbing gums. I cleared my throat to make them aware of my approach.

Maynard sat at the table. "How is your mother?" he asked.

"Not so well, Maynard."

"Is she still asleep?" Lorraine asked.

I nodded and put on the water for tea. "So, what are you two young people up to?" I asked.

They giggled like young people. "We might as well tell you," Maynard said.

"Maynard," Lorraine complained.

"He's going to find out anyway."

I looked at Lorraine, then back at Maynard. "Find out what?"

"We're getting married," Maynard said.

The news made sense, but was no less shocking for that fact. "You're kidding me."

"No sir, I'm not," he said.

I looked at Lorraine and I was filled with sudden panic. "And where will you live?" I asked them.

"Here in my house," Maynard said.

"Thank god," I said.

"Excuse me?" Lorraine said.

"I meant 'of course.' I'm really happy for you Lorraine. I really am. Congratulations, Maynard, you're getting a fantastic partner."

"I know that all right," the old man said. He reached over and took Lorraine's hand.

"Is it going to be a big ceremony?" I asked. "Or an intimate, special, small thing." *For which I will not pay and perhaps not attend.*

"Small," Lorraine said.

Maynard looked at me with his ancient, milky eyes and said, "I'd like you to be my best man."

"Really?" *Are you crazy? I don't know you from shinola.*

"Your family has been so kind to my Rainey and you mean so much to her. I just want you to be a part of it."

"Don't you think you should ask a good friend?"

"Friends all dead," he said.

So, what do you say to that? I said, "I'll be honored."

"And I want your mother to be my matron of honor," Lorraine said.

"Okay."

"We're tying the knot on Saturday," Maynard said.

"That's two days away."

"We're old. We don't have time to waste." Maynard laughed and then Lorraine laughed with him.

Their laughter was genuine, sweet, beautiful and I felt happy to hear it from Lorraine. Listening to it, I realized that I had never heard the same quality in the laughter shared by my parents, though I'd no doubt they loved each other very much.

"Saturday," I said.

It was Christmas break of my freshman year in college. Father was excited to have me home and telling him about my classes and my professors. Ever since I began reading serious literature, he had forced the rest of the family to endure our discussions at the table. When I was eleven, he would prod me with simple questions, get me tied up and laugh a bit at me. When I was fourteen, he would bait me, twist me up, confuse me, then laugh a bit at me. At eighteen, he honestly seemed to believe I could add something to his understanding of novels and stories. I told him that I had read Joyce in a class. Bill moaned. One would have thought that his second year in medical school would have proved a more normal common ground between physician and son. Lisa was about to graduate from Vassar and had adopted a kind of death-girl attitude in spite of her being off to medical school the next year.

"We read *Portrait* and *Wake*," I said.

"I see they've refrained from using complete titles in university these days."

I laughed and Father laughed, but the rest of the family, I'm sure, read his comment as contentious and condescending.

"What did you think of *Finnegan's Wake?*" Father asked. He turned to Bill. "Have you read it?"

Bill shook his head.

Father took a quick bite of potatoes and returned his attention to me. "So?"

"I think it's overrated," I said.

He stopped chewing

"Or not rated correctly, anyway."

"That's youth talking," Father said. "The word play alone makes it a remarkable book."

"Yeah," I said. "And it's multilingual and all that, but still."

"I'd think that you'd never consider fiction the same again after reading that book."

"Well, you don't actually read it," I said. "You look at it for a long time, but you don't really read it."

"My point exactly." He laughed and drank some wine. He offered a nudge of his elbow toward Lisa as if to include her.

"Okay," I said. "This is what I wrote in my paper." I looked at Mother and my siblings and felt sick, like I had been seduced into slitting their throats. I looked at my father's excited eyes. "In spite of the obvious exploitation of alphabetic and lexical space in the *Wake* and in spite of whatever typographical or structural gestures one might focus on, the most important feature of the book is the way it actually conforms to conventional narrative. The way it layers, using such devices as metaphor and symbol. What's different is that each sentence, each word calls attention to the devices. So, the work really reaffirms what it seems to expose. It is the thing it is, perhaps twice, and depends on the currency of conventional narrative for its experimental validity."

Father looked at me for a long time. He then looked at his other two children and put his fork down. "I hope before you go to bed this evening, you kiss your brother." Then he stood and left the table.

Of course I felt bad for my brother and sister, but I felt worse for myself. I didn't enjoy being so set apart and I was well aware, painfully aware, of the inappropriateness and incorrectness of Father's assessment of me.

At eighteen, I realized I was eighteen and not so smart or special, and that might have been the only way that I was in fact special. I found my own ideas poorly formed and repugnant, my self awkward and, more or less, for lack of a better word, geeky. In fact, my brother, second-year medical school student that he was, revisited his childhood and, when he passed in the hallway, muttered, "Geek."

"It's not my fault," I said.

Lisa hit the top of the stairs as I said this, gave me an almost sympathetic look, shrugged and stepped into her room. The closing of her door was just ever so slightly louder than a normal closing of a door and so she too managed to slap me about some.

But how bad Lisa and Bill must have felt. They were far more accomplished than I at the time (and later). I had done nothing yet. I viewed my father's favoritism as irrational and saw myself as being saddled with a kind of illness, albeit his.

Numbers 23, 24

Wilde: I'm afraid for the voice.
Joyce: What do you mean?
Wilde: The way writing is moving. All voice will soon be lost and what will we be left with?
Joyce: Pages.
Wilde: And story?
Joyce: What is story anyway? Just a way to announce the last page.
Wilde: Have you ever walked through a thunderstorm carrying a long metal pipe?
Joyce: No, I haven't.
Wilde: You should try it.
Joyce: Are you upset?
Wilde: No, just announcing the last page.

X X X

Marilyn had never looked more beautiful to me. We were sitting in her kitchen and, from all appearances, Clevon was not present. Marilyn poured the coffee.

"I looked at a place for Mother yesterday."

"How was it?"

"Fine. Clean. Neat. Cheery. What do you say about a place where people go to expire."

"I'm sorry about not calling yesterday."

"I figured you were busy," I said.

"Clevon and I are now officially broken up."

The news pleased me but I was unsure how I was supposed to take it.

After a brief pause, Marilyn said, "I have to tell you, though, that we slept together that night."

Why did she have to tell me that? I didn't need to know it and I could have done quite well without knowing it. Had I not known, I would not have cared, but now all I could do was care. I cared about what he meant to her, about what I meant to her, about whether she was on top or he, about whether she had had an orgasm, more than one?, about the size of his penis, about the size of mine, about why she had told me. I studied the aged wood table, warped white pine slats with a mitered border of what I thought might be maple, an odd combination. I ran my fingers along the rounded edge in front of me. "Well, those things happen, I guess," I said.

"I realized he doesn't mean anything to me."

I nodded. "A good thing to realize." *However late.*

She got up from her chair and came to me, bent at her waist and kissed me on the lips. She pulled me to my feet and led me by the hands into her bedroom, where again she kissed me. We rolled around a bit, gyrating and rubbing body parts with a level of arousal that was both refreshing and, sadly, stale, my understanding that the excitement was partly, at least, simply a function of newness. While kissing her neck, which was slightly salty, I glanced at her night table and saw a copy of *We's Lives In Da Ghetto* by Juanita Mae Jenkins. I stopped moving.

"What's wrong, baby," she said. I liked the way her voice sounded, especially as she called me *baby*, but the sight of that book had called back the troops.

"Have you read that book?" I asked.

She looked back over her head to see. "Oh, that? Yeah, I just finished. It was pretty good."

"What was good about it?" I rolled off to lie beside her.

It was clear she was confused that we were having this conversation. "Is something wrong? You can just come out with it. I shouldn't have told you about Clevon."

"What did you like about the book?"

"I don't know. It was a good story, I guess. Lightweight stuff, but it was fun."

"It didn't offend you in any way?"

She stared at me for a couple of seconds, then said, with an attitude, "No."

"Have you ever known anybody who talks like they do in that book?" I could hear the edge on my voice and though I didn't want it there, I knew that once detected, it could never be erased.

"What's wrong with you?"

"Answer the question."

"No, but so what? I just read through that dialect shit. I don't like the way you're talking to me."

"I'm sorry," I said, feeling genuinely bad for having sounded like I was attacking. "It's just that I find that book an idiotic, exploitive piece of crap and I can't see how an intelligent person can take it seriously." So much for changing my tack.

Marilyn pulled the nearest pillow to her chest and rested her chin on it. "I think you should leave."

"I'm sorry," I said.

"Just go."

As I left the room and approached the front door I could hear her crying. But there was nothing to say.

Since Lorraine spent the night and the morning at Maynard's getting ready for her wedding, I was left alone to care for Mother. I had not known the extent to which I depended on the servant, and I learned that reality knows neither subtlety nor kindness when it decides to "get in your face," as it were. Mother was having a particularly difficult morning. She knew who I was and who she was and that there was a wedding to attend, but had forgotten how to dress. And so I dressed her. My maleness meant nothing to her as she asked me to help her with her bra and her slip and her hose. I felt as if I were stranded in some surreal, poorly dubbed, Italian film, but finally it was all too real.

"This bra cuts into me," she said. "Find me another one."

I imagined this was the way she had come to talk to Lorraine. I brought her another and helped her on with it, having to adjust her sagging breasts in the cups

"That's better." She looked around. "My shoes. The black ones with the straps. And my pearls. The double strand."

"I can't find the black shoes," I said from her closet.

"They're there, Lorraine. You simply have to look."

"Mother, I don't think you packed them."

"They're right in front of you," she snapped. She stepped over in her stocking feet, lowered herself to a knee and grabbed a pair of ox-blood pumps. "Right here."

"You look nice, Mother," I said, standing behind her as she sat facing her vanity mirror.

Father had returned from a dinner, the pre-departure discussion of which aroused my curiosity. He kissed Mother at the door and then walked up to his study. I followed in his wake and plopped down on the leather sofa across from his desk.

"And how was your dinner?" he asked.

"Standard," I said, using a term I'd gotten from him. "Lorraine put too much salt in the vegetables. As usual."

Father laughed.

"How was your dinner?" I asked.

"It was very good. But I'm afraid I'll pay for it later." He sat at his desk and began to sift through his stack of mail. "We had oysters and lemon pie for dessert."

"I like oysters."

"I know you do. Perhaps we'll all go to Crissfield's later in the week."

"Lisa will like that," I said. "What was the dinner like? What did you talk about?"

He looked at me for a couple of seconds. "Well, it was a group of my old friends. A couple of them have been away for years. They're all gray now. We talked about the days when we were not gray, about the things we used to do and how we used to laugh." He paused. "It was the talk of the dead, Monk."

I just looked at him.

He studied my ten-year-old face, then smiled. "I'm not as old as it sounds, I believe." He opened another letter, read it and tossed it. "It would of course be a shame to get too old. There's no virtue in living too long. Living shouldn't become a habit." By now he was talking more to himself than to me. "Tomorrow night. Tomorrow night, we'll go out and get you some oysters."

We are told that the subject of the statement should not be taken as synonymous with the author of the formulation—*either in substance, or in function.* This is, my theoretical friends have told me, a characteristic of the enunciative function. The statement with which I was concerning myself was the box containing the letters of my father. Was it something my mother was attempting to tell me about my father? Or rather, was it more ingenious, as brother Bill would have had me believe, a message from my father, his knowing that Mother would not in fact burn the box and would somehow get it to me? As I got Mother ready to go to Lorraine's wedding I went over and over again the contents of that box, wondering what if anything I was supposed to do and at whose behest. Knowing Father, perhaps I was only supposed to learn some lesson about life, not take literally any concern about tracking down some lost half-sibling. Indeed, I knew him to be short-patienced when it came to, as he put it, "vulgar, common and simple-minded devotion to rudimentary biological relationships."

"So, Mother, what do you think of Lorraine getting married?" I asked as we walked to the car.

"A bit sudden."

"She seems happy."

"I don't think she knows what she's doing. What does she know about relationships? She's never had one. And this boy."

"He's almost seventy, Mother."

"Oh, well, he looks young. I don't know, Monksie. I guess it's a good thing. I won't be around forever to care for Lorraine."

"Let's not talk like that," I said as I closed her door.

I was putting the key in the ignition. We were taking the car even though Maynard's house was just a quarter mile away, just outside the community.

"I think they're having sex," Mother said.

I said nothing.

"What do you think?"

"I think it's their business."

"Hmmmph."

Wittgenstein: Why did Bach have to sell his organ?
Derrida: I don't know. Why?

Wittgenstein: Because he was baroque.

Derrida: You mean because he composed music marked by elaborate and even grotesque ornamentation?

Wittgenstein: Well, no that's not exactly what I was getting at. It was a play on words.

Derrida: Oh, I get it.

When we arrived at Maynard's house, Lorraine was standing in the yard and yelling back at her husband-to-be who was standing on the porch. "How dare you call me old, you fossil!" is what she yelled.

Nothing's easy. Least of all being confronted with one's own question-able agenda, however unworked out or articulated. In a flash, I was washed with guilt as I considered that on some level, this was all my plan, that I wanted to marry off Lorraine and commit Mother and get on with my life. Indeed, I did want to marry off Lorraine and indeed I wanted to do so, so that I would not have to look after her in her remaining years. But I truly did not want to commit Mother. That was a lie to myself. On some level, given her condition, I wanted very much to commit her and for as much my sake as hers. I was also troubled by the word *commit*. One *commits* murder or suicide, permanent things. The finality of my admitting her to the *retreat* in Columbia loomed large in my thinking and feeling.

Mother remained seated in the car while I approached Lorraine, ask-ing the stupid but appropriate question, "Is there something wrong?"

"Yes," she cried. "That old coot called me old."

"That ain't what I said," Maynard said, calmly. He leaned against a post. "I told her to let my nieces take care of the food because she needed her rest."

"He said it again," Lorraine said.

"Said what?" I asked.

"He called me old."

"No, he called his nieces younger," I said.

"He called me old," she cried.

"Damnit, Lorraine, you are old," I said.

The look on Lorraine's face cannot adequately be described and that is description enough.

"Hold on there," Maynard said, walking to Lorraine. "That's awfully rough, what you said to my bride. Who are you to call her old?" He put his arms around her. Lorraine hugged him back.

Mother had gotten herself out of the car now. "If Lorraine is old, what does that make me?" she asked.

I looked at each of their faces, then settled on Maynard's. "Where's the preacher?"

"Everybody's in the house," he said.

"Well, come on," I said, cheerfully. "Let's have ourselves a wedding."

D. W. Griffith: I like your book very much.
Richard Wright: Thank you.

Somewhere in Hollywood, Wiley Morgenstein smoked a cigar and contemplated the commercial value of *My Pafology*. He sat poolside with a big man from New Jersey with whom he attended two years of school at Passaic Junior College thirty years earlier.

Wiley smiled and relit his cigar. "They go to the movies now, these people. There's an itch and I plan to scratch it."

"Feel like some shuffleboard?"

"It's a damn good book, too. This one will get me taken seriously."

"Who's the blonde in the jacuzzi?"

"I've gotta meet the writer though. I want to know the hand that wrote this book. You know what I mean?"

"I'm going to ask her her name."

The dynamics of the joyous occasion were all too apparent upon our entering the house. The faces of those who bore resemblance to Maynard were unsmiling and easy to read. The faces asked, *Why is this old maid marrying poor old Maynard? For his meager savings?* Still, there was an attempt at cordiality which was slightly more than admirable and somewhat less than fully hypocritical. There were six of them, a daughter and her husband, three nieces, and a sister-in-law. There was a table of food and a television tuned to a baseball game. The son-in-law sat eyes fixed on the game. I asked him who was playing and he said he didn't know and it became clear that he was not watching the game but seeking to seep into the screen, away from the scene at hand. I sat beside him and watched my mother engage rather comfortably in small talk.

"This ain't gonna happen," he said.

I looked at him.

"This wedding, it ain't happening."

"Why do you say that?"

He pointed across the room. "See her? That's my wife. She's Maynard's daughter. She hates Lorraine. I was up all night listening to how much she hates Lorraine."

I studied the daughter, the way she cut glances at Lorraine.

"I'm Leon."

"Monk." I shook his hand.

"So, you're related to Lorraine?"

"She works for us."

He looked at me.

"She's our housekeeper."

"Your maid?"

"She's like part of the family," I said, trying to recover. "She's been with us for years, my entire life."

"She's been with you," he said, slightly (not-so-slightly) mocking. "What are you, rich or something?"

"No, we're not rich."

"I'm an electrician's helper. What do you do?"

"I'm a novelist." I read the blank expression on his face. "And a professor. Actually, I'm on leave right this year."

"On leave. And they're paying you?"

"Well, no."

"So, you're telling me you're not working and it doesn't matter. That makes you rich in my book. How many other servants your family got?"

"Only Lorraine."

Leon laughed to himself and looked back at the television.

"So, what kind of wedding present you gonna give your servant?"

His question was both odd and forward, but it caused a flood of thoughts in me. What was I going to give Lorraine? What did I owe Lorraine? What did my family owe her? Had she saved for retirement? Had she ever filed her income taxes? "As a matter of fact," I said to Leon. "I'm giving the bride ten thousand dollars."

Leon looked at me, then at the game, then back at me. He got up and walked across the room to his wife where I am sure that he told her what I had just told him. The daughter then told the nieces and the sister-in-law, who by all appearances was already drunk, and there seemed to be a new air of joy and repose. I was left with a bad feeling, not because I saw the family Lorraine was marrying into as mercenary, not because I had just then decided on my gift, but because I truly didn't understand how anyone could get so excited over a mere ten thousand dollars. I saw myself exactly as I had never wanted, but always did, awkward and set apart, however unfairly and incorrectly. I turned my attention to the screen and saw a ball sail over the left field fence. I considered that Leon would have no trouble with my having money, no matter how much a figment of his imagination it was, if I were that ballplayer. The problem was the one I had always had, that I was not a *regular* guy and I so much wanted to be. Can you spell *bourgeois*?

My mother stood near a large window and raised a glass of wine above her head. Everyone responded by raising their glasses. But I could see her eyes filling with the vacancy that frightened me so. I stood and walked toward her. She turned those empty orbs to me and hissed.

My grandfather was very bright, but was not notably funny. He realized this and was famous for the funniest line of our family history. He said, "My claim to having a sense of humor is a singular demonstration of such." I was ten when he said it and even then the layers of logical play thrilled me. I remember my father near rolling. My grandfather was more playful than my father and had a softer hand with Bill. Bill took it hard when the old man died a month later. He was very old, well past eighty.

Father was actually tender that day and much of his tenderness was directed at my brother. He sat us down in his study, sat next to Bill on the sofa and put a hand on his knee. I think Bill and Lisa knew what was coming, but I surely didn't. I watched my father's face. "Children, your grandfather has passed away," he said.

I remember hanging on the expression *passed away*. Perhaps I was simply trying to avoid the news. Lisa cried. Bill's face became vacant, hollow and he fell against Father, his head on his shoulder. I would never see them so close again, without barriers, without tension. I didn't know enough to cry, but I understood that Grandfather was dead.

At dinner that evening, Lorraine paused in the dining room and asked if Father would like her to say a prayer.

"Hell no," he said. When Lorraine was gone, he looked at Mother and the rest of us. "My father loved these lines. *'And the fisher with his lamp / And spear, about the low rocks damp / Crept, and stuck the fish who came / To worship the delusive flame: / Too happy, thy whose pleasure sought / Extinguishes all sense and thought / Of regret that pleasure cease / Destroying life alone not peace.'*"

Father cast an eye to the door through which Lorraine had exited. "I ask that grief not push us to the irrational belief in some god. We do not need to believe that Father has gone on to the good light. He told me often that he was not afraid of the dark. Neither am I. And neither are you." His eyes seemed to find me.

I did not understand why my father chose that moment to affirm his atheism. Perhaps he felt his foundation shaking. Perhaps he was angry. Perhaps he was simply passing on to us what little he knew about life and death.

Mother, whose silence was impossible to miss throughout these opening minutes of the meal, cleared her throat and said, "This is not about you."

To which Father replied, "Quite right."

And we ate.

Mother snapped. "Who are these people?!" she shouted. "Lorraine, you little strumpet, how dare you let these—these hooligans in here."

"Come, Mother," I said. I tried to guide her away. "She's sick," I whispered to Maynard and the others.

"I've never trusted that Lorraine. Only after money, that girl."

"See, I told you," Maynard's daughter said to the others.

"How dare you," Lorraine said to the daughter. "You simpleton."

"That simpleton is my wife," Leon said.

"They're all thugs," Mother said. She twisted away from my grasp and stood on a foot stool. "All of you, out of my house!"

"Your house?" a niece said.

"I'm sorry," I said.

Lorraine was crying now. I was encouraged by the sight of Maynard attempting to comfort her. I apologized again, but when I turned and tried to collect my mother, she bolted across the carpet and into the bathroom. I do not remember hearing a sound as loud as the clicking of the lock on that door.

I knocked. "Mother?"

"Who are you?"

"It's me, Monksie."

There was no response. I knocked again. "Mother?"

The minister took this opportunity to arrive, swinging open the door and saying, "Shall we begin the joyous event?"

"Mother?"

"I knew she was a golddigger."

"Shut up, you witch."

"That witch is my wife."

"Everyone, please calm down," from Maynard.

I could hear Mother pulling things from the cabinets and I became afraid. I put my shoulder to the door and broke the lock. Mother had her pantyhose halfway down and screamed when she saw me. I pulled up her clothes and carried her crying out of the bathroom and away from the house. At the car, she began to come around.

"Are we late?" she asked.

"Actually, it's over. It was a nice service," I said.

Somehow Lorraine and Maynard ended up married. Lorraine came by to collect her things that night on her way to a honeymoon in Atlantic City and didn't say a word to Mother. She barely spoke to me, saying only, "This is the thanks I get."

I handed her an envelope and said, "I'm sorry Lorraine. I hope this helps."

Maynard offered me a weak smile, an understanding smile.

I called Bill and told him that Mother would be committed the next day. He said he would fly in. I told him not to bother, that he wasn't needed. He said he would come anyway.

"I wish you wouldn't," I said. "This is going to be difficult enough as it is." I heard music in the background. Nina Simone, I think. "It's all arranged. I'm going to take her and stay the day with her."

"We can both visit with her."

Some water is so clear that trout will swim to your fly, your silhouette all too visible to them as they gaze up and through the water and air, and will inspect your tying job, the amount of head cement you applied, observe whether you used a good stiff hackle or whether you used natural or synthetic dubbing material, nose the thing, then swim away. Occasionally, one will take the fly, not caring that a bit of thread is visible where the tail is tied down, not even caring that your tippet is corkscrewed. A trout hiding behind a rock in fast, muddy water might or might not take a nymph fished deep through the riffle. For all the aggravation a trout can cause, it cannot think and does not consider you. A trout is very much like truth; it does what it wants, what it has to.

I was exhausted, my eyes burning from having been open and staring at either Mother or the book in my lap all night. The backs of my legs had gone numb from sitting in the round-rimmed wooden chair. I was completely distrustful of any measure of stability the old woman exhibited that evening of Lorraine's wedding. I was terrified that I would wake and find her bed empty, then, after a brief search, her lifeless body floating in the creek or simply laid out at the bottom of the stairs. The business of committing her seemed so much more urgent now. I was desperate to know that she was safe and I was desperate to discontinue my feeling of desperation.

When Mother awoke, she took me in for a few seconds, then said, "Good morning, Monksie."

"Good morning, Mother. How did you rest?"

"Fine, I suppose. I had dreams I didn't like." She sat up, smoothing the sheet and light blanket around her. "I can't recall any of them."

"I can never remember my dreams either."

"You weren't in that chair all night, were you?"

"No, Mother." As I lied, I wondered how I was going to bathe and dress for the day. I didn't have Lorraine to watch her now. "Mother, if you wait right here, I'll bring you some tea."

"That would be nice, dear."

She began to hum as I left the room. I believe it was Chopin, a polonaise, but I could only place the quality of the melody and not the piece itself. I hurried to my room where I washed up at the sink and threw on a clean shirt and socks. I returned to her door and listened. She was still humming. I could hear her turning the pages of a magazine. I ran to the kitchen, put on the water and sat at the table to catch my breath. My eyes must have closed and sleep taken me because I woke with a start, finding Mother removing the whistling kettle from the burner.

"You're tired," she said.

I watched as she poured the water into the pot and dropped in the ball that I had already filled with tea. She put the cups and saucers on the table and set the pot between us.

"Isn't this nice," she said.

"Yes, Mother."

"My favorite time is always waiting for the tea to steep." She looked past me to the screened porch. "Where is Lorraine?"

"Lorraine was married last night."

"Oh, yes." She seemed to catch herself. Then she appeared very sad.

"Will you miss her?" I asked.

She looked at me as if she'd missed the question.

"You were just thinking about Lorraine, weren't you?" I asked.

"Of course. I hope she will be very happy." Mother poured the tea.

"I'd like you to pack a bag this morning," I said.

"Why?" She held the cup in her hands, warming them.

"I have to take you someplace. It's a kind of hospital."

"I feel fine."

"I know, Mother. But I want to make sure. I want to be certain that you're all right."

"I'm perfectly fine."

"Your father can give me a pill or something." She sipped her tea, then stared at it.

"Father's dead, Mother."

"Yes, I know. There was a cardinal outside my window this morning. A female. She was very beautiful. The female cardinal's color is so sweetly understated."

"I agree."

Mother looked at my eyes. "I must have spilled something in bed last night."

"I'll take care of it."

"Shall I pack a small bag?"

I nodded. "A small bag will be fine."

X X X

I could feel the leaves wanting to change color. But still the days were warm. I talked Mother into strolling with me down to the beach. The morning was clear, just a few clouds searching for each other out over the bay. Mother had managed to dress herself; however, her sweater was on inside out. This was a mistake that even I could make, but it gave me a much-needed nudge to keep perspective. That morning, while picking up her room, I had found some stained underwear she'd attempted to hide.

She wore khaki trousers and sneakers and I could tell she was trying to walk briskly. "When you were a little boy the bay wasn't so dirty," she said. "You used to dive off the back of the boat and swim around like a fish. You'd go down and disappear under the bottom and my heart would just stop."

"I'm sorry about that. I didn't mean to scare you."

"Oh, I know. You were just so small. Actually, I enjoyed watching you, Bill and Lisa having fun like that." We were at the community dock now and she stopped to stare at a line of weathered boards. "I can't believe Lisa is gone."

I put my arm around her. "Neither can I. Lisa was special. She loved you very much, Mother."

"I know. I loved her too."

"Lisa knew that."

She rubbed my arm. "Why aren't you married, Monksie?"

"Haven't found the right person, I guess."

"I suppose that's the important thing, finding the right person. Still, life is short." She paused. "I wish I were closer to Bill's children. The distance has been so difficult."

"I know."

"Do you talk to Bill?"

"Occasionally."

"I think I haven't talked to him in months. Poor Bill. Bill and your father never got along. Sad thing."

"Yes, it was."

"I don't think Ben was fair to Bill."

"I think you're right."

"But you. Your father was crazy about you. He'd talk about you when you weren't around. Did you know that? Well, he did. You were his special child."

"I suppose I knew that. Lisa certainly believed it. Bill, too. Actually, I appreciated your evenhandedness more than his attention."

"You would." She smiled at me. "He was right to consider you special."

"Thank you, Mother."

The conversation was unraveling my resolve. She was so lucid, so reasonable, so much herself.

Pollock: You first.
Moore: No, you.
Pollock: No, I insist.
Moore: You.
Pollock: You.
Moore: Very well.

As I stood there with Mother, the breeze off the bay filling my shirt and chilling me, I tried to consider her coming loneliness, waking in a strange bed, with strange faces, strange food, but instead I thought of my own loneliness. I had allowed the letters of friends to go too long unanswered and I imagined they had written me off. I felt small for regarding myself, for being so self-centered in the face of Mother's coming day and life.

"Should we be going?" she asked.

"Mother, I have to tell you what's going on."

"Yes, dear?"

I held her close and looked at the water while I talked. "Lately, your condition has been getting worse. The doctor said it would happen this way." I took a breath. "Do you remember standing in the boat out in the middle of the pond."

Mother laughed. "What?"

I could see she did not know what I was talking about. "You rowed yourself out into the pond and I had to swim out and get you." I let her silence settle. "You locked Lorraine out of the house and came to me in the study with Father's pistol. You locked yourself in the bathroom at Lorraine's wedding. Mother, I'm afraid you're going to get lost and hurt. I'm taking you to a new place to live today."

She pulled the edges of her sweater. "Is it time to go?"

"I guess so."

"I trust you to do what's best, Monk."

My first table saw had a plastic guard on it. I would faithfully lower it and let it protect me every time I slid a piece of wood through the machine, happy when it cut easily, cursing when the awkward shield caused me to have to switch off the power or bring back the half-sawn wood. But the high whine of the blade, frankly, scared me. I could measure with my eyes and hear the destructive capabilities of the disc and even smell it when a piece of wood would linger against the blade and get burned. Then I learned to remove the guard for larger boards, then screw it back on. I screwed it back on less often, then less often still until I could not say where the thing had been put. I would push the boards through without a thought that I might lose a finger or that the blade might fly off and carve through my cranium. I began to enjoy the burning smell, the whine of the machine, the sight of the first notch the blade made in the bottom corner of the board.

And so we made the trip to Mother's new home in Columbia. She was so clear-headed throughout the admissions process that I was ready to take her back to the beach. But the administrator showed no pause, only asked the questions and filled out the forms. We walked to Mother's suite, an apartment more than a room, though it lacked a kitchen. Mother touched the institutional furniture and frowned slightly.

"Would you like me to bring some things from the house?" I asked.

"That would be nice. You decide what."

We walked outside to the grounds and the real sadness of the place took me. An old woman reached to me with her eyes as I passed her wheelchair, asking if I could tell her something, tell her that I knew her, anything. They were all old, all waiting. Some seemed in good enough spirits. Most were women. Outside, the sun was warmer, the expanse of green lawn leading to a wrought iron fence negating the earlier hint of fall in the air. I turned to Mother to find her wandering away toward the fence.

"Mother?" I chased after her. "Mother?" I turned her around.

Her face showed no recognition. I was a blank space in her universe. She let me lead her back to her rooms. The young nurse who had been guiding us and trailing back a proper distance seemed to all too well understand what was happening. She helped me put my mother to bed, backed me out of the room and said that she would sit with her a while. As I left I realized that all the furniture had rounded edges and was soft wherever possible. I would bring no furniture from home.

Bill and I were over at Eastern Market, wandering through the aisles of produce and fish. Bill was a teenager and I was pretending to be one. Father had charged us with finding a nice late-season bluefish. School was about to begin for us and we were enjoying the last days of summer break. Bill was talking with a friend of his who worked at a crab stand while I looked over the fish. Two letter-jacketed boys from Bill's school swaggered down the aisle toward us, making their kind of animal noises to announce their presence.

"Hey, it's Ellison," the shorter one said.

"Hello, Roger," Bill said.

"Ready for school?" Roger asked.

The taller of the guys looked at his watch, then out the far door. "Come on, Rog."

Roger smiled. "In a minute." He looked at the skinny kid behind the counter. "What about you, Lucy?"

"Don't call me that," the kid said.

"So, what were you two talking about? Is there a party somewhere I shouldn't know about?" Roger laughed, nudged his friend. His friend laughed weakly, disinterestedly. "Is this your brother?" he asked Bill.

"Yeah."

"You one, too?" Roger asked me.

I looked at his face, then at the letter G sewn onto his blue and white jacket. I understood it was an award for wrestling, because it had pinned to it a medal, two figures posed one behind the other in close contact.

"What are those guys doing?" I asked.

Roger was thrown. "What?"

"On your jacket. Is that what you got a letter for? What sport is that?" Bill and the kid behind the counter started to laugh.

"What?" Roger said. "It's for wrestling."

"You mean rolling around on the floor with another boy."

Roger's brown skin turned purple and he took a step toward me. His friend caught him and said, "Let's just get out of here, Roger."

Bill and I watched them leave. Bill then flashed me an awkward smile, then seemed to fold up. But I was pumped up, wanting to talk, jump around. "Did you see his face?" I asked.

"Yeah, I saw it."

"Are you mad at me?"

"No, I'm not mad at you, Monk."

"Then what is it?"

"Nothing. You wouldn't understand."

"I understand a lot of things."

"Like what?"

"Like—" I stopped and looked at the fish. "This is a good one. Father will like this one."

I drove back to D.C., back to what had been my mother's home, what had been my parents' home. The inside of the house was stale and hot. I switched on the large air-conditioning unit in the dining room and sat at the table. I sat where I had always sat during meals and regarded the other chairs. Mother and Father had sat at the prominent ends and I was placed on a side alone, facing my brother and sister, an empty chair beside me. The occasional guest would occupy that seat, but otherwise it was always there, empty, never removed to be against the wall like the other auxiliary chairs. I listened to the house, recalling my parents' voices and footfalls, but I couldn't hear them. I heard the hum and periodic rattle of the air conditioner, the switching on of the refrigerator in the adjacent kitchen, the ringing of the phone.

It was Bill. "I'll be there in a bit."

"Where are you?"

"National. I'm about to walk over to the Metro."

"Would you like me to pick you up?"

"No, that's all right."

"I'll pick you up at Metro Center."

"I'll take the Blue to the Red and I'll meet you at Dupont Circle at," I could hear him looking at his watch, "four o'clock."

"See you there."

My brother's hair was blond. I recognized his face as he sat on a bench near some conga players, but I thought only *That guy looks just like my brother.* My brother had blond hair. It was my brother and his hair was yellow. His skin was still light brown. He called to me.

"Bill?"

"It's me." He hugged me, an event in itself, and I appreciated the gesture, but it was as stiff as if he hadn't touched me at all.

"Hey, your hair is blond," I informed him.

"Like it?"

"I guess. It's different." I felt like an old fuddy-duddy, as my mother would say of herself. "I found a parking space up on Connecticut." I reached down and picked up his soft leather bag. "It's good to see you," I said as we started to walk.

"You're looking well," he said.

"A little out of shape. But not you."

"I'm in the gym every night."

I made a kind of congratulatory sound that I hoped didn't come off as patronizing. "I should try a little of that."

"How's Mother?"

"In and out." As I said it I wondered which was the bad way: in or out? Was she lost when she was in her mind or out of it? And I wondered if the symptoms I had been observing were in fact not those of her disease, but of her coping with deterioration, a retreat to a safer place.

"Does she know who you are?"

"She did today," I told him. "How are the kids?"

"Fine, I think." He watched me for my reaction and when I gave it to him, he said, "We'll make it through. It's hard to hear *your daddy's a fag.*"

"Would you like to go the house first or to see Mother?"

"The house. I need a shower. I was up early to catch the plane."

I drove us home. Bill fiddled with the radio.

"How's work?"

"Good."

"How's—" I searched for his friend's name.

"Gone."

I have often stared into the mirror and considered the difference between the following statements:

(1) He looks guilty.

(2) He seems guilty.

(3) He appears guilty.

(4) He is guilty.

"Are you all right?" Bill asked. He was out of the shower and had returned downstairs to join me in the den. I was lighting a cigar. "You shouldn't do that," he said.

"Yes, I know." I watched the tip glow orange and shook out the match. "Are you about ready to go?"

"It's sort of late now, don't you think?"

It was in fact nearly six. "It's a little late," I said, "but it is her first day there. I'd like to check up on the old lady."

Bill nodded.

Mother had not eaten, we were told. She did not recognize Bill, pulled away from him when he took her hand and tried to look at her eyes. She did not recognize me. She might have if we had stayed another sixty minutes, another fifteen, another five. But we didn't.

"About the money," Bill said.

"I've got it covered," I told him.

It had become my practice (at least I wanted it to be) to let such conversations wither and die of their own accord, to not offer any appropriate or inappropriate comment, but to simply shut up and let the words become vapor.

Only appearances signify in visual art. At least this is what I am told, that the painter's work is an invention in the boundless space that begins at the edges of his picture. The surface, the paper or the canvas, is not the work of art, but where the work lives, a place to keep the picture, the paint, the idea. But a *chair*, a chair *is* its space, is its own canvas, occupies space properly. The canvas occupies spaces and the picture occupies the canvas, while the chair, as a work, fills the space itself. This was what occurred to me regarding *My Pafology*. The novel, so-called, was more a chair than a painting, my having designed it not as a work of art, but as a functional device, its appearance a thing to behold, but more a thing to mark, a warning perhaps, a gravestone certainly. It was by this reasoning that I was able to look at my face in the mirror and to accept the deal my agent presented to me on the phone that evening.

"His name is Wiley Morgenstein and he wants to pay you three million dollars for the movie rights," Yul said. "Monk? Monk?"

"I'm here."

"How's that sound?"

"It sounds great. Are you crazy? It sounds terrific. It makes me sick."

"He insists on meeting you."

"Tell him I'll call him."

"He wants to meet you. He wants to pay you three mil, the least you can do is have lunch with the guy. I haven't told him that there's no Stagg Leigh yet."

"Don't. Stagg Leigh will have lunch with him."

Yul laughed. "You've lost your mind. What are you going to do? Dress up like a pimp or something?"

"No, I'll just put on some dark glasses and be real quiet. How's that?"

"Three million for you means three hundred thousand for me. Don't screw this up."

"Yeah, right. Gotta go."

"Wait a second. Random House says there's so much excitement about the book that they're going to try to bring it out before Christmas."

X X X

Bill asked if everything was all right when I walked into the kitchen after having been on the phone. I told him that all was well and he told me that he was going out with an old friend. He told me that his friend was coming to collect him shortly. He told me not to wait up.

X X X

I hadn't noticed before the box containing the letters from Fiona to my father smelt of lavender and rose-leaves. This time, without actually reading the letters, I attended to the script, the hand at work, and found a purity there that perhaps reflected the depth of feeling. I imagined that nurse had had small but strong hands with trimmed nails, a weaver's hands perhaps. I opened each letter, then thumbed through the pages of the curiously chosen novel. With *Silas Marner* I found a slip of paper and on it was written the lower East Side Manhattan address of Fiona's sister. Her name was Tilly McFadden.

Editor: What a surprise.

Stagg: I just called to ask if I need to make any changes in the manuscript since you plan to bring the book out earlier.

Editor: No, it's just perfect as it is.

Stagg: Will I see galleys soon?

Editor: No need to bother with that.

Stagg: There is one change I'd like to make.

Editor: Certainly.

Stagg: I'm changing the title. The new title is Fuck.

Editor: Excuse me?

Stagg: Fuck. *Just the one word.*

Editor: I so love My Pafology *as the title.*

Stagg: We'll call the next book that. This one is called Fuck.

Editor: I don't think we can do that.

Stagg: Why not?

Editor: The word is considered obscene by many.

Stagg: The novel has the word fuck *all through it. I don't care if* many *find the word obscene.*

Editor: It might hurt sales.

Stagg: I don't think so. If you like I can give you back the money and take the book elsewhere.

F U C K

A   N o v e l

Stagg R. Leigh

The fear of course is that in denying or refusing complicity in the marginalization of "black" writers, I ended up on the very distant and very "other" side of a line that is imaginary at best. I didn't write as an act of testimony or social indignation (though all writing in some way is just that) and I did not write out of a so-called family tradition of oral storytelling. I never tried to set anybody free, never tried to paint the next real and true picture of the life of *my* people, never had any people whose picture I knew well enough to paint. Perhaps if I had written in the time immediately following Reconstruction, I would have written to elevate the station of my fellow oppressed. But the irony was beautiful. I was a victim of racism by virtue of my failing to acknowledge racial difference and by failing to have my art be defined as an exercise in racial self-expression. So, I would not be economically oppressed because of writing a book that fell in line with the very books I deemed racist. And I would have to wear the mask of the person I was expected to be. I had already talked on the phone with my editor as the infamous Stagg Leigh and now I would meet with Wiley Morgenstein. I could do it. The game was becoming fun. And it was nice to get a check.

Jelly, Jelly
Jelly
All night long

Behold the invisible!

X X X

Bill did not come home that night, but came in the following morning, smiling and talking fast. I had collected some of Mother's favorite recordings and was taking them to her with a CD player. He seemed high to me, but I couldn't imagine on what and I had never been good at making those kinds of calls. I asked if he was all right.

"Yeah. Why?" was his response.

"I don't know," I said. "You just seem different."

"Different? Like how?"

"Never mind."

"No, I want to know how I seem different." The edge on his voice was amplified by its suddenness.

"There was no subtext," I said. "If you want to know, I thought that maybe you were high."

"High on what?"

"I don't know. I don't care."

"This is because I've been of no help regarding Mother, isn't it?"

"No."

"You're mad because I stayed out all night. Should I have called?"

"I'm going to see Mother."

"That's why I'm in town." Bill tried to look like he wasn't high. "But I can see that my presence isn't urgently required."

"I was on my way out when you came in. I waited around this morning for you and so I decided to leave. Now, you're here. So, I'm asking you, would you like to go with me to visit Mother."

"I need to shower. And it's my business where I've been "

"I'll wait."

"No, that's okay. You go on. She's probably wondering what's keeping you."

I watched his lips and realized I understood nothing he was saying. His language was not mine. His language possessed an adverbial and interrogative geometry that I could not comprehend. I could see the shapes of his meaning, even hear that his words meant something, but I had no idea as to the substance of his meaning. I nodded.

"What's that supposed to mean?" he said.

He was mocking me. That was it. He understood my confusion and was using it against me. I nodded again.

"Go on." As I reached the door, he said. "I was wrong to think you'd understand. Actually, I didn't expect you to at all. You're just like Father. You always were and you're growing up to be him."

I nodded.

"Go on. Go see Mother without me. Time has *a way of deflating purpose and becoming all those things that the center of our being would rather reject. Be that as it may though, my center is far more centered than that tainted middle of yours. I'm true to myself in spite of the detours and interruptions I have encountered beyond the shelf of what is my beach.*"

I didn't nod this time, but left.

Sitting in the attending physician's office, awaiting a report on Mother's first night's stay, I was able to examine the small shelf of books behind the doctor's desk. There were books by John Grisham and Tom Clancy, a paperback of John MacDonald and things like that. Those books didn't bother me. Though I had never read one completely through, I had peeked at pages, and although I did not find any depth of artistic expression or any abundance of irony or play with language or ideas, I found them well enough written, the way a technical manual can be well enough written. *Oh, so that's tab A.* So, why did Juanita Mae Jenkins send me running for the toilet? I imagine it was because Tom Clancy was not trying to sell his book to me by suggesting that the crew of his high-tech submarine was a representation of his race *(however fitting a metaphor)*. Nor was his publisher marketing it in that way. If you didn't like Clancy's white people, you could go out and read about some others.

> *Where fo' you be goin?*
> *Mis'sippi.*
> *Why fo' you gone way down dere?*
> *I gots to get 'way from this souf-side Chicago.*
> *Shit, Mis'sippi aint nofin but da souf-souf-side Chicago.*
> *(They laughed together.)*

The doctor was a fat, unhealthy-looking man, but a natty dresser. His wingtips were polished to a shine and the sweater vest (despite the warm weather) he wore blended perfectly with his suit. He sat behind the desk and I imagined him to look like Tom Clancy, though I had never seen as much as a newpaper photo of the man. Then I imagined him trying to squeeze through the small hatch of a submarine.

"Your mother is not having a good day so far. We've had to sedate her. We have a nurse at her bedside now. I don't really know what to say, Mr. Ellison. Sometimes patients take a sudden turn. Perhaps tomorrow she'll have a better day."

Then the fat doctor was my sister Lisa. She leaned back in the chair and lit that imaginary cigarette and said my name. I allowed my awareness of my hallucination to serve as evidence that I was not in fact insane, but I had to note that coming on the heels of my brother's linguistic show I was a bit concerned.

"There's nothing to do, Monk," Lisa said. "Go home. Make a home. Relax in the knowledge that Mother is not suffering. In fact, to her each moment is new. Think of it like that. You know the joke: What's the best thing about Alzheimer's? You get to meet new people." Lisa laughed. "So, run along. And don't let Bill get you down. He's trying to find his way. He can't help it if he's not likeable. At least, I never much liked him."

"How do you know Mother's not suffering?" I asked.

The fat man, whose desk plate read Dr. H. Bledsoe, said, "Pardon me?"

"I'm sorry," I told him. "I was talking to someone else."

"Are you feeling all right, Mr. Ellison?"

"Yes, just fine. Here I brought some of the music my mother loves." I put the bag on his desk and stood to leave. "Do you think familiar things like the music will help?"

"I doubt it. It's possible."

Bill was not at the house when I returned. On the dining room table I found a note, which read:

Upstairs in the study you will find a note which explains everything.

I went up to the study and found an envelope on the desk. Inside was a note, which read:

FUCK YOU!

Bill

✗ ✗ ✗

Ain't you Rine the runner?

Wiley Morgenstein flew into D.C. to meet Stagg Leigh. Stagg was a little nervous about the lunch and so he spent extra time preparing. He stood in front of the bathroom mirror and practiced frowning, carving a furrow into his forehead, above the bridge of his nose. He shaved off his mustache and made his apologies to its original owner. He tried on a hat, but couldn't bring himself to leave it on for more than a few seconds at a time.

"Who are you trying to fool?" he asked the mirror.

Should he wear knob-toed shoes? Sneakers? County jail flip-flops? He decided on brown weejuns, khakis and a white shirt with blue stripes and a button down collar. The clothes were available.

He was to meet Morgenstein in the restaurant on the roof of the Hotel Washington. Stagg put on his dark glasses and went there late.

The balcony of the restaurant overlooked the east lawn of the White House, but Morgenstein had taken a table inside, a booth in fact, in a dimly lighted corner of the main room. Stagg was shown to the producer's table. There was a young woman seated with him and they both rose when Stagg arrived. They shook hands.

"Pleased to meet you, Stagg," Morgenstein said. "This is my girl Friday, Cynthia."

"Oh, I can't tell you what a privilege this is. To meet an author of your notable station." She giggled a high-pitched giggle.

"Well, sit down, have a seat, have a seat."

Stagg sat and tried to see the man in the dim light from behind his shades. Morgenstein was heavier than he had imagined, dressed casually in a tee-shirt beneath a blazer. And Cynthia was no more his assistant than Stagg was a real person. The young woman was nearly wearing a strained piece of fabric around what were, no doubt, enhanced breasts.

"Sorry about the table inside here and all, but, hell, I'm fat and I need air conditioning." Morgenstein laughed.

Stagg did not.

"You're not all that fat, Wiley," Cynthia said.

Morgenstein ignored her comment. "Your editor was shocked that I was getting a meeting with you. Thanks for coming. Would you like something to drink?" He was already summoning the waiter. "Hey, I love that damn novel. I laughed my ass out. Oh, it's sad too, don't get me wrong. And real as hell. We can just lift the dialogue right out of the book." The waiter arrived. "What'll you have?" Morgenstein asked Stagg.

"A Gibson," Stagg said.

Morgenstein struggled through a frown and continued. "You know I would have paid for the damn novel even if you refused to meet with me. I just decided to see what would happen. Three mil talks, don't it?"

"Yes, indeed," Stagg said.

Morgenstein offered a puzzled look to his young friend. "You know, you're not at all like I pictured you."

"No? How did you picture me?"

"I don't know, tougher or something. You know, more street. More . . ."

"Black?"

"Yeah, that's it. I'm glad you said it. I've seen the people you write about, the real people, the earthy, gutsy people. They can't teach you to write about that in no college." He turned his face to Cynthia. "Can they, sugar."

Stagg nodded a cool nod.

"Hey, look at the menu and see what you want," Morgenstein said. "This is all right, isn't it. I had a hell of time picking a place. I was reading the book again on the plane and I thought about meeting at Popeye's." Morgenstein laughed. Cynthia wrapped her fingers around his arm and laughed, too. "See anything you like?"

"I think so."

The waiter came back with the Gibson and waited for their orders.

"Me and the lady will have big steaks, medium and whatever else you bring with that. But no butter on the potatoes. Ranch dressing on the salads. Stagg?"

"I'll start with the carrot and ginger soup. That's served cold, isn't it?"

"Yes, sir."

"I don't see it on the menu, but I'd like just a plate of fettucini and a little olive oil and Parmesan."

"Not a problem, sir." The waiter looked to Morgenstein. "Wine?"

Morgenstein looked to Stagg.

"Anything you like," Stagg said.

"Bring us a red wine," Morgenstein said. As the waiter collected the menus and left, the fat man turned to his date with a troubled expression. To Stagg, "You know, you really ain't at all what I expected."

"We went over that. Why did you want to meet?" The tough act was working. Stagg saw a slight recoil of fear in Morgenstein.

"No reason in particular."

They sat quietly for a while. Cynthia whispered something to Morgenstein, then giggled again. She played with a lock of her blonde hair and looked at him, her head tilted.

"So, you've done some time," Morgenstein said. "I almost went to the joint, but my Uncle Mort got me off. It was a bum rap anyways, some kinda interstate commerce shit. What'd you do?"

Here Stagg was faced with a dilemma. So far, his only lie had been to answer to his name. Even owning up to having written the *damn novel* was honest enough. "They say I killed a man with the leather awl of a Swiss army knife." The qualifier *they say* was a stroke and Stagg smiled to himself, a move that served to underscore the quality of his crime.

Morgenstein stiffened briefly, then seemed relieved. "Here I was about to think you weren't the real thing." He laughed with Cynthia, who was now eyeing Stagg quite differently. She seemed to crawl behind the fat man, but at the same time smiled coyly at Stagg, her gaze focused on, no doubt, her reflection in his dark lenses.

"I'm the real thing," Stagg repeated. "Cynthia knows I'm the real thing. Don't you, Cindy."

Cynthia squirmed.

"Yeah," Morgenstein laughed nervously.

The salads and Stagg's soup came. Stagg took two tastes of the soup and pushed the bowl aside.

"Don't you like it?" Morgenstein asked.

"Yes, it's quite good. It's exactly what I wanted." Stagg smiled again at Cynthia, then to Morgenstein, "I'm afraid I have to run now. I have to pay a visit to a convalescence home."

"Community service? I had to do that once. What a pain in the fucking ass. Little brats."

"It was a pleasure." Stagg reached across the table and shook the man's fat paw, nodded to Cynthia.

"Hey, do you have a number here in town where I can reach you?" Morgenstein asked.

Stagg looked at the man for a couple of seconds, then laughed a cool laugh before walking away.

Behold the invisible!

Stagg found that the world changed for him during the elevator ride down to the lobby and in the lobby he was confronted with a huge poster, a colorful confusion of shapes which asked the question:

Did Julian Schnabel Really Exist?

He wandered to a next sign:

What does the Avante Garde?

To another:

One Man's Graffiti is Another Man's Writing on the Wall

Stagg was confused, angry. Outside, he scratched the dark glasses from his face and disappeared.

The afternoon turned cool and a gentle rain fell. I watched people make their way into the building while I sat by Mother's bed. She was asleep. We listened to a Brahm's symphony, number 2 or 3. She always liked it more than I.

I thanked my parents on more than one occasion for not raising me Catholic. I was thirteen the final time and they finally responded to me by saying, "We're not Catholic, dear." The *dear* was supplied by Mother.

"Oh, I know that," I said. I stopped at the door and turned back. "That was a different thank you from my thank you for not raising me as a Christian."

"Oh, we know that," Father said.

"Why do you thank us for that?" Mother asked.

"Le coeur a ses raisons que la raison ne connaît point," Father said.

"I know my reasons," I said.

"Good boy," Father said.

"Vive le roi," I said.

Father laughed. Mother had already turned back to her book.

I recalled the stupid fight that had ended my brief, and no doubt short-lived-anyway, relationship with Marilyn. It was not her lack of taste or possession of questionable taste that caused me to make a scene upon finding that awful novel by her bedside. I reacted because the book reminded me of what I had become, however covert. And that was an overly ironic, cynical, self-conscious and yet faithful copy of Juanita Mae Jenkins, author of the runaway-bestseller-soon-to-be-a-major-motion-picture *We's Lives In Da Ghetto*.

Not only my situation but my constitution seemed to make me an unsuitable candidate for the most basic of friendships, new or old, and romantic involvement seemed nearly ridiculous to me. Perhaps my outburst with Marilyn was as much a well-timed retreat as it was an expression of snobbish literary outrage.

My agent was not so much angry as he was amazed by my demand that the title of the novel be changed to *Fuck*. He asked me if I was crazy and I reminded him that he thought I was crazy when I first suggested he send *My Pafology* out.

"You've got a point," he said. "Still, don't you think you're pushing it just a bit?"

"Not really. This thing is in fact a work of art for me. It has to do the work I want it to do."

"That's bullshit."

"Maybe."

"I don't think they're going to let you do it. Why not *Hell* or *Damn*? Why *Fuck*?" I could hear him shaking his head.

"That's the title I want."

"What if their lawyers say no."

"They won't say no."

After a pause. "And what did you say to Morgenstein?"

"Nothing really."

"Well, the guy's in love with you. He's scared to death of you, but he said, '*That fuckin' guy's da real thing.*'"

"He's right."

Rothko: I'm sick of painting these damn rectangles.

Resnais: Don't you see that you're tracing the painting's physical limits? Your kind of seeming impoverishment becomes a sort of adventure in the art of elimination. The background and the foreground are your details and they render each other neutral. The one negates the other and so oddly we are left with only details, which in fact are not there.

Rothko: But what's the bottom line?

Resnais: The idiots are buying it.

Rothko: That is it, isn't it?

Resnais: I'm afraid so. They won't watch my films and believe me, my art is no better for the neglect.

Rothko: And no worse, Alain.

Yul: They say you can have the title change if you spell it with a PH.

Me: P-huck. Why would I spell it with a PH?

Yul: They say it won't be as offensive on the jacket.

Me: The hell it won't. Fuck with an F or they can p-huck off.

(LATER)

Yul: They said okay.

Me: That's fucking great.

X X X

I visited Mother every day for the first three weeks. The drive to Columbia wasn't so long and it made for a healthy break in my boredom. I would awake each morning, piddle around in the garage-turned-workshop, go for a long walk, sit down at my desk for several hours and try to construct a new novel that would redeem my lost literary soul, then get in the car to go see Mother. Once I was back home I would read, then torture myself about work. I was lonely, angrier than I had been in a long time, angrier than when I was an angry youth, but now I was rich and angry. I realized how much easier it was to be angry when one is rich. Of course, there was the accompanying guilt and the feeling stupid for feeling guilty, what I was told was one of two common intellectual's diseases—the other being diarrhea.

Mother was more out than in lately, but the staff kept a close watch and I was confident that she was safe. The irony was that as her mind failed, her body became healthier, she even put on a few pounds and her hand strength was greater than it had been in years. The doctor told me that it would be a short-lived irony. Of course, he didn't put it that way. He said, "Her body won't be that way for long." He said it as if to reassure me, as if the incongruity of her mental and physical states should be more offensive than her complete and total decay.

When she was herself, we listened to music and talked fancifully about going into the city to hear something at the Kennedy. Then she would drift, rather peaceably, off to sleep. It was all very sad and I more than once sat behind the wheel of the car and cried.

X X X

The call came in the morning and it was basically what I needed—something to do. Carl Brunt was the director of the National Book Association, the NBA, which sponsored the so-called major award in fiction each year, called simply and pretentiously *The Book Award*.

"Your name came up as a possible judge for the award," Brunt said.

"I'm flattered."

"Personally, I'd really like to have you as a judge. There will be five of you and about three hundred novels and collections of stories."

I listened.

"We don't pay much. A couple of thousand and travel to New York for the ceremony. Your library will be greatly fattened."

"That's fine."

"Are you interested?"

I detested awards, but as I complained endlessly about the direction of American letters, when presented with an opportunity to affect it, how could I say no? So I said, "Yes."

"Well, that was easy."

"Who are the other judges?"

"I haven't lined all of them up yet, but Wilson Harnet has agreed to be the chair of the committee. Do you know him?"

"Yes, I do. He should be good."

"Well, this is great," Brunt said. "I'm looking forward to working with you. And of course keep this to yourself until we announce the panel."

"Certainly."

"Great."

The Judges

Wilson Harnet (chair): Author of six novels. His most recent book was a work of creative nonfiction called *Time is Running Out*, about his wife who was diagnosed with cancer. As it turned out, his wife did not die and all the secrets of theirs that he revealed led her to divorce him and so the literary community eagerly awaited his forthcoming book titled *My Mistake*. A professor at the University of Alabama.

Ailene Hoover: Author of two novels and a collection of short stories. Her book of stories, *Trivial Pursuits*, won the PEN/Faulkner Award. Her novel, *Minutia*, reached four on the *NY Times* bestseller list. A resident of upstate New York (apparently all of it).

Thomas Tomad: Author of five collections of stories. Among them, *The Night They Came, A Night in Jail, The Night Has Eyes*. His work was praised by the American Association of Incarcerated People Who Write.

Also the senior editor of an imprint of St. Martin's Press, Living Cell Books, specializing in books by lifers. From San Francisco, California.

Jon Paul Sigmarsen: A Minnesota-based writer. Author of three novels and three books of nature writing. Won several awards for his *Living with the Muskellunge.* Host of a literary talk show aired on PBS in St. Paul called *With All This Snow, Why Not Read?*

Thelonious Ellison: Author of five books. Widely unread experimental stories and novels. Considered dense and often inaccessible. Best known for his novel *The Second Failure.* A lonely man, seemingly having shed all his friends. Visits his mother daily though she cannot remember who he is. Cannot talk to his brother because he is a nut. Cannot speak to his sister because she is dead. Too mystified to actually be depressed. Likes to fish and work with wood. Looking for single woman interested in same. Lives in nation's capital.

We five judges were introduced during a teleconference and the other four were decent and reasonable enough, as people are wont to seem at first meetings, especially over the phone.

Harnet, the chair, sounded as if he were smoking a pipe, not that something was in fact in his mouth, but as if he were tasting his breath. "We have an arduous and taxing task facing us, colleagues," he said. "They tell me we've more like four hundred books coming to us."

"Oh, good heavens," Ailene Hoover said. Her voice that of an older woman. "I'm just finishing a book myself."

Thomas Tomad said, "Surely we're not expected to read every word of every book. We do have lives. I can't be cooped up in the house all winter long."

"I think a lot of the books you'll be able to dismiss after the first couple of sentences," Harnet said. "Of course, if one of those books ends up on another judge's list, you'll have to go back to it."

"I'm not reading any of that experimental shit," Hoover said.

"I'm sure we'll discover each other's tastes and show due respect," Harnet said.

Jon Paul Sigmarsen laughed and said, "I plan to do a lot of my reading while ice fishing."

"How much ice do you usually catch?" Tomad said.

Tomad and Sigmarsen laughed.

"What's so funny?" Hoover asked.

"I have a question," Sigmarsen said. "How does one judge a novel against a collection of stories? I mean, if a novel has a bad chapter, then it's a flawed novel. But if all the stories in a book are great except one, then it's still a great book. Do you see what I mean, what I'm getting at?"

"That's a good question," Tomad said.

"What question is that?" Hoover asked.

"About stories and novels," Harnet said.

"Oh, yes, I suppose we're to read them both," Hoover said.

"Ellison, you haven't said anything," Hoover said. "Ellison?"

"I'm here."

"What do you think?"

"Nothing yet. I haven't seen any books. How often are we supposed to meet, on the phone or otherwise?"

"They've left that up to us," Harnet said. "But I have a plan. I suggest we talk in three weeks just to compare preliminary notes."

"We should meet in a couple of weeks to see if anything great has shown up," Hoover said. "I hear Riley Tucker has a book coming out. And Pinky Touchon."

"You know, somebody got a picture of her the other day," Tomad said.

"Who?" Hoover asked.

"Touchon," Tomad said. "In was in the Chronicle. It seems Pinky lives here in San Fran and no one even knew."

"I heard it's a big book," Hoover said.

"I heard that as well," said Sigmarsen.

"In a couple of weeks then?" I said.

What some people would have you believe is that Duchamp demonstrated that art could be made out of anything, that there is nothing special about an *objet d'art* that makes it what it is, that all that matters is that we are willing to allow it to be art. To say, *This is a work of art*, is a strange kind of performative utterance, as when the king knights a fellow or the judge pronounces a couple man and wife. But if it turns out that the marriage license was incorrectly filled out, then the declaration is undone and we will say, "I guess you're not husband and wife after all." But even as it's thrown out of the museum, what has been called art, it is still art, discarded art, shunned art, bad art, misunderstood art, oppressed art, shock art, lost art, dead art, art before its time, artless art, but art nonetheless.

I'm reminded of the parrot in the house, which when he hears a knock at the door says, "Who is it?" The man knocking answers, "It's the plumber." The door remains closed and so he knocks again. "Who is it?" the parrot asks. "The plumber." Knock, knock. "Who is it?" "The plumber!" This goes on until the crazed knocker breaks through the door, falls onto the carpet below the parrot's perch, has a heart attack and expires. The residents of the home return to find the man stretched out on their floor. "Who is it?" the wife asks. The parrot says, "The plumber."

The question is of course, does the parrot answer the woman's query? And of course he does and he doesn't. He's a parrot.

Rauschenberg: Here's a piece of paper, Willem. Now draw me a picture. I don't care what it is a picture of or how good it is.
de Kooning: Why?
Rauschenberg: I intend to erase it.
de Kooning: Why?
Rauschenberg: Never mind that. I'll fix your roof in exchange for the picture.
de Kooning: Okay. I believe I'll use pencil, ink and grease pencil.
Rauschenberg: Whatever.

(4 weeks later)

Rauschenberg: Well, it took me forty erasers, but I did it.
de Kooning: Did what?
Rauschenberg: Erased it. The picture you drew for me.
de Kooning: You erased my picture?
Rauschenberg: Yes.
de Kooning: Where is it?

Rauschenberg: Your drawing is gone. What remains is my erasing and the paper which was mine to begin with.

(Shows de Kooning the picture)

de Kooning: You put your name on it.

Rauschenberg: Why not? It's my work.

de Kooning: Your work? Look at what you've done to my picture.

Rauschenberg: Nice job, eh? It was a lot of work erasing it. My wrist is still sore. I call it "Erased Drawing."

de Kooning: That's very clever.

Rauschenberg: I've already sold it for ten grand.

de Kooning: You sold my picture?

Rauschenberg: No, I erased your picture. I sold my erasing.

The books began to arrive, boxes of them. At first I could not open a single one, but was taken by them as objects. The covers were all so attractive. The jacket copy made each one sound great, blurbs from established literary icons told me why I should like it. The fat books were praised for being fat, the skinny books were praised for being skinny, old writers were great because they were old, young writers were talents because of their youth, every one was startling, ground-breaking, warm, chilling, original, honest and human. I would have found refreshing:

> *Jo Blow's new novel takes on the mundane and leaves it right where it is. The prose is clear and pedestrian. The moves are tried and true. Yet the book is not so alarmingly dishonest. The characters are as wooden as the ones we meet in real life. This is a torturous journey through the banal. The novel is ordinary but not insipid, pointless but not meaningless, savorless but not stale.*

> *Jo Blow is a middle aged writer with a family and no discernible special features. He lives in a house and is about as smart as his last novel.*

So, I opened the first book and I loved it. Actually, I enjoyed reading. The book sucked. But I did enjoy reading it and so I read another and another. I read three in one night and the better part of the next day. All

three were sterile, well-constructed, predictable fare. I decided that perhaps I was jaded. I was familiar with novels the way a surgeon is familiar
with blood. I would have to contact my innocent, inner self, the part of me
that could be amazed by the dull and commonplace.

As I was leaving the house to visit Mother, the telephone rang
She said, "Wanna fuck?"
"Linda?"
"How'd you guess?"
Linda Mallory. I considered her name. And as she spoke, saying things
that I could not remember because I was not listening, I realized that my
life was in need of a gratuitous sex scene. My mind required a new source
of guilt, as Mother's failing condition had justified her placement. And
even as I decided to pursue that guilt, I also sought to assuage it by re-
minding myself that Linda very much was using me. I caught in her
stream of language that she was in Washington.
"Where are you staying?" I asked.
"What?"
"Where are you?"
"I'm at the Mayflower again."
"I'll be there at seven. How's that for you?"
"That's fine," she said, skeptically. "Monk? This is Monk Ellison, isn't it?"
"Yes. Seven."
"Seven is great."

X X X

Mother's incontinence had become more pronounced and though she
seemed strong enough to move herself around, she chose not to. When I arrived, the attending nurse and an orderly were changing the sheet while my
mother lay in the bed. She was uncovered from the waist down and while
the orderly pulled away the soiled sheets, the nurse wiped the mess from my
mother's skin. I turned away and stepped back into the corridor, still seeing
Mother's head rolling toward me and her vacant eyes pointing my way. She
was so far from the woman who had told me once that listening to Mahler

made her see colors right before she cried. "I see autumn in the fourth symphony," she said. "Ashen greens giving way to reds and ochre while the sky darkens and the night feels cool." The same woman whose shitty ass was being wiped by a woman who didn't know who Mahler was had said that.

Linda Mallory was the postmodern fuck. She was self-conscious to the point of distraction, counted her orgasms and felt none of them. She worried about how she looked while making love, about how her expression changed when she started to come, whether she was too tight, too loose, too dry, too wet, too loud, too quiet and she found need to express these concerns during the course of the event.

"Does my hair look nice splayed out across the pillow?" she asked.

"It looks fine, Linda."

"Am I moving all right, too fast, too slow?"

"Move however it feels good to you."

And so I suspected she did, as she screamed into my face, startling me somewhat and my reaction must have shown, because she said, "Was that too loud? Was I ugly? Oh, my god, I can't believe I did that. Oh, my god."

"It's okay, Linda. Are you all right?" I asked.

"Why, don't I seem all right? Did you come?" She leaned after me as I rolled off her.

"No."

"I can't believe I screamed like that." She turned to the nightstand and grabbed a cigarette, lit it.

"Don't worry. So, you screamed when you came. That's good, isn't it?"

"I think I came. Yes, that would be good, right?"

She put her cigarette-free hand down on my penis. I was still hard, but far from excited.

"Mister Ready," she said.

Paying a visit to Linda had been a bad idea and it was still one. I could not simply get dressed and leave, though guiltily I must admit that is exactly what I wanted to do. I harbored no ill feelings toward Linda and in fact respected her enough not to pity her. Oddly, her anxieties were coming across as endearingly comic. Even then, when I first considered that awkward thought I understood my judgment to be mere rationalization, not to have me think better of her, but of myself.

"Shall we watch a movie?" I asked.

"Don't you want to make love again?"

"I'm afraid you've worn me out," I said. "You're really quite athletic."

"Really?"

"Yes."

I used the remote control to turn on the television. Linda nestled her head onto my chest and I was saddened by the fact that I disliked the coconut fragrance of her shampoo. The first image on the screen was a wildcat tearing apart a rabbit. "Change," she said and I did. "Change." I did. "Change." I did and offered her the controller. She refused, said, "No, you hold on to it. Change." Finally, she had me settle on some noir film with actors I didn't recognize. She squirmed playfully, as to get more comfortable, then promptly began to snore.

It was the season of the absent or lazy editor. So many of the novels were needlessly fat. Six were more than nine hundred pages, twelve were better than seven hundred and any one of them would have and could have been, with a modicum of editorial attention, a good four-hundred-page novel. There was an incredibly dense novel from a well-known, reclusive writer of dense novels. There was a nicely crafted and notably lean novel from a writer whose reputation was astonishingly well made. There was a volume of collected stories from a dead writer, a shelf of first novels about fatherly abuse and motherly alcoholism (and the reverse), a mid-list author's new (but dreadfully old) take on the academic novel, twenty-eight middle America, domestic, where-will-the-children-live novels, forty coming-of-age novels, thirty-five new-life-after-the-wrecked-marriage novels, thirty crime novels, forty so-called adventure novels and six yeah-we're-Christians-with-chips-on-our-shoulders novels. For the most part the titles received more consideration than the stories or the writing. Still, I found thirty I wished I had written—ten because I would have done a better job. Of ten others I was saddened to admit I could not have written them better. The other ten were simply good, well-crafted, serious, thoughtful.

At the first conference, one of the judges, I am not to say which one, said, "I'd like to see Rita Totten's *Over My Body* on the short list." When asked why? she said, "For two reasons: because Rita is a good friend of mine and because she got such a scathing review in the *New York Times*."

I pointed out that one could argue that either of those reasons might be enough to keep her off the list.

Thomas Tomad sighed, "This is Tomad speaking—" (as it was a telephone conference it was kind of him to identify himself) "—and I believe that Totten's novel is just so much fluff. Filthy fluff, but fluff none-the-less."

Another judge: "I'd like to see Richard Wordiman's book on one of the lists."

"Don't you work with him?" someone asked.

"Why yes, and although I don't think it's his best book, I'd like for him to know that I take his work seriously."

"Why don't we wait until all the books come in?" I asked.

"Sounds reasonable," Wilson Harnet said. "This is my suggested course of action. We each compile a list of twenty-five books. Then we see if there's any overlap. We'll discuss the list and any book with at least two mentioners goes to the next round. From there we'll wing it."

Tomad: "Sounds good. I've already got a couple I'm willing to go to the mat for. There is some gritty stuff out there."

Sigmarsen: "Ya, sure. The nature writing is skinny by my standards, but still there are a couple good ones. Toby Lancfugen's book is remarkable."

Hoover: "I didn't get all of that. Yes, of course. I was surprised to see so many books by such big names. Shouldn't we just go ahead and put them on the first list?"

Ellison: "Okay."

X X X

Christmas came and went. Mother's body became more fit as her mind failed completely. My editor called my agent with the exciting news that *Fuck* was going to be released earlier because of the great interest. And even then, when I heard that I would see the book in March, I did not suspect that in January I would open a padded envelope addressed to Thelonius Ellison and find a bound galley of *Fuck* with the request that it be considered for *The Book Award*.

Dilemma: I refused to admit that I, Thelonius Ellison, was also Stagg R. Leigh, author of *Fuck*. But yet here was the book. I could not disqualify myself, because I would betray my secret.

Solution: Ignore it. Who in his right mind would consider giving that novel an award?

Yep.

I had become a hermit. I had a stack of mail from friends, which I had not opened. I had a stack of letters from people at various universities either requesting letters of recommendation for applicants seeking employment or students seeking admission to programs—such was my conjecture, as all of them remained sealed. I felt guilty about those, more so than the personal ones. From a couple of institutions there were three or four letters and I guessed that they were invitations to give readings. I gave few enough readings, as I found the whole custom rather idiotic. "Read the damn book," I always wanted to shout and just sit down. Once I considered taking a couple of boxes of books and having the audience read silently while I read silently, then point out that they didn't need me after all. I was not a popular reader, a fact that never hurt my feelings, but now I could imagine that my failure to even respond to the invitations made me that much more desirable.

I sat back on the sofa in the study, closed my eyes and imagined a reading given by Stagg Leigh:

Site: East St. Louis Public Library or the Lansing Public Library or the Worcester Public Library or Borders Bookstore in Philadelphia, Dallas, Jacksonville or Waterstone's Bookstore in Boston, New York, Chicago.

Stagg's outfit: Yellow, baggy, draping wool pants. Black silk shirt with loose sleeves and several buttons at the cuff. A gray, sharkskin blazer, double vented, double breasted with a yellow kerchief peeking from the breast pocket. Gray hose. Tasseled loafers, black.

or

Black pants, black shirt, black watch cap, dark glasses, black army boots.

or

A colorful dashiki, white trousers, sandals, red fez.

Stagg is to be introduced by a young white woman, a representative of the Friends of Books Society, Becky Unger. "I'm just so pleased you could come and read for us," she says privately. "We'd heard that you're very shy. Oh, I didn't mean anything by my use of the word 'shy.' Private, I meant to say private."

"I prefer 'reclusive,'" Stagg says, his voice barely audible.

"Reclusive. Okay, then." The friend of books gets up and steps to the lectern. She clears her throat and the room comes together "Thank you all for coming," She clears her throat once more. "It is my pleasure to introduce our guest, Mr. Stagg Leigh. I know that many of you have been as eagerly awaiting Mr. Leigh's reading as I have, so I'll make this short. Mr. Leigh is the author of an exceptional first novel," looks at the audience, catches her breath, looks at her hands, then, "Fuck." Mixed giggles and muttering erupt in the audience. "This first novel is a runaway bestseller and is presently enjoying its third week at number one. I believe that Mr. Leigh lives in Washington, D.C. This book meant so much to me when I read it. It opened my eyes to ways of black life and helped me understand the pain of those people. So, please join me in welcoming Mr. Stagg R. Leigh."

Stagg stands and steps to the lectern, acknowledges Ms. Unger with a nod and faces the audience. There are a couple of blue-haired older white women in the front row, nervous-seeming, eyes darting, Stagg says, "Thank you for having me." His voice is barely audible. The audience leans forward, collectively, hanging on his voice, staring at him. Stagg takes a breath and says,

"Fuck!" *The audience is knocked back into their seats. "—is a true story." Again his voice is barely loud enough to hear, but they do and they moan their approval. "This novel is not true factually, but it is the true story of what it is like to be black in America. It ain't pretty."*

"Here, here," from a white, bow-tied man in the back.

"During my time in prison," a look at the blue-haired ladies, "I learned that words belong to everybody, that I could make my place in this bankrupt society by using my God-given talent with language."

Applause.

"Fuck! *is my contribution to this wonderful country of ours. Where a black ex-con can become rich by simply telling the truth about his unfortunate people."*

Applause. Applause. Applause.

Stagg opens his book. **"Fuck!"** *The audience falls back, then forward to listen. "'Mama look at me and Tardreece and she call us human slough . . .'"*

Fuck, despite its title, was chosen by Kenya Dunston, or whoever made those kinds of decisions for her, to be a selection of her book club. There was much excitement at the publisher's offices as it meant that somehow we would split a huge chunk of money. One of the conditions, however, was that Stagg Leigh would appear on the Kenya Dunston Show. This was a bad thing and it filled me with fear and hate. The fear was of being exposed. The hatred, of myself. But the money was more than significant, nearly doubling my advance. *Il faut de l'argent.*

"What are you going to do?" Yul asked.

"You mean what is Stagg Leigh going to do," I said.

"I suppose I do mean that."

"I suppose the author will show up at the studio at the specified time."

"Good lord."

I returned home from visiting Mother with the thought that I had only imagined her body remaining in good condition. It was by contrast to her mental failure that I of course was misled. My mother was dying. I felt what I assumed to be normal guilt at the consideration that she might be better off dead. It sounded as awful in my head as it looks on paper. How was I to know what pleasures she was enjoying in her own world. But of course I knew—the fleeting, solitary moments of comprehension must have been punishing and brutal. That night I put on my sneakers and went for a run, resolving to keep my own body fit.

Corpora lente augescunt, cito extinguuntur.

It was easy, difficult, anxiety-making, welcomed, and frightening to forgo a visit to Mother. I had been the dutiful son, the good man, the family rock, but I had to create a little space. In a way it was a trial run, as I would be going to New York soon for a meeting of the award committee and for Stagg Leigh's appearance on television. I paced the house, believing that this would be the one lucid day for Mother out of the last twelve, that she would turn sad-faced to the young nurse who changed her diaper and say, "Where is my Monksie?" I consciously shrugged off the guilt, as much as one can shrug off guilt. Guilt made for poor cologne. I hated three things on people. I hated the heavy humor of public men. I hated overt and indulgent self-deprecation. And I hated conspicuous guilt. I prided myself in the fact that I had only ever been guilty of the latter two.

I drove out to Columbia the next day. Mother was perhaps worse, certainly no better, and if she had been lucid the previous day, there were no residual effects and the room held no echoes. She held her knotted hands in her lap as she sat in her chair and stared into nothingness.

I stopped by the market on my way home to pick up what had become my diet, yogurt and fruit and those cups of dehyrated soups. I carried three bags, one containing a single honeydew melon as I walked out and toward the parking lot. There was a man standing at the edge of the sidewalk, a man perhaps my age, but still he was older, injured by life. He pointed at me and sang,

> *Bread and Wine*
> *Bread and Wine,*
> *Your cross ain't nearly so*
> *Heavy as mine . . .*

I stood just five feet from him. I could smell the wear on his soiled topcoat, count the wrinkles about his eyes. I think I scared him slightly. He stepped back and hunched almost imperceptibly, as if ready for flight. I nodded to him, said, "You're right." And I gave him my bag with the melon. I handed him that weight and he walked away, glancing back suspiciously twice. I looked for my keys, then back to the man and he was gone, as if sucked down a hole.

X X X

Thelonious and Monk and Stagg Leigh made the trip to New York together, on the same flight and, sadly, in the same seat. I considered that this charade might well turn out of hand and that I would slip into an actual condition of dual personalities. But as I nursed my juice through turbulent skies I managed to reduce the whole thing to mere drama. I was acting, simple and plain, and my pay was substantial and deserved. So, *we* were there dressed as myself, once Monksie in my mother's eyes, once artist in my own eyes. I checked into the Algonquin as was arranged by the staff of the National Book Association, put down my bags and took a nap.

At the meeting of the committee that afternoon, I sat between Ailene Hoover who smelled of garlic and Jon Paul Sigmarsen who somehow smelled of fish. We were in a spacious conference room with a window overlooking a courtyard. We discussed book after book, Sigmarsen and Tomad being the most emotional in their likes and dislikes. Wilson Harnet was almost annoyingly diplomatic and Ailene Hoover was there on and off. Perhaps my participation was the most problematic, as I listened carefully and spoke very little. About an hour into the discussion, a terrible thing happened and it happened like an ambush, as if staged, rehearsed, prepared solely for me; Ailene Hoover brought up *Fuck*.

"Have you all read *Fuck* yet?" she asked.

All had, except Sigmarsen.

"What about you?" Harnet asked me.

"I looked at it," I said. "It didn't capture me."

"Oh, I thought it was just marvelous," said Hoover.

"A gutsy piece of work," from Tomad.

"I have to agree," Harnet said. "I think it's the strongest African American novel I've read in a long time."

"I look forward to reading it," Sigmarsen said.

"I suspect it will at least be on our list of twenty," Harnet said.

"I should think so," Hoover said.

"I guess I'll have to give it a reading," said I. My spirit could not have been more deflated. My feet felt leaden, my stomach hollow, my hands cold. Nothing could have been more frightening or objectionable to me. I would rather have included the screenplay to *Birth of a Nation* on the list than that novel.

I went back to my room fit to be tied. I paced. Then I watched *Imitation of Life*. Then I paced. I ordered dinner to my room, but ate none of it.

X X X

The following morning, after no sleep, I showered, dressed and took a cab to the address I'd found in Father's papers, to what was, at least at one time, the apartment of Fiona's sister, Tilly McFadden. The name on the box was still McFadden and so I rang the bell. The door buzzed and I entered the stairwell. The brownstone had seen better, cleaner days, but still the building was not in bad repair. I walked up the four flights and found the door ajar. I knocked.

"Come on in," a man called. Upon seeing me, he said, "Who you?" He was a shirtless, bald white man with a ring in his lip and a large tattoo covering his left shoulder and left side of his chest. He was fat as well, one biscuit shy of three hundred pounds. He had one boot on and was laboring to dress the other foot. Frankly, he scared me.

"My name is Thelonious Ellison."

"So the fuck what?"

"I was hoping you might be able to help me." I stared at his tattoo. It was a scene, a wooded place with a tiger fighting a snake.

"If you ask for money I'm going to beat the shit out of you."

"Are you a skinhead?" I asked. The question just popped out. I was curious.

"Get the fuck outta my house," he said and hauled himself up onto one boot and one sock.

"I'm looking for Tilly McFadden," I said.

"Well, you're ten years too late," he said. "She's dead."

"I'm sorry."

"Fuck you." For whatever reason he sat back down. Perhaps he was tired. "Are you her son?"

"Why the hell you want to know?" He gave me a hard stare.

"Actually, I'm looking for her sister, Fiona."

"Dead, too," he said. "Shit, boy, you too late for everybody." Now, he seemed amused. "What you want them for?" He acted like he smelled money.

"I'm looking for your cousin Gretchen. Is she dead as well?"

He stopped lacing his boot and sat up straight. "Naw, she ain't dead. Why you want her?"

I decided to come right to the point. "It appears that she's my half-sister."

"I knew," he said and rocked his head a little. "I knew she had nigger in her. My mother wouldn't own up to it, but I knew it."

"Do you know where she is?"

"I might. Why you looking for her?"

I looked at the crucifix on the wall, right next to the swastika. "Actually, it's personal."

"Hey, I know where she is, you don't."

"Maybe you could just tell me her last name."

He smiled at me and said nothing.

"How much?" I asked. "A hundred?" I had my money out of my pocket. "Two?" His face didn't change. "I've got two-fifty. I'll give it to you if the address is correct."

"What if I just kick your ass and take it."

"That wouldn't be as easy as just taking me there."

A nasty, wicked smile filled his ugly face and it made me hate him. I wasn't sure if he was finishing his boot tying so that he could beat me up or to take me to Gretchen's.

"Let's go," he said.

And so we walked from his building several blocks to another brownstone. For a fat man his pace was decent, though he panted alarmingly. I bristled at the thought of trying to resuscitate him should he collapse. The while I worried that he would turn and punch me or that we would happen onto some of his neo-Nazi pals and that I would be left for dead. Just a pause here to point out that if my mood before this was dark, by now it was pitch and dour, and I perceived it as pernicious itself, attacking me as much as the situation. This man was in fact related to me. He was the cousin of my half sister, which by my reckoning made him my half-cousin-by-law-once-removed, granted not a close relation, but close enough to sicken me some considerable measure.

"She's on the third floor," the skinhead said. "Her last name is Hanley." He held his red-knuckled hand out open for the cash. I gave him the money and watched him walk away. At the corner he glanced back at me with that grin.

Up the steps, I found the name *Gretchen Hanley* on the box and pressed the bell.

"Who is it?" a woman answered through the intercom.

"Ms. Hanley?"

"Yes?"

"My name is Thelonious Ellison. I'd like to talk with you."

There was a long pause, then the door buzzed. I reached for it quickly and entered the building, which had fallen into a sadder state than her cousin's building. I hadn't noticed before, but the day had turned hot and so with all the walking and climbing I had become rather sweaty and somewhat disheveled. I tucked in my shirt, took in a deep breath and knocked.

If there was a family resemblance, it was lost to my eye. Gretchen was in fact an attractive woman, wide in the shoulder and hips and tallish, with light brown hair which fell past her shoulder and hazel eyes. A baby cried in the corner and after opening the door, she turned to see to it.

"Gretchen?" I said.

"Yes, that's my name." There was an edge on her voice. "What can I do for you?" I could hear her accent.

"My father was Benjamin Ellison," I said.

She was holding the child now so that its face was at her shoulder. She looked at me. Her back was to the window and I could not read her expression.

"Your mother's name was Fiona?"

"Yes." She stepped closer and looked at my face. "So, you're my brother." She smiled and I could detect ever so faintly a likeness to her skinhead cousin. "So, is our old man dead yet?"

"Yes, he is."

That seemed to unscrew her slightly and she sat down at the table, rocked the baby.

"If it makes any difference," I said, "my father never knew where you were. He died about seven years ago. I didn't know about you and your mother until I found some letters."

She stared at me. Then I realized she was looking at my clothes. I looked around the apartment and saw that she was living badly. The place was clean enough, but it wore the scars of hard times. The Formica-topped table might have seemed chic in a bright, suburban kitchen, but there it served as merely a log, the dents and blemishes marking memories. Just looking at the sofa, I knew that the reverse sides of the cushions were even more stained.

"This is my granddaughter," she said. "I watch her while my daughter works. Then I go to work. Tomorrow will be the same and the day after even more the same. What do you do, Mr. Ellison?"

"I'm a writer."

"How wonderful." She looked at the baby's face, touched it with her finger. "A writer. Did you go to college?"

"I did."

"How nice. I suppose you learned a lot in college." The baby made a another crying sound and she shushed him somewhat roughly. "Support the Negro College Fund, I always say."

I didn't like the woman, but her bitterness didn't and shouldn't have surprised me. "Anyway," I said, "my father wrote you this letter before he died. I recently found it and so I tracked you down." I put the letter on the table in front of her.

She looked at it, but did not reach for it.

I sat down in the chair closest to me and studied her face. A terrible sense of loneliness came over me and I was hard put to understand whether it was an empathetic response to Gretchen or simply my own feeling. I also felt responsible, however wrongly, for the poverty in the room with me.

"So, you're my brother."

I nodded.

"Do I have other brothers and sisters?"

"You have another brother. Your sister is dead." I looked at the dirty window. "I didn't mean to come and stir up bad feelings for you. My father left his letters to be found and I was the one who read them. From what I can see, he loved your mother very much. I think he wanted to find you, but didn't know how."

"You found me."

She was quite right and to that I had no satisfactory reply.

"Father wanted you to have this money." I took out my checkbook and pen.

"Money?"

I could not tell if she was surprised or offended, but I twisted the point of the pen out and continued. "Yes, Ms. Hanley, my father left you some money." I wrote out a check for one hundred thousand dollars and handed it to her, to my astonishment without hesitation. I'd never before written a check near that large and it felt strange, dizzying.

"My goodness," she said, not looking at the check. "Money, how about that? And that makes it all okay, does it?" She glanced about her home, seeming to take it in, seeming to draw my attention to the conditions of her life.

"I don't think so." I stood. "But that's all I'm here to do. Well, good luck," I said, turned and walked out of her apartment.

She came to the door and opened it after me. "This is real?"

"Yes."

Now, if you pitch your little tent along the broad highway
The board of Sanitation says, "Sorry, you can't stay."
"Come on, come on, get movin'," it's the ever-lasting cry
Can't stay, can't go back and can't migrate so where the hell am I?

I chose to walk back to the hotel, having no money left for a taxi, and refusing to sink even lower to the tunnels of the subway. The exercise, however, did little to clear my head. The consideration of my newly found branch of the family generated new levels of irony and resonance to my plight as Stagg Leigh. Sitting in Gretchen's apartment, I was reminded of my sister's clinic, of the women seated in the waiting area, of the babies in their laps, of the toddlers picking at the nap of the carpet. I stopped at the window of a small gallery and looked at the photographs in the front display, dreary photos, wide-angled, cold depictions of a typical though anonymous waterfront. There were no people in the pictures, only ships and cranes and concrete and water. The photographer's name was Brockton and I wondered what he had done with the people, how he had cleaned his canvas so completely.

I walked on and above a warehouse I saw a billboard, which attracted my attention only for its spanking newness:

KEEP AMERICA PURE

X X X

Stagg Leigh leaves his hotel room, 1369, dressed casually in black shoes, black trousers, black turtleneck sweater, black blazer, black beard, black fedora. Stagg Leigh is black from toe to top of head, from shoulder to shoulder, from now until both ends of time. He bops down the carpeted hallway to the elevator, down again, farther down, down.

precibus infimis

The elevator doors close, metal doors meeting edge to edge. Inside is an older black man dressed in a modest, brown suit. He presses the lobby button, then regards the lighted panel in front of him, watching the floor badges illuminate in descending sequence. Without looking at Stagg, he asks, "Are you an engineer?"

"An *engineer?*"

"Yeah, that's what I asked you," he says, challengingly.

"No, sir, I'm no engineer."

"Too bad," the old man says. The doors slide open.

As the man steps out of the car, Stagg says, "In fact, in a way, I am." But the man is gone.

ridentem dicere verum quid vetat?

Ailene Hoover boards the car, presses the button, though it has obviously already been pressed. She does not look at Stagg's eyes, but he feels her making note of his color, his one color, his size, his long fingers, his large feet. She wears too much perfume, smells of gardenias. She touches the heart-shaped pendant which hangs around her neck. Then she turns a suspicious smile to Stagg, asks, "Do I know you?"

"I don't believe so."

"'There is something familiar about you."

"Really? I suppose I have one of those faces."

"Yes that must be it."

The doors open.

medio tutissimus ibis

Stagg takes the subway, the underground, to the studio, realizing as the train rumbles that so does his stomach. He is starving. Other stomachs rumble. He is encased with other black men. Though it is a golden day outside, they cruise below the world to their destinations.

At the studio, Stagg is met by a man named Tod Weiß, a young man, dressed nicely, his hands soft when they shake. But Weiß is sure of himself. He is the producer and when he snaps his fingers, somebody jumps. He wears a large smile and runs his fingers through his hair.

"We're so glad you're here," Weiß says. "If you hadn't made it I don't know what we would have done. We were told that maybe you wouldn't show up, but here you are. It's wonderful. Love the book. Come on, I'll take you to makeup."

"No makeup," Stagg says, his voice flat, black.

"But this is television."

"I'll be behind the screen anyway."

"That is very true. You know I hadn't considered that fact." Weiß grabs a passing assistant, "Go find a screen, pronto." Then to Stagg, "I've got a thousand and one things to take care of. Dana will take care of you."

Dana has been invisible up until now. She is younger than Weiß, black, slight. She appears, ready to take Stagg to the holding room. Weiß walks away. Dana leads Stagg down a corridor, her heels clicking against the wooden floor. She does not mention the book, but opens the door, then closes it when Stagg is inside. Stagg sits.

The door opens.

"Monk?" It was Yul. "Is that really you?"

"Shut up," I said.

Yul sat beside me on the sofa and stared at my beard. "It's not a very good disguise."

"It's good enough. I'll be off camera."

Yul shook his head. "You're walking the thin line, buddy."

I held my bearded face in my hands. I wanted to cry. I felt so lost, so alone. I looked at Yul. "You're still the only one who knows?"

"No one in the office even knows. Well, Isabela, the accountant knows, but she hardly speaks any English anyway. She hasn't put anything together."

"All this for money," I said.

Yul nodded, laughing.

"Maybe not," I said.

He paused and looked at my eyes.

"Meaning?"

I shook my head. "I don't know."

"Mr. Leigh, ten minutes," Dana says from the other side of the door.

I turned to Yul and asked, "Is it too late to jump into my hole and hide?"

"It appears so. Later, when it's all out, you'll look back at this stuff and laugh. The irony, and I know it will kill you to hear this, is that this will probably help the sales of your other books."

"When it's all out?" I shook my head. "No one is ever going to know that I wrote that piece of shit. Do you understand?"

"Okay, okay, calm down. You'd better get into character."

And he was right, Stagg Leigh had slipped away from me in my concern about discovery. I closed my eyes and conjured him again. I reached into my pocket, pulled out my dark glasses and put them on.

"*Fuck!*" I said.

"I want order!" someone shouts.

Dana leads Stagg to a chair behind a screen. Kenya Dunston approaches. She looks just as she does on televison, no more real than that. She is perhaps heavier.

"Stagg Leigh, chile, I'd know you anywhere," Kenya says. She hugs Stagg like she knows him, loves him as a friend. "That's some book, some book."

"Time, Ms. Dunston," a young woman says.

"It's time," Kenya says. "It's time." And she walks to the other side of the screen.

Had I by annihilating my own presence actually asserted the individuality of Stagg Leigh? Or was it the book itself that had given him life? There he was for public scrutiny and the public was loving him. What would happen if I tired of holding my breath, if I had to come up for air? Would I have to kill Stagg to silence him? And what did it mean that I was even thinking of Stagg as having agency? What did it mean that I could put those questions to myself? Of course, it meant nothing and so, it meant everything.

Theme music blares. The audience sings along. Kenya Dunston is introduced. The audience roars. Kenya is excited, so excited. She is smiling broadly, beaming. "I am pleased to have on the show today Stagg Leigh, author of a novel that is just about to be released. It will be a bestseller and I understand that the movie rights have already been sold. Can you believe it? This is Stagg's first novel. But I must tell you that our guest is rather shy and that he agreed to be with us only if he could remain behind a screen. So, please join me in welcoming the silhouette of Stagg Leigh, author of—" She stopped. "What am I supposed to say? I'll go ahead and say the title and let the chips fall where they may. Stagg Leigh, author of *Fuck*."

Applause.

"How are you, Stagg?"

"Fine."

"That's some book."

"Yes."

"Would you like to tell us how this story came to you?"

"No."

"Come on. Is it a true story? Share with us what in your life prompted you to write such a gripping and truly realistic tale?"

"I don't think so."

"Well, the language is certainly vivid. I felt like I was right there. And exciting? I thought I was going to bust several times while reading."

"Thank you."

"Is Go Jenkins based on anyone in particular?"

"No."

"It's not easy to get you talking, is it?"

"No."

"Well, perhaps when we come back from this commercial break, you'll take some questions from the audience."

"What the hell is going on?" Kenya says. "That son of a bitch won't say a goddamn thing. What the hell kind of interview is that?"

Weiß is kneeling beside Stagg. "Please, you've got to try to open up a little. Tell us anything. Tell them to buy the book for crying out loud. Anything."

5

4

3

2

1

"We're back. Our guest today is the writer Stagg Leigh. He's here to *discuss* with us his first novel, *Fuck*. Stagg, are you feeling a little more like talking now?"

"Not really."

General panic. Awkward silence. Restless audience noises. Dana giggles into her fist. Camera pans audience and comes back to Kenya.

"Well, we were warned that our guest is extremely shy and so he is. This would be a good time for me to read a passage from this brilliant novel." Kenya opens *Fuck* and reads:

I love Cleona and I hate Cleona. There be two lil' niggers in my head. Nigger A and Nigger B. Nigger A say, Be cool, bro, you know you ain't gots no money, so just let this girl go on back to school and through maf class and English class and socle studies so she can get out and be sumpin. Just let her have a chance, one chance to be that nurse she always talkin bout bein. But Nigger B be laughin, say, Shit, take this

*bitch home to her house and hit it one times, two times. She got the nerve to be talkin
to Jeep-nigger in front of you.* **Beep** *that shit. If she gone dis you like that, nail her
ass. Later you can go out and find that Jeep-mutha***Beep** *and* **Beep** *him up. Right
now, take this* **Beep** *home and get a taste. You remember how good that* **Beep** *was,
the way she whimpered, like she be crying, like it hurt. Nigger be hurtin a* **Beep**.
Beep *school. She ain't gone be no nurse. She ain't gone be nuffin.*

*When we walk to her house I see some guys playin ball. I ain't played no ball in
a long long time, I thinks to myself. At one time I was real good I could dunk from the
top of the key and all like that. I had me a nice jumper too, but* **Beep,** *how you gone
get into college and get all that big money when you ain't nuffin to begin wif and
when the mutha***Beep** *make it so you cain't stay in school. And I wasn't bout to suck
no coach's* **Beep** *for a chance to play. I shoulda gone over there when I was good
and tried out for the Lakers. I woulda fit right in. Showtime. Me and Magic. I didn't
even need no practice, that how good I was.*

*Cleona unlocks the door and we goes inside and she turn to me and say, "Now
give me the money."*

*"Slow down, baby," I say in my smooth voice. "Why don't you show me where
the baby sleep."*

*"You know where the baby sleep. The baby sleep in my room and we ain't goin in
there. Now, give me the money."*

"Well, could you get me some ice water?" I ax.

She sigh real heavy and stomp them big feet off in the direction of the kitchen.

*I sits down on the sofa and I see that the thing be new. I run my hand along the
cushion beside me and I'm thinkin, shit, where this mutha come from. Brand new.*

*Cleona come back into the room with the glass of water and hand it to me and
then just stand there.*

"You got a new couch," I say.

"So?"

"Where you and yo mama get the money for this here?"

"That ain't none o' yo business," she say.

*"I think it is," I say. "If my baby's mama gone out sellin her ass fo money to buy
furniture, that be my business. Maybe you don't need no money."*

"You s'posed to give me money every monf for Rexall."

*"S'posed to ain't the same as got to," I say. I looks around the room. "***Beep,**
y'all got a lot of nice **Beep.***" I sips my water and it be warm. "I said ice, bitch."*

She just stare at me.

"I'm sorry, baby," I say. "That just come out all wrong. C'mon here and sit down beside me."

She still just lookin at me.

"Sit down," I say again.

She plop her big ass down heavy next to me and I put my arm round her and she get all stiff.

"C'mon, Cleona, loosen up some. Ain't nobody home." I touch one of them big **Beep** *with my finger and say, "That's where my baby be havin dinner."*

Cleona don't want to but she let out a giggle.

I touch her **Beep** *some more. "That's a big ol'* **Beep,***" I say. "I wanna taste what my baby be drinkin. You want me to taste what my baby taste?"*

*Her eyelids be flutterin closed now and I think she say yes and I pull her shirt and look at that big-ass bra she be wearin. I try to undo the mutha***Beep** *in the back, but* **Beep,** *I cain't get it loose and I say, "Hep me out, damnit."*

Cleona reach her hands back, one from over her head and through her collar and the other up the back of her shirt and she open it up. Those giant jugs just flop there like big pillows, like bags of sand. I grabs on to them and sucks 'em real hard till she moans and I whispers a lil' sumpin, I don't even know what the **Beep** *I be sayin, but I squeeze and suck and squeeze and suck. The clock cross the room says one o'clock and I remember that I'm s'posed to meet Yellow and Tito over at the pool hall, so I gotta pop it quick. I push her back and undoes her pants, all the while I'm suckin on them* **Beep** *and she's moanin. It's hard to get her pants over her big ass, but I do it and then I puts it in her, all of it. Wham! Just like that and she cry out and man I feel so powerful. I bang it, man, I bang it and she start cryin, openin her eyes and seein me and she be cryin, sayin for me to get off her. But I be hittin it now and I smile at her.*

"God, I just love that," Kenya says, shaking her head. "Now, I know some of you at home are thinking that some of the language is kinda rough, but let me tell you, it doesn't get any more real than this. With this kinda talent, chile, don't you think we ought to forgive our guest's intense bashfulness?"

Audience applause, approval, endorsement, blessing.

I looked out from the house that was my disguise and saw Yul standing backstage. He applauded lightly, nodding to me, shrugging slightly, then he gave me a thumb-up that caused me to sink. I looked down at my feet, imagined my reflection in the leather of my shoes. Kenya Dunston was jabbering on the other side of the screen. What she was saying mattered none. I got up and walked away.

Hard luck Poppa standing in the rain
If the world was corn, he couldn't buy grain,
Lord, Lord, got them Brown's Ferry blues.

I returned to Washington defeated and feeling as near suicide as I had ever felt. I considered putting my head in the oven, but as Mother had always exercised a preference for electricity over gas, I could only hope to cook myself to death. I contemplated putting my father's pistol to some use, but years of reading led me to understand that there were just too many not-quite-fatal places a piece of metal might lodge itself, leaving me where? *Just as I was.* And there was the nagging fear that upon waking from a three-year coma I would find the identification bracelet on my wrist reading *Stagg R. Leigh.* I shuddered at the notion and the woman beside me thought that I was responding to her offer of a mint. She was Australian, I believe, and she said, "You only need to say no, mate."

I apologized. "I was somewhere else," I said.

"I don't like flying either," she said. "You look low."

I nodded, not wanting to chat, but I had already been rude once.

"Yeah, you look low, all right. You seem like you wanna put your head in a croc's mouth."

"Is that an efficient method?"

She laughed. "Clean off," she said, then leaned back to regard me. "You're all right, mate."

"How do you mean?"

"I mean, I like you. Course if you go off and kill yourself, then I'll say I liked you. Past tense, you know."

"I know."

"You should come to Australia," she said. She was not a large woman, but she sounded big. "There are some places in the desert that you'd think are just hell. Then you could come back here and everything would be right as rain by comparison."

"You think so?"

"My daddy used to say, *There isn't anything so bad that seeing something worse won't make better.*"

"A poet, your father."

"A bit of a bastard, he was. Made me love life though. Just by being there, if you catch my meaning."

"I do."

She again offered me a mint and this time I took it and thanked her. She said, "These are just god-awful," as I put the thing in my mouth.

"Not so bad," I said.

The phone discussions with the judges turned out to be disheartening, infuriating and stultifying. To a person, they had all fallen in love with Stagg Leigh's *Fuck.*

"The best novel by an African American in years."

"A true, raw, gritty work."

"So vivid, so life-like."

"The energy and savagery of the common black is so refreshing in the story."

"I believe it will be taught in schools, despite its rough language. It's that strong."

"An important book."

> **Of all them black-faced crew**
> **The finest man I knew**
> **Was our regimental bhisti, Gunga Din.**

The house was cold. Mother was the same. Life was the same. I had a new book out, but no one, thank god, knew it was mine. And the damn thing was doing well, very well, enormously well. I read many books that I thought were fine, but my fellow judges would hear none of it. Because we had to, we came to five finalists.

They were:
  (1) *Traditions,* by Zeena Lisner.
  (2) *Monte Cristo,* by J. Thinman.
  (3) *Exit the Moon,* by Jorge Jarretto.
  (4) *Warrior's Happiness,* by Chic Dong.
  (5) *Fuck,* by Stagg R. Leigh.

We would sift through the finalists and shake out a winner at a final meeting right before the awards ceremony in New York in February.

Das Seitengewehr pflanzt auf! The scream came to me in a dream, but as much as it frightened me, I did not wake, but instead continued dreaming, understanding in fact that I was dreaming. The idea that Nazi soldiers were after me was scary enough, but my fear was compounded by my knowledge that I was aware of it all being a dream and my inability to actually awake. I was hiding in dense brush at dusk. There was a French farmhouse in the distance, across a pasture, and beyond that was an orchard of some kind. The Germans were coming through the orchard, bayonets fixed as ordered. They burned the house and came across the meadow, poking their weapons into mounds of hay. A woman ran from the burning house, falling, crying. I could not see her face, but she was carrying a canvas. I could see the picture well in spite of the distance and the failing light. It was *Starry Night.* The soldiers took the painting from the woman and lanced it. I felt a sharp pain in my middle, grabbed my stomach and when I looked down at my hand I found it covered with blood. But I kept telling myself, "This is a dream. This is a dream." Behind the

soldiers a male chorus sang "The Horst Wessel Song." Then the painting
was aflame and the heat I felt made me scream out and the soldiers heard
me, reckoned my position and came toward me. I then realized that I was
sitting in a foxhole with a .50 calibre machine gun. I forgot my bleeding
and my burns and started shooting, mowing down the soldiers like so
many cans. One soldier, though shot, crawled bleeding all the way to my
foxhole while "Horst Wessel" was replaced by "Stars Fell on Alabama."
The wounded man looked at me, at my own blood on my shirt, and said,
"Wie heißen Sie?" And I didn't know.

I called Bill, but Bill was not home. Bill was never home, never at his office, never anywhere. He never called back, never left a message, never
wrote. I wondered if Bill was dead. I wondered if it mattered.

One Tuesday, Mother seemed herself for a couple of minutes near the
end of my visit. She gazed up at me from her darkness and said, "Monksie, we are all such vain creatures. The hard part is seeing myself, what I've
become. I see for a couple of seconds and then I don't know where I am. I
wish I could tell you I'm in here looking out. Thursday I plan to have a
good day. Be sure to be here on Thursday." The nurse told me as I was
leaving that a couple of Mother's old friends had come by to see her.

"They stood at the foot of her bed, but she just stared past them out the
window," the woman reported. "Then they left. One of them had been by
before. Same thing happened."

"Does my mother know who you are?"

The nurse nodded her head. "Much of the time. That's not unusual
though. I don't mean anything to her. I'm just furniture."

On Thursday, just as she predicted, she smiled to me with a smile that
was indeed hers, asked me to put on some music. "Something nice," she
said. "Some Ravel." She floated her hands in the air. "Ravel is so dan-
cey." I put the music on and she closed her eyes. "At times, I believe your
father was bored with me. I think I annoyed him. But he never said any-

thing, never let it show on his face or in his tone, but I believe I saw it. In the way he moved, the way he would turn a page. I know he loved me, because why would he have hidden his feelings so. Oh, we had good times, Monksie. Your father and I got along beautifully, but still there were those moments, moments when I felt so small." She sighed, but kept her eyes shut. "Once I mentioned to him that I thought he was wearied, but he shook his head and smiled and wondered where I got such an idea." She breathed in a deep breath and smiled sadly. "I always promised myself I wouldn't become old and smell of mentholated spirits. But I do, don't I, Monksie."

"I can't smell it, Mother."

"You're sweet. Like your father."

"We promise ourselves all sorts of things during our lives," I said.

"What have you promised yourself?"

I looked at her quiet face. "I promised myself once that I would not compromise my art."

Mother's eyes opened and she said, "What a fine promise. Are you sure I don't smell of mentholated spirits?"

"Yes, Mother."

Mother's eyes closed again.

✗ ✗ ✗

I tried Bill again. Left a message. No response.

✗ ✗ ✗

So, I had managed to take myself, the writer, reconfigure myself, then disintegrate myself, leaving two bodies of work, two bodies, no boundaries yet walls everywhere. I had caught myself standing naked in front of the mirror and discovered that I had nothing to hide and that lack was exactly what forced me to turn away. Somehow I had whacked off my own

willy
stick
dick
doink
rod

pecker
poker
member
prick
putz
schmuck
tallywhacker
johnson
thing
little friend

and now had to pay the price. I had to rescue myself, find myself and that
meant, it was ever so clear for a very brief moment, losing myself.

Another list of keywords (phrases):

echoes
dead
clock
thunder
obstupefactus
poached eyes
arabesque
nightmaze
et tu Bruno?
species
nocturnal
cad
$C_5 H_{14} N_2$
moral cement
London Bridge's Fallin' Down
Maybe it's the heat
dancing doll
lynch
Hahal shalal hashbaz

I had the strangest of thoughts. I reasoned, for lack of a better word, but perhaps no word is better, that if I were to go out into the streets of Washington, say around 14th Street and T, I might find an individual who by all measure was Stagg Leigh and then I could kill him, perhaps bring him home first for a meal, but kill him after all. But there was no such person and yet there was and he was me. I had not only made him, but I had made him well enough that he created a work of so-called art. I felt like god considering Hitler or any number of terrorists or Congressmen. I resolved that I could not let the committee select *Fuck* as the winner of the most prestigious book award in the nation. I had to defeat myself to save my self, my own identity. I had to toss a spear through the mouth of my own creation, silence him forever, kill him, press him down a dark hole and have the world admit that he never existed.

Christmas and New Year's passed the way I had always wanted them to, without note. In the middle of January *Fuck* was number one on the *New York Times* bestseller list, had been picked up by two more book clubs.

I sat up all night for several nights, pretending to look over my notes for a *real* novel.

When I was near delirium, I recalled the Icarus myth and pointed out to myself that whereas Icarus did plummet to earth, Daedalus in fact flew. I decided that Zeno was too slow getting to his point and that Thales' theory didn't hold water. I also determined that there is no alternative to mudness, that if you take all the blue out of purple, you aren't really left with red; it just looks that way.

New York Times 17 January

Fuck
by Stagg R. Leigh
Random House. 110 pp. $23.95

by Wayne Waxen

There is so much excitement over this new novel by unknown Leigh that it is difficult to write a review which approaches objectivity. But that is the point. This novel is so honest, so raw, so down-and-dirty-gritty, so real, that talk of objectivity is out of place. To address the book on that level would be the same as comparing the medicine beliefs of Amazon Indians to our advanced biomedical science. This novel must be taken on its own terms; *it's a black thang.*

The life of Van Go Jenkins is one of sheer animal existence, one that we can all recognize. Our young protagonist has no father, is ghetto tough and resists education and reason like the plague. It is natural, right for him to do so. He is hard, cruel, lost and we are afraid of him; that much is clear. But he is so real that we must offer him pity. He is the hood whom Dirty Harry blows away and we say, "Good, you got him," then feel the loss, at least of our own innocence.

Van Go has *fo* babies by four different mothers. He pays no child support, has no job, and no ambition except that he is on the verge of becoming a criminal. His mother, whom he stabs in the novel's opening dream sequence, arranges employment for him. He goes to work for a wealthy black family with a beautiful daughter who soon becomes the target of Van Go's burgeoning criminality.

The characters are so well drawn that often one forgets that *Fuck* is a novel. It is more like the evening news. The ghetto comes to life in these pages and for this glimpse of hood existence we owe the author a tremendous debt. The writing is dazzling, the dialogue as true as dialogue gets and it is simply honest. *Fuck* is a must read for every sensitive person who has ever seen these people on the street and asked, *"What's up with him?"*

Call it expediently located irony, or convenient rationalization, but I was keeping the money.

New York. Lunch with my fellow judges was had in a little, but expensive, Italian restaurant not far from the hotel where the awards ceremony would be held later that evening. I hardly ate, having left my appetite behind some months earlier, but the others seemed particularly grateful for free meal and drink. We made small talk and I came to understand that they all had been accompanied to the event by their wives, girlfriend and husband and so I felt even more conspicuously alone.

I listened at first rather patiently to their dismissal of the four finalists that were not *Fuck.* I became more disheartened as it became clear that their pathetic discussion was ranking that most disgusting of novels as clearly superior to its opponents. I began by mentioning the strength of one or another of the other books, but soon I had turned to a pointed attack against *Fuck*.

"It's not that it's a bad novel," I said, sipping wine, then placing down my glass. "It's no novel at all. It is a failed conception, an unformed fetus, seed cast into the sand, a hand without fingers, a word with no vowels. It is offensive, poorly written, racist and mindless."

Wilson Harnet, Ailene Hoover, Thomas Tomad and Jon Paul Sigmarsen just looked at me, none of them speaking.

"It's not art," I said.

Ailene Hoover said, "I should think as an African American you'd be happy to see one of your own people get an award like this."

I didn't know what to say, so I said, "Are you nuts?"

"I don't think we have to resort to name calling," Wilson Harnet said.

"I would think you'd be happy to have the story of your people so vividly portrayed," Hoover said.

"These are no more my people than Abbot and Costello are your people," I said, considering that I had perhaps offered a flawed analogy.

"I learned a lot reading that book," Jon Paul Sigmarsen said. "I haven't had a lot of experience with color—black people—and so *Fuck* was a great thing for me."

"That's exactly what I'm talking about," I said. "People will read this shit and believe that there is truth to it."

Thomas Tomad laughed. "This is the truest novel I've ever read. It could only have been written by someone who has done hard time. It's the real thing."

"I agree," said Harnet.

"Oh, my god," I said. I leaned back and looked out at the day.

"I say we vote," Sigmarsen said.

"I second," from Hoover.

"I don't want to vote," I said.

"I'm afraid we have a second," Harnet said. "All in favor of *Fuck* as our winner for this year's Book Award, raise a hand."

Of course, all four of them did.

"I believe we have a winner."

"That's democracy," I said and offered what might have been construed as a smile.

They smiled back, then ordered dessert.

In my room, I stretched out on the bed and contemplated my course of action. Stagg Leigh would in fact be awarded the Book Award. I considered my motivation in creating Stagg in the first place, felt again my anger and dissatisfaction with my world and my course of action became clear to me. I dressed and as I did I hummed. I had not hummed in a very long time; music had left me. I felt the spirit of Mother in my humming. I felt the spirit of my sister in my pithiness and that of my father in my playful arrogance. I even felt something of my brother and I knew that tonight I would be exposed.

Tarski: Don't I know you?
Carnap: You might.

The Ceremony

We judges, not only of fiction but of poetry, nonfiction and children's literature, were all seated at tables with *important* guests. It was a good thing, because I could no longer stand the sight of my *colleagues*. I was seated with the Director of the Board of Boston General Hospital, the CEO of General Mills, a vice president from General Motors and head of marketing from General Electric, all with their spouses.

After introductions, I said, "I feel generally out of place."

This made them laugh.

I was sitting between the wife of General Motors and the husband of General Electric and to my dismay, they wanted to talk to me. Finally, General Mills looked across the table and in a stage whisper said, "So, are you going to tell us who wins the big prize?"

"I do," I said.

They laughed again.

"The process wasn't all that grueling, was it?"

"Nearly four hundred books to read," I said.

"Whew. I don't think I've read half that many in my life."

"Sure you have, dear."

"I don't know."

"Was it a tough decision?"

"It was quite easy actually," I said. "I'd say it was decided over a month ago."

"I know which one it is."

I look at the wife of Boston General.

"Will you tell me if I'm right?"

"No, I won't," I said. "This has to be done correctly."

"Oh, you artists and your integrity."

That made me burst out with a short laugh which caused them to look at me.

"It's the word *integrity*," I said. "It always tickles me."

They all nodded, as if to say, "A writer." Then they shared glances and seemed more soothed as they perhaps shared the thought, "A *black* writer." But that observation was no doubt my anxiety getting the better of me.

The awards were given for the other categories and people applauded, but as always they waited for the fiction. Wilson Harnet stepped from his table to the front of the room and smiled. He said, "I know something you don't know."

The audience roared.

I looked across the room and saw my agent, Yul. He spotted me and with his eyes asked me what was up. With mine, I told him to stick around.

"It was an onerous task," Harnet said. "I'm told that we received more submissions this year than ever before. I can believe it. We read over five hundred novels and collections of short stories."

The audience let go a gasp, *tutti*.

"But it was a labor of love. Our decision was a difficult one, but one I believe will meet with much approval. The finalists of course are the cream of the crop in our eyes. Each of these books is remarkable in its own way. Sadly, however, four of them came up against a monster of a work, a real beauty, we writers like to say."

"Do you say that?" Mrs. General Mills asked.

"All the time."

Harnet laughed for no apparent reason. "I'm sure I could bore you by going on, but I will simply tell you the name of the winner. This year's committee for the Book Award in fiction has chosen *Fuck* by Stagg R. Leigh."

Whistling, cheering, applauding. "Here, here!"

"I hope Mr. Leigh was able to make it," Harnet said.

I stood and began to approach the front of the room.

But somehow the floor had now turned to sand . . .

My steps were difficult and my head was spinning as if I had been drugged. Cameras flashed and people murmured and I couldn't believe that I was walking through sand, through dream sand. Off to the right were members of the *Noveau Roman* Society along with Linda Mallory and perhaps my high school librarian. To my left were my father, my mother and the woman I knew to be Fiona on either side of him and behind them my brother, sister and half-sister. There were others I knew but failed to recognize and they all pressed around me, urging me forward and the camera flashes blinded me and made the room black during their moments of absence.

"Ah, here comes one of my fellow judges," Harnet said. "Perhaps Mr. Ellison has heard something about the whereabouts of our winner."

I was halfway there.

"It's a black thang maybe," Harnet said.

Laughter.

The faces of my life, of my past, of my world became as real as the unreal Harnet and the corporations and their wives and they were all talking to me, saying lines from novels that I loved, but when I tried to repeat them to myself, I faltered, unable to recall them. Then there was a small boy, perhaps me as boy, and he held up a mirror so that I could see my face and it was the face of Stagg Leigh.

"Now you're free of illusion," Stagg said. "How does it feel to be free of one's illusions?"

"I know those lines," I said aloud, knowing I was saying them to no one.

Harnet covered the microphone when I was next to him and asked me what I thought I was doing.

"The answer is *Painful and empty*," I said.

"This man needs help," Harnet said.

I looked at the faces, all of them, from time and out of time, but it was my mother to whom I spoke most directly. "The roses will forever smell beautiful," I said. Then the lights were brighter than ever, not flashes but constant, flooding light. I looked at the television cameras looking at me.

I looked at the mirror, still held by the boy. He held it by his thigh and I could only imagine the image the glass held.

I chose one of the TV cameras and stared into it. I said, "Egads, I'm on television."

X X X

hypotheses non fingo

Percival Everett is Distinguished Professor of English at the University of Southern California. His most recent books include *James*, *Dr. No* (finalist for the NBCC Award for Fiction and winner of the PEN/Jean Stein Book Award), *The Trees* (finalist for the Booker Prize and the PEN/Faulkner Award for Fiction), *Telephone* (finalist for the Pulitzer Prize), *So Much Blue*, *Erasure*, and *I Am Not Sidney Poitier*. He has received the NBCC Ivan Sandrof Life Achievement Award and the Windham Campbell Prize from Yale University. *American Fiction*, the feature film based on his novel *Erasure*, was released in 2023. He lives in Los Angeles with his wife, the writer Danzy Senna, and their children.

Manufactured by Versa Press on acid-free 30 percent postconsumer wastepaper.